Rock Starr Baby Daddy

A Flip or Flop Mystery

Lynda Rees

The Murder Guru

ROCK STARR BABY DADDY

A Flip or Flop Mystery

by

Lynda Rees, The Murder Guru

Email: lyndareesauthor@gmail.com
Website: www.lyndareesauthor.com
Original Edition
Copyright © 2025 by
Publisher:
Sweetwater Publishing Company
6612 Ky. Hwy. 17 North,
DeMossville, KY 41033
Editor: Sarah M. Hart
www.sweetwaterpublishingcompany.wordpress.com

Email: lyndareesauthor@gmail.com
Website: http://www.lyndareesauthor.com
Facebook: @lynda.rees.author
Copyright © 2025

DEDICATION:

*I dedicate this story to my
incredible daughter,
Brandy M. Nelson
You have blessed me with
the gift of having you, and angel on earth,
in my life and as
my
best friend.
You are so very special.
Hold your head high.
Keep your crown on straight.
My love for you is eternal.*

*MomMe
Lynda Rees*

PREAMBLE

The cocktail waitress arrived at work and swapped greetings with the day-shift bartender as she left. She hung her purse and coat on a rack and donned the apron over her uniform. "Hey, Boss," she greeted her manager. "How's it going today?"

He looked up from the grill where he was preparing food for patrons they anticipated. "Same old, same old. You know the routine. It ebbs and flows with flight landings and takeoffs." He went back to his cooking.

She left the kitchen through swinging doors to the bar room. A customer was nursing a drink at one end of the bar. She stopped by, introduced herself, and asked if he needed anything. He didn't.

She checked the stock of liquor, beer coolers, clean glasses, and noted the bar was clean. Then she went to a woman in a corner booth with her feet resting on top of a suitcase. The gal was deep into conversation with someone on her cell and waved the waitress away. She had a half-glass of what looked like an old-fashioned Tom Collins or a gin and tonic, so the server made a mental note to check back with her when she got off the phone.

She cleaned a table that had recently been vacated and sat the dishes on the bar near the kitchen door. A gentleman at one table stood, so she strode to him. He handed her his bill and a wad of cash. She checked the amount and smiled. "I'll be right back with your change."

He smiled and grabbed his luggage. "Not necessary. Keep the change."

She smiled. "Thank you, Sir. Have a pleasant day." She shoved the money and tab into her apron and groaned. A well-dressed gentleman had passed out on his table. A double-old fashion cocktail glass sat nearly empty beside his manicured hand. He wore a designer suit and outrageously expensive shoes.

A waste of a wealthy, fine-looking male.

She'd hoped this job might be her way to meet a man of substance. This handsome dude sure wasn't him. Glancing around, she tried not to draw attention to the over-served fella as she tapped him on the back. "Mister, you can't nap here. You'll have to find somewhere else to sleep it off. Try your loading gate."

The guy didn't stir. She shook his shoulder. "Sir, you need to leave."

She slipped the tab and bills on top of it out from beneath the guy's hand, where they rested on the table, and stuffed them into her apron. His hand slipped off the surface and dangled loosely at his side. Oh snap! That can't be good.

Her heart froze. Breathing halted. She jerked, then glanced around to see if anyone took notice of her panic. No one appeared aware of the situation. The waitress's icy hand trembled as she pushed the guy's collar down enough to gain access to his jugular. Steadying two fingers there, she tried calming herself enough to focus on what she was feeling—or in this case, what she didn't feel. *No pulse.*

Son-of-a—

The gal in the corner acted as though in her own world. She stowed her phone away and downed the last of her drink. Then she gazed around her table, as she gathered her personal items. Looking up, she caught the server's eye and jerked her head back to call her over.

The waitress stilled her breathing, forced her hands to stop quivering and walked casually to her. The woman shoved her tab and credit card toward. "Can I get you anything else?"

"No thanks." The woman fumbled with her purse, ignoring the servant. "Just a copy of the receipt please."

"Sure thing. I'll be right back with that." Sophie's words trailed behind her as she strutted away, hoping her voice hadn't cracked with emotion welling inside her.

Sophie pushed the card and tab into her apron and walked as calmly as she could muster, around the bar. She stopped briefly to collect the bar customer's credit card and bill. "I'll be right back with your receipt."

She ambled to the exit door and clicked it locked. Not meeting the eyes of the man at the bar, she strutted past him, carrying the tray of dirty dishes collected from the various customers, and carried them into the kitchen.

"Boss, we've got a problem."

CHAPTER ONE

Charli Owens and her fiancé, Eli Lange finished breakfast, trying to ignore the argument going on at a table across the dining room at the Sweetwater Hotel. The meal was supposed to be relaxing to take their minds off the coming project they had just begun, renovating a large estate house. It wasn't a big project, but they all had their issues. The half-full restaurant was known for great food and even better service. Today it had been slow, and the food was not up to their normal standards. To top it off, a strange couple had been loudly bickering since they sat down.

The elderly man was about the age of Charli's grandmother. He was handsome with tints of silver at the ears of his lush raven hair. His navy, well-fitting, designer suit gave the impression of affluence without being pretentious. A pale blue shirt was unbuttoned at the collar and worn without a tie, giving him a casual but businesslike appearance. Throughout their disagreement, he had remained calm and kept his voice low.

The female appeared a few years younger than her companion, also in business casual dress, wearing dark slacks and a tan tunic. Her brown hair was fashionably coiffed in a French twist. The only jewelry she wore was a set of large pearl earrings. Her brown leather tote hung from an adjacent chair of their four-seated table. Several times she raised her voice as her fist smacked the table. Silverware bounced and clanged. She glared with anger and frustration, but their words were muted from where Charli and Eli sat, so they couldn't hear the gist of the conversation. Whatever they were discussing had riled the female.

Their waitress, Carla Sanford, and a bartender Charli didn't recognize had been watching the argument, probably gauging whether to intervene or leave their angry guest to it. Carla strutted toward them, as she pulled a black folder from her apron.

Carla laid the check file on the table, giving Charli and Eli an apologetic smile as she glanced over her shoulder. "I'm so sorry about this. Hopefully those two will settle down . . . or leave. I apologize that they have disrupted your peaceful meal and for any delays in service."

Eli reached for the check. "It's not a bother. You do appear to be busy though."

She nodded. "Yes. We're woefully understaffed. Ralph and Howard are training two new maids, a security guard, a mixologist, and a bakery chef. It's a madhouse around here, but we're doing everything possible to ensure our guests are comfortable." That explained the new bartender.

Charli was familiar with Ralph Bacon and Howard Cummins. Ralph not only owned but managed the hotel. Howard wasn't just the head desk clerk. He was Ralph's top man.

Howard had a cute but silent crush on Gran. He lit up and fidgeted whenever she made an appearance. The shy fella had never gotten up the nerve to ask her out.

Eli inserted several bills, enough for their tab and a hefty tip, into the folder and handed it to the waitress. "Thanks, it was fine."

Charli knew the ins and outs of staffing from running her company Owens Construction. She specialized in remodeling homes for resale. Both she and Eli had years of experience and were multi-skilled, and she held a real estate license. "I completely understand. We've had our own issues with contractors and vendors. You'll be back to normal in no time."

The waitress winced. "I sure hope so. Thank you for your business. Enjoy your day." She stuffed the tab in her apron.

He stood and pulled Charli's chair out. "You too, thanks."

As Charli stood the ruckus across the room got her attention. The heated disagreement escalated. The woman was royally pissed off. Her loud tone held the attention of other diners and hotel personnel.

The spiky-haired, blonde bartender stationed behind the back bar counter whispered something to Carla as she returned to the station. The two of them leaned together acting as though they were discretely listening. A tattoo or birthmark showed above the collar of the strange barkeep's uniform.

The female at the table jerked to a stand. Clearly, she didn't care she caused a scene. She snatched her bag. "How could you do this to me? I've done everything to help ensure your success. I've been totally devoted to you, and you're leaving me . . . deserting me like this. I will never forgive you." Her arms flailed as she spit out the words. "I don't know why I'm in this miserable, hick town. I could've met you in Nashville. That is, if you ever finish with your monkey business here." Obviously, this was not her choice of places to be. "I'm going for a swim. Stay far away from me."

Charli and Eli walked toward the exit. With a sharp turn she whizzed past like a whirlwind, and then sped through the hotel lobby to disappear along a hallway.

Eli put a hand to Charli's back. "Geez, that guy sure knows how to pick them."

Charli giggled. "Hope he's a good tipper."

CHAPTER TWO

Feet curled beneath her jean-clad bottom, Irma Owens threw her arms in the air and cheered uninhibitedly. The cardinal on the red sweatshirt bobbed up and down as her breasts rose and fell in excitement. Her grandson passed his first ever touchdown scoring ball as the rookie quarterback for Louisville university. The red and white clad receiver stepped across the line into the endzone.

"That's my boy!" She beamed at her companion perched on the sectional sofa.

Sam Baker grabbed the bucket of popcorn between them to keep it from toppling to the floor and shot her a glowing grin on his pleasant, chubby face. "That boy has talent."

The doorbell interrupted their celebration. She sat her beer bottle on the coffee table and padded barefooted to the door. Opening it, she gasped. Her throat tightened, blocking the air.

Before her stood the one person who had haunted her dreams, ruined her for other men, and hurt her more than anyone else ever had. Her mouth eased open, and her forehead edged into a frown.

The handsome, silver-haired man wore a wry smile. *Of course, he did.*

His voice flowed robustly, like golden, honeyed Kentucky bourbon from perfectly-formed, luscious lips that had once granted such pleasure she had never found a replacement for them.

Her heart reacted as though they'd only parted as lovers yesterday—not forty-something years ago. The body knew what the mind had blocked. Sensory reactions were beyond her control. Her heart sang the song of passion she'd written only for him when she'd believed he'd loved her as she still loved him. In those days, she'd sang every day.

No more.

He snickered, clearly amused at her shock. "You going to stand there like I appeared from my grave? Or you going to let me in?" That deep, sensuous melody coated the scars on her soul, like balm on gnawing wounds.

She let the healing happen, glad for it and smiled. Gaining control of her senses, she chuckled. "Of course," stepping back to make way for her unexpected guest. "Get that sweet ass of yours in here." It was probably a mistake, but she would never turn him away.

What the hell?

She was a sucker for this guy. Unfortunately, he knew it.

Guffawing like it had only been days—not years— many, many years—since she'd laid eyes on him anywhere other than in the pages of a magazine, he stepped into her domain. A clearing of a male throat behind her reminded Irma she was not alone with the love of her life.

She turned. Her original invited guest stood and slipped into his shoes before walking toward them at the entryway. The shorter man's hand stretched to the newcomer.

She waved toward the handsome male who had just arrived. "Sam, I'd like you to meet Wesley Drake. Wesley and I worked together when I was in show business."

The two men shook heartily. Each surveyed the other up and down like two stallions with a mare in heat at stake.

Her lips twisted at the humor of it. Then she took control of the situation again. "Wes, this is my dear friend, Dr. Sam Baker. Sam is our county's coroner. We were watching my grandson, Kyler's first football game of the season. He's a freshman and their second-string quarterback. He just scored a touchdown."

Wes winked, as though they shared a secret.

If only he knew . . . Nope, never mind.

He glanced at the big-screen television mounted over the fireplace that Sam had put on 'pause.' "You must be very proud."

She couldn't help but compare the men physically. Tall, stylish, and handsome, Wes stole her breath away. Sam's five-foot-four frame sported a round belly not hidden by bagginess of his red sweatshirt and comfort-fitting jeans.

Wes's thick, silver-trimmed dark hair contrasted with the ring of barely-there, grey that circled the sides and back of Sam's head.

Sam was sweet, affectionate, and attentive. She was comfortable with him and enjoyed his company. On the other hand, Wes' presence could make her heart sing, and he hadn't lost that power.

She inhaled deeply, powering her resolve to remain friendly . . . but not overly. "Extremely proud. I've always been in awe of both of my grandchildren."

Wes beamed, as though oblivious to his effect on her emotions. "I envy you the family you've built here in this lovely town. I haven't toured Sweetwater, but I like the quaintness of what I've seen so far."

Sam eyed her with an unspoken question then slid a comforting hand down her arm. He knew her well, and she could tell he sensed the change in her Wes's arrival caused. "It looks like you and Mr. Drake need alone time to catch up. I've got work at the office. I'll get out of your hair." He bent toward her and planted a soft kiss on her lips. "Talk tomorrow. Okay."

"Oh, Sam, I hate for you to leave without catching the rest of the game. You're welcome to stay."

"Yes," Wesley interrupted. "I had no intention of running off Starr's company. Please, stick around, Dr. Baker." To the untrained ear, his words sounded sincere.

Knowing him better than he probably knew himself, Irma was aware Wes's tenor didn't back up his words. He obviously wanted to be alone with her.

What the heck?

She couldn't have dreamed this nightmare up had she still been drugging on LSD, or whatever was handy at the time. The good old days—*yeah, right. Not!*

"No really. It's okay." Sam stepped around her and opened the door. "No worries, Sweetie. I'll see you soon."

She held the door for him. "Of course." She gave him a peck on the cheek.

His chubby hand touched hers as he exited, an understanding smile on his lips. "Alrighty, then." The lock clicked shut behind him.

Wes seemed to study her face. "I'm sorry about that. I had hoped to catch you at home, but I didn't mean to screw up your date."

Shaking her head with an eye roll, she turned and walked to the sofa. She snatched the bowl of popcorn and walked it to the bar. "You want a beer?"

At his nod, she pulled two icy brews from the fridge, popped the tops, and sat one in front of a barstool. He accepted the amber bottle with a hand that sported a bandaged finger and sat at the stool she indicated. Navy blue slacks of his silk suit concealed long, slim legs. Black Italian leather shoes gleamed as he perched them on the footrail.

Her fingers itched to unbutton the ocean-blue oxford dress shirt draped casually across his rippling chest and flat abdomen, its top three buttons opened. The sight of him took her breath away.

"To what do I owe this personal appearance? Sweetwater, Kentucky isn't exactly on your celebrity circuit." Taking a long swig of beer, she ambled slowly around the island and sat in the barstool beside him, feeling every bit like a lioness wary of her prey. Was he the prey? Or was she?

He smiled guilelessly. "I'm here to see you. I owe you an apology, long overdue."

Bottle poised, neck pointed in his direction, she cocked one brow and glared. "You think?"

He chuckled. "You never were one to mince words. Your plucky moxie is part of why I loved you."

Easy with the words there, big boy. My heart might believe you mean them.

Pursed lips blew air out, turning her head away then back. "You had a funny way of showing it. Exactly what are you apologizing for?"

Staring at the floor, he heaved a sigh then met her eyes. "I ended things between us badly. It was a huge misunderstanding. I jumped to conclusions and gave you no opportunity to explain. I'm sorry for my actions and for hurting you. There is no excuse. I don't expect you to forgive me. I just wanted you to know. I've come to realize I did it because of my own issues, not because of you. It took me many years of making worse mistakes; repeating a misguided cycle of self-destruction; and spending a fortune on divorces, alimony, and therapy, to figure out I can't fix my own life unless I at least tell you how sorry I am for hurting you—for everything."

Shockwave.

"You know I didn't sleep with Jimi that night."

What had happened to the selfish, short-sighted man she'd loved? The Wes who'd left her sobbing in a New Jersey parking lot in August of 1970 wouldn't be caught dead admitting to being mistaken. He certainly wouldn't apologize.

Wes touched the side of his nose with the bandaged digit. "Yeah, I got that when I ran into him at a concert a couple of months later. He strutted up to me and, without a word of warning, clocked me one that broke my nose and knocked me on my ass. Then he proceeded to tell me what an asshole I was. No. I believe it was *M . . . F . . . er* to be exact. He explained you'd been ill and had spent the night in his bed . . . alone. He even asked me where the hell I was while my woman was sick as a "Songbird in a cat's bed," were his exact words."

She chuckled at the image, stood, and collected their empties, then went for another round from the refrigerator. "Wish I'd seen that. He never told me about it."

As she returned to her stool, she took a sip. "He and I only had that one short fling at Woodstock. '*Free love*,' peace, drugs, and rock and roll. You know how it was. I stopped drugging after that wild trip, but we remained the best of friends. He always had my back . . . like a brother." That familiar ache always hit when she thought about and missed her wild, crazy but loyal, loving friend.

A slight nod and he smiled. "Yeah, I knew it. Guess I was always a bit jealous of your close relationship . . . especially knowing you'd bumped uglies together."

His scent too close for comfort, drifted the distance to her nostrils. Raw, earthy sandalwood and a dash fresh ocean breeze hinted at the man who enjoys finer things in life. With eyes closed she envisioned windows thrown open, bluegrass beginning to thrive in the meadow and blossoms renewed after a fresh spring rain. It was intoxicating, and she basked in it.

She laid a hand over his broad one on the countertop. Cool to the touch but oh, so familiar in hers. "You had no need to be. I was blind, stupid in love with you and faithful until the day you tossed me to the curb without a backward glance."

He winced at the barb and bent his head. "I know that now. You were my first experience with a serious romance—of any kind. It frightened the hell out of me. I didn't see it then. Looking back, experience had already taught me all good things come to an end. So, I jumped at the chance to finish it on my own terms, instead of waiting for the inevitable."

She eyed him over her nose. "Because your mother dropped you off at the fire station and left you to be raised by the system?"

A weak, grateful, closed-mouthed smile met her glance. "Something like that. You would've made a good therapist, you know."

"Oh, really?" She cocked her head. "Maybe, but I was just so damned talented and determined to become a rock 'n roll legend." Her laugh must've been contagious.

He joined her, seeming to come out of momentary despair her comment and his reminiscing had caused. "That you were, my sweet-assed Starr Bright. That you were. Still are." He squeezed her hand and let go.

They sat like that for a few minutes, tempering sizzling emotions, quietly sipping cool drinks. She broke the silence separating them. "I understand how you misread the situation. I only wish you'd given me a chance to explain."

Their eyes met. She recognized raw honesty and something else in them. *Pain? Remorse? Hope?* Wishful thinking on her part.

She shrugged. "Jimi found me upchucking in a trash can backstage after my performance. I was supposed to drive to the city and stay a couple of days with my assistant friend, Esi Baxter; but I was too sick to drive that far. He and the boys were heading out for a round of afterparties, so he offered me his bus bed." She paused for a refreshing sip. "I only meant to lie down for a little while until the nausea passed. I got comfy in that big, black satin waterbed. Next thing I knew, the sun was up. The smell of coffee brewing drew me to the living quarters. I helped myself to a cup. The guys were sprawled about on every possible surface in different stages of zombie-ism. There was no place to sit. Jimi was lying on the sofa, so he moved his feet to accommodate me."

"I'll never forget that scene. When I arrived with his new tour contract, there you were, wearing his tee shirt, his face covering your titties. Those bare, silky legs of yours were crossed beneath you; and his big, bare feet plopped possessively in your lap. You still smacked of sleep, and your jet-black hair was haphazardly piled in a messy bun on top of your head. God, I loved that shiny mop of ebony that fell all the way to your luscious ass." He paused.

She didn't dare interrupt his interpretation of that day. A twinge of heat nestled in her groin at his tone as he spoke about her, stirring an instant contraction.

She shoved that baby back into hiding where it belonged. This man was pure torture to her libido. As much as she wanted him, always had; she couldn't afford the indulgence. It had proved nearly fatal in the past and had changed the course of her life.

Shaking his head, he avoided her gaze. "It was such an intimate scene. I let that green-eyed monster take control. I just couldn't handle it." He heaved a heavy exhale. "I didn't realize it at the time, but it was probably the precise situation I'd been expecting. I didn't admit it to myself, but I'd always assumed at some point you would desert me. No one could love me enough to stick around. Not my ma. Not even you. So, I took the easy way out. I'm sorry I did." His eyes lifted to meet hers.

Was he sorry for his treatment of her or for himself and the loss? The tug came as those beautiful pale green eyes pulled her in, like they always had. It seemed they could reach inside her to her very core and coax her soul to surrender to him.

She let it happen, let the connection between them struggle free of ties she'd bound it with and uncover itself from the depths it had been buried in for so long. Love for this man filled her being with joy. Her heart swelled, and she relished the sensation she'd deprived herself of for decades. Her lids closed, savoring the vision in her mind. Surely, partaking of a fantasy could do no harm. *Or could it?*

With an exhale, a breath of reality reminded her he was only here for redemption—not to pacify her addiction to him. His confession had nothing to do with her. It was about him, liberating himself from guilt.

She looked him in the eyes, trying not to become mesmerized by them the way she had been in the past. "No worries. I forgave you many years ago. It wasn't worth the effort to continue hating you."

Surprise showed on his handsome face. "Oh?" Didn't he realize he'd had such power over her?

Apparently, he still did. She nodded nonchalantly, forcing her face not to reveal turmoil her insides were in. "Yes, hating you was only hurting me—not you. It was like drinking poison and expecting you to die from it."

His head tilted in affirmation. He took a few minutes, likely rolling that notion around in his brilliant brain. His smile warmed with what appeared to be understanding. "You're much wiser than I. Always have been. I didn't deserve your forgiveness."

Truer words had never been spoken. *No matter.* She wouldn't grant him the knowledge of how difficult it had been to release the torture he'd put her through. His apology didn't justify revealing that.

"No, you didn't; but I did." Her mouth quirked to the side. "That was the past. It's over. I'm glad to see you're getting your life in order. That is what this visit is about, right? You're looking for redemption of some sort?"

He probably had a long list of females he'd offended in the past that he was apologizing to. Was he working some sort of AAA-type of program?

He snickered. "I'm not so sure about that. I've really screwed the pooch, so to speak."

Undoubtedly. She gave him a friendly smile. "At least you had the guts to try. You moved on with your life. I read that you married not long after we . . . broke up. I tried to be happy for you when I saw your engagement and then wedding photos posted in the industry rags." *Tried* being the operative word.

He glanced away as he began, "Thank you for that." His gaze returned to her. "You know, I heard rumors that you'd found someone, too. Some said you and your new fella were expecting, but on television it didn't show."

Good. He had bought the idea that she moved on quickly to another lover after he left her hanging.

She scoffed. "Yes, Gloria, my dresser was a genius at designing stage costumes to hide my baby bump. Styles then were full, mini-dresses, which made it easy."

"I'm very impressed. How on earth did you manage to raise a kid while constantly on tour? It must've been difficult." He seemed to study her face.

"Not really. A nanny traveled with us. Between me, the nanny, and my assistant, Esi, I had all the help I needed. The guys in the band were awesome with Tucker. It was a boy, you know. I think my son helped them not miss so much, their own children back home with their wives and girlfriends. Tucker was a sweet, well-mannered child. I loved having him with me."

"I envy you that. I never had children of my own." His mouth quirked up and down, hinting that he might regret that decision now that he was older.

CHAPTER THREE

Wes stood. "I've done what I came for and screwed up your day too much already. I'd best be getting back to my hotel. I've got work to do before we move on to Nashville."

"We?" Irma asked, gathering their empty bottles.

"Yes, my assistant travels with me. We're on our way to Nashville to get a tour contract signed by one of my agency's country singers." He dropped the name of a well-known celebrity Irma wrote a couple of songs for in the past few years.

Did he know that? Probably.

He pulled a phone from his jacket. "I'll call a ride share."

"You don't have a car?" She dropped the empties into the trash.

"I do, but I left it for my assistant. She's rather peeved at me right now."

"Oh?" Her brows shot up. *Lover's quarrel?*

His lips pursed. "Yes, I broke the news to her that I'm retiring. She just signed a contract to purchase her condo and recently bought her first car."

She chuckled. "First car? How old is this little flame of yours?" Did she sound snarky? Oh well. He'd deal.

He laughed. "You know how it is. Living in New York, having a car is expensive. Not only do you have the usual expenses, but you needed a conveniently located place to park it. That costs an arm and a leg. I have no idea why she wanted one. Driving is a headache in the city. It's a waste of money and time, if you ask me."

"But why is she mad?"

"She went on a rampage about me deserting her when she has all these new obligations. She's under a lot of stress right now. I think it has something to do with her mom, too. She's losing it—dementia, you know. She and her sister are footing the bill to cover care for Mom."

"A facility?" That would be outrageously expensive, especially in New York City.

"No, I think she lives with the sister. She works from home." He frowned. "It's that, her new mortgage that she's not used to yet, and the vehicle expenses. She jumped to the conclusion that she'll be out of a job when I retire. That's ridiculous. If I sell the company, and if she doesn't want to stay on, I plan to give her several years of salary as a parting bonus. That should give her plenty of time to find another job. I could help with that. She's a devoted, excellent assistant; and I couldn't have done what I have with the agency if it weren't for her. If the new owners don't keep her on, they would be losing an extremely valuable asset. It would be a tremendous loss."

"Doesn't she understand all that?"

"She will . . . eventually. She didn't give me the chance to explain."

Irma marched to the counter and picked up her keys. "No worries about a ride. I'll take you to your hotel. I assume you're at the Sweetwater Hotel. It's the best in town."

"Starr, you don't have to do that. I can call a ride."

"Nope, and it's Irma these days. I'm no longer Starr Bright of the Terrestrials. Just plain old Irma Owens."

"Damn, woman, you could never be plain old anything." He winked and followed her to her garage.

CHAPTER FOUR

His eyes widened at the sight and scanned the sleek design of her baby blue 1957 Ford Thunderbird with awe. "Wow, this is some ride. Did you know this was the final model of the original two-seater sports car? The Corvette was popular back then, but this baby was a serious rival." He examined shiny chrome around the removable hardtop, porthole window, and a distinctive rear bumper with integrated exhaust tips. "What's she carrying under the hood?"

She climbed into the driver's seat. He shut the door, rounded the rear, and climbed in next to her. Satisfaction filled her lungs as he stroked the luxuriously soft, two-toned blue and white, leather seat.

She held the door, grateful to have segued into a more comfortable subject. "Yes, it's the rare E-code version with dual four-barrel carburetors. They say the 270 horsepower produces a top speed of one-hundred miles per hour. I've personally had it at one-thirty. Lord only knows what it would top at."

He chuckled, as she roared the engine. "You always did have a lead foot." He stroked the padded dash with admiration. "Nice."

She pulled out of the garage onto and made her way toward the town center. "Thanks. It's my one great indulgence. If a girl's got to drive, she needs a set of fantastic wheels. Check it out. The Dial-o-Matic power seats adjust automatically when the ignition is turned on or off."

"Awesome. This car is a highly sought-after classic. I'll bet it would go for . . ." He rubbed the side of his nose. "I don't know. Maybe fifty-thou?"

She glanced to the side at him. "Try seventy-five . . . in this condition and these options. I wouldn't sell her for a hundred thousand."

He beamed "I don't blame you. Well done."

His admiration did nothing to help ease Irma's anxiety. She was torn between dragging Wesley to his hotel room for a heated afternoon of sheer passion and the knowledge that such an encounter with him would destroy her.

Chatter between them on the short ride was easy, regardless of her nerves. She and Wes had never had issues talking about anything and everything—except for one thing.

A short ride later they'd entered the center of town. Irma drove them along a street several blocks long where they passed on the right a couple of banks dueling it out on opposite corners, a real estate company housed on the next corner, facing another bank, then the sheriff's office and jail just before the end of the street did a U-turn at a four-story, red, brick courthouse boasting it had taken up residence in 1862, well before the Civil War.

The lane rounded the end, and they came to the other side. The center park housed immaculately kept grounds, tree shaded benches where people read books, newspapers or their phones. A statuesque water fountain in the park's middle, characterized some historical figure in bronze. A round, wooden gazebo gave the appearance of a lacy crown and held benches around the railing of its interior. People milled about. Some chatted. Others rested on one of the many seats. An elderly lady led a white poodle at the end of her leash.

Brick buildings were a mixture of circa 1900 and modern-day construction. The vast number of them from the former.

They passed a retro, turquoise and white tiled front theatre, capped with an old-fashioned marquee featuring one of the latest movies he'd seen advertised. To either side of the center ticket window were heavy, ornate double doors flanked to the outside with large glass-enclosed posters advertising films that were 'Coming Soon.'

"This town is so quaint. It looks like a scene out of an old Jimmy Stewart movie."

She chuckled deeply. "It sort of is. I love it here. To me, it's just home." They rounded a corner, and his hotel came into view. She pulled the car into the lot and parked.

He turned to her. "How about a drink? I could use a bourbon."

Was he anxious to get her alone too?

"There's a nice lounge in the hotel." *It should be fine. I can't get into too much trouble there. Right?* Surely, she could control her inner impulses. She'd managed to do so for many a year so far. Besides, she could use a strong drink about now. "You can have your liquor. I'll have an iced tea." *Better safe than sorry.*

She walked him inside, not wanting to part with Wes. Tomorrow, he and his assistant would be on the road to

Tennessee and then who knew where. It might be her last opportunity to spend with Wes.

Sheriff Wyatt Gordon's truck was parked at the curb, and behind it two others were nearby. "That's odd."

As they entered the hotel, the desk clerk nodded toward the door, and the sheriff walked from there to the center of the lobby where he met up with Irma and Wes. "Wyatt, what on earth is going on?"

Wyatt cleared his throat, standing as tall as Wes, and eyed her curiously. "I'm surprised to see you here . . . in this situation." He turned to Wes. "Howard at the desk told me you are Wesley Drake." Surprisingly, Wyatt didn't extend a hand for a shake.

Wes's voice held a guarded tone. "I am. Is there some issue?"

Wyatt stared at Wes without expressing what was on his mind. "I'm afraid there is. I understand you're traveling with a woman."

Wes nodded cautiously. "Yes, my assistant, Tara Bonner, is accompanying me. We're on a business trip. Is Tara okay? Did something happen to her?"

Wyatt's expression didn't change. "What business do you have in Sweetwater?"

Wes cleared his throat. "Actually, my business is in Nashville. We're on our way there."

Wyatt continued to glare. "You rented a car in Louisville. Why didn't you fly directly to Nashville from New York?"

Wes grew agitated. "I don't see as how that's any of your concern, but I wanted to stop by here and visit my old friend." He looked at Irma with an attempt at a grin that looked more like a plea for support. He was clearly confused.

Irma intervened, "Yes, Wyatt, Wesley and I are friends from when I was a touring singer. We had a nice, little visit."

One of Wyatt's brows lifted. "It seems a drastic detour for a couple of hours to drop in on a friend."

Wesley's growl showed his frustration. "Listen, Sheriff, I don't know what's going on here but I'm beginning to resent this rude interrogation."

Wyatt grunted. "Mr. Drake, I assure you, you'll know it when I interrogate you."

Irma gushed out a breath, shaking her head and looking up. Her gaze met Wyatt's. "Wyatt Gordon, what the hell is going on here?" The two of them had been friends since she was a teenager, and Wyatt was the toddler son of a past sheriff.

Wyatt snickered at her outburst. "I apologize, Irma." Turning to Wes, his expression wasn't as remorseful. "Mr. Drake, I regret to inform you that your assistant has been found dead in your room."

Wes's brows froze together, and it was clear he held back tears. "Tara's dead? But how? What happened to her?"

Wyatt's stone-face expression was familiar. Irma had worked with him before on cases. It was his lawman gaze—one that gave nothing away he didn't want you to know and hid his personal emotions. "The front desk tells me she stopped by after a swim and requested that a maid bring fresh towels to the room in a couple of hours. Later when the maid service arrived, there was no response to the knock. She let herself in. Finding Ms. Bonner in bed, she told her she'd placed the towels in the bathroom. When no response came, she walked closer to the bed and touched Ms. Bonner's foot through the sheet. Again, she spoke, but there was no response. She moved closer and felt no breath. The maid rushed to the desk and reported the incident."

Irma's jaws dropped. Her mouth flew open, and her tented eyebrows. "That poor woman." Poor Wes, he obviously cared for this woman. "What happened, Wyatt? Did she have a heart attack in her sleep?" She turned to Wes. "Was Tara sick?"

A grimace on Wes's face showed his perplexed state. "No! I mean, I don't think so. Tara was very active. Far as I know, she's in great physical shape. What happened to her, Sheriff Gordon?"

Wyatt kept his stone face. "I'm hoping you can shed light on that. I'm afraid we're going to need you at our office for questioning." He spoke into the com attached to his shirt. "Jaiden, can you join me in the lobby?"

Seconds later, Deputy Jaiden Coldwater entered from the first-floor hallway. The exotic half-Irish, half-Choctaw woman stood shoulder high to the tall sheriff. Her thick, raven hair rested in a bun at the back of her head.

She looked up at Wyatt. "Hotel employees, except for Howard and Ralph, are waiting for questioning in the dining room. I've assigned a team of deputies to take their statements. Leo and I questioned Howard and Ralph. Leo is in the bar questioning guests who were staying in rooms along the crime scene hallway. Howard and Ralph are arranging to move those people to other accommodations."

Wyatt nodded. "Thanks. This is Wesley Drake. Please, take Mr. Drake to the precinct and make him comfortable.

I'll be right there once I do a run through to make sure everything is in order here."

Irma's words shot out, "Crime scene? What in the blazes?"

Wes's voice sounded desperate. "Who would want to harm Tara?"

"We're hoping you can help with that." Wyatt gazed from Wes to Jaiden with a head nod.

Jaiden stepped forward and put a hand on Wesley's forearm. "Would you please come with me?" She urged him toward the door.

"Do I need a lawyer?" His stare moved from Jaiden, to Wyatt, to Irma.

Irma gasped. "Wes, don't say anything until your lawyer gets there."

"My attorney is in New York and specializes in corporate law. I don't know anyone licensed to practice in Kentucky or versed in criminal law."

Irma winked, hoping to bolster his spirits that clearly had hit rock bottom. "No worries. I will call Carlton Farmer. He and his partner handled many high-level criminal cases in Boston. They moved their practice here to be near family. They're the best of the best."

Wes's nose curled up. "From Boston? That must've been an impressive firm. Why would he leave it so his partner could be closer to family?"

Irma's head tilted. "Sorry, Carlton's partner is also his husband."

Wes gave her an open-mouthed nod as he allowed Jaiden to nudge him through the exit doors. Wyatt excused himself and strode toward the barroom. Irma whipped her phone out, found the contact number and hit SEND.

"Carlton, it's Irma Owens. I have a friend who needs your help." She gave him the specifics and agreed to meet him at the sheriff's office.

CHAPTER FIVE

Irma met Carlton at the sheriff's office. After she briefed him on everything she knew so far, he spoke with Jaiden. "I'll escort you to the room where Mr. Drake is waiting. Can I get you all some waters or a soda?" "Can I go too?" Irma was desperate to see how Wes was holding up.

"No." Carlton took her hand. "It's best that you remain here. I need to talk with Mr. Drake alone first." He glanced at Jaiden and back. "Irma, it's likely they are going to need a statement from you as well."

It hadn't occurred to her, but since she was the reason for their visit to Sweetwater, it made sense. "You will represent me. Won't you?"

Carlton nodded. "Of course, unless there's a conflict. We don't know if you need representation at this point. Let's find out what's happening and take it one step at a time."

Carlton and Jaiden moved along a short hallway and through a door. It closed behind them. Moments later, Jaiden reappeared, leaving Carlton with Wesley in the closed room. She strode to where Irma stood waiting. "How about we get your statement while we wait? Sheriff Gordon will be here in a few minutes, and he'll want to talk with Mr. Drake."

She showed Irma to her desk and waived her to the chair beside it. Pulling up her computer to a form, she smiled at Irma and asked her for her personal information. "Tell me everything you can about your relationship with Mr. Drake and Ms. Bonner."

"I have never met Ms. Bonner, though Mr. Drake . . . Wes told me she was an excellent, dedicated assistant and had worked for him for several years. She travels with him as he meets with clients around the globe. He is a co-owner of a very large entertainment agency. When I began my singing career, Wes was my agent until the early 1970s. We had a falling out, and I switched agencies."

Jaiden typed as Irma spoke and gazed at her as she stopped. "Tell me about this falling out."

Irma sighed. She might as well be forthcoming. It would come out one way or another. "Wes and I were lovers. We had a lover's spat and broke up. He went one way. I went the other. I dropped him as my agent." She winced. "It doesn't pay to mix personal and business."

Jaiden frowned. "What contact did you have with Mr. Drake between this breakup and now?"

"Let's see . . . not much. He brought his wife to one of my shows back in the 80s. I'm sorry. I don't recall the date. It was in London. They were in town visiting friends. His wife had told him she was a fan and wanted to meet me. Honestly, I don't think that was the case. He brought her to my dressing room after the concert and introduced us. She was polite but distracted and left quickly to ensure they didn't miss a late dinner planned with their friends. Wesley was apologetic and nice. It was good to see him doing well."

"So, Mr. Drake is married."

"I don't believe so. He has been married . . . several times. I'm not clear on his marital status now, but I got the feeling he is single."

Jaiden's brows rose. "Why? Did he hit on you?"

Irma rolled her eyes. "One could only wish." She chuckled.

Jaiden laughed along. "Ah, you still have a thing for Mr. Drake."

Irma shook her head. "Let's just say, he's the one that got away. But no. Mr. Drake and I have nothing going on currently and nothing in the works."

Jaiden snickered. "He's a very handsome man. I wouldn't blame you if you were hot on his trail."

"Well, sweetheart, I'm too old to chase men. I've been burned before and have no expectations a white knight is going to ride his hearty steed into my stable—not at this age."

"Ah, Irma, you're a very attractive, vivacious female. Don't give up the ghost just yet."

"Honey, I'm the same age as your gorgeous mother. Would you give that same advice to Brightleaf?"

Brightleaf Coldwater was an older, silver-haired version of Jaiden. Ater her husband's death, she retired her Texan veterinarian hospital and moved to Kentucky to be near her son. As Calvin Coldwater's Navy Seal career ended, he became a racehorse trainer at Land's End Farm.

Jaiden chuckled. "It wouldn't be such a bad thing for Mom to find another man. I sometimes think she's lonely."

Irma snickered. "I don't know. She's pretty active. We play cards once a week. She's involved in activities at church and comes to the same water aerobics class I do. I think she helps Rose out at Parsley, Sage, Rose, Mary &

Wine farm sometimes. I know she's hoping Rose and Cal will produce a grandchild for her to spoil sometime soon. I wouldn't worry about your mama, honey."

Irma and Brightleaf belonged to the same poker group. Truth be known, it was the source of most of the Sweetwater grapevine, that originated gossip that circled the town. They meant no harm, only looking out for their neighbors, often helping before it was requested. Some called it meddling. Others referred to it as southern hospitality.

Rose and Cal had been married for a few years, soon after he moved to Sweetwater. She was a partner with Sheriff Gordon's wife Lemon Sage, who owned the organic farm, Parsley, Sage, Rose, Mary & Wine. Rose was a purple-haired mystery to most residents, but she'd struck up a strong relationship with Sage when she'd first arrived from New York, and it had morphed into a strong bond.

Jaiden pulled them back to the subject at hand. "So, how long did Mr. Drake intend to stay in Sweetwater?"

Irma shook her head. "I have no idea. I assumed they'd be moving on by tomorrow. He didn't speak of anything that might keep them here."

"Were you aware they were coming?" Jaiden stared blankly.

"No, not at all. I just opened the door, and there he was."

"The purpose of his visit? Did he want you to reignite your singing career? Did he attempt to renew your love affair? Was it personal or business?"

Irma's shoulders lifted. "It seemed personal, but no. He didn't want any of that. He said he came to apologize for the way he acted when we split up. He wasn't asking for forgiveness and only wanted to make amends."

Jaiden's head rocked up . "How did you react?"

Irma scoffed. "I forgave him years ago. I didn't see the point of holding a grudge. Yes, he acted unreasonably at the time. I'm sure he had his reasons. Whatever they were, it was what it was. I couldn't stay angry with him. I needed to give it up and go on with my life."

Jaiden. "That doesn't completely answer my question."

Irma thought a second. "I was happy to see him and invited him in. We talked. Wes apologized. It was good. He said he and his assistant were driving to Nashville to get a contract signed, so I assumed they'd leave right away, at least by tomorrow. He'd taken a ride-share to my house and left their vehicle for Ms. Bonner, so I gave him a lift back here. I only came inside because he invited me to the bar for a drink."

Wyatt arrived. He went into his office and dropped his cap on the desk. Returning to the bullpen, he worked his way to Jaiden's desk.

The deputy eyed her boss. "I've taken Irma's statement. Mr. Drake's attorney, Carlton Farmer, is with him now."

"Good, thanks." He stepped behind her and read what Jaiden had captured on the screen. To Irma, "Look, I'm going to interrogate Mr. Drake."

"Can I be with Wes while you question him?" It was a longshot, but Irma had to try.

"I'm afraid not, Irma. Only his attorney can be there." He turned to Jaiden. "You're observing, right?" With Jaiden's nod he turned back to Irma. "Join Jaiden in the observation room, if you wish."

Relief flooded Irma's chest with air. "Oh, gosh, Wyatt, thanks. That would be great." She hadn't hoped for such a concession. Apparently, Wyatt wanted her to listen in. Perhaps he thought it might spur more to come from her.

She followed the two officers. Jaiden opened the first door on the left, and Wyatt entered the second. She settled into a chair beside Jaiden facing the one-way mirror. On the other side, Wyatt's back was to them. A metal table separated him from an exhausted-looking Wesley and his all-business, red-headed lawyer. He explained their talk would be recorded and pushed a button on a machine on the desk. He recited who was present and the reason for the discussion.

Wesley's stark expression made her heart bleed for him. Facial features visibly tightening, as he listened to what Wyatt had to say and braced himself with a hand against the table. Wyatt explained again the circumstances of how Tara Bonner's body was found.

"Have you notified her family?"

"We have not. What can you tell us about them?"

"She has a sister and mother in New York. Her mom is suffering from early onset Alzheimer's. After she got lost in her apartment building, the girls decided she shouldn't live alone. Tara's sister moved in with her. With Tara's traveling constantly for her job, it was best for everyone. Blakely works from home, so she can be with their mother most of the time. They have a paid care-giver that comes in when Blakely needs to be away for long."

"Do you have their contact information?"

"No, I'm afraid I don't. I'm sure they're in Tara's cell phone."

"We have that. Sage Gordon, our technical expert, is trying to access Ms. Bonner's cell phone."

Wes's brow crunched together. "Tara was very close to both of them."

"She is unmarried?"

"Yes, and there's no boyfriend at this time . . . far as I know." His face went stone white.

"Fine. We should have those numbers soon. Sage will then contact her next of kin."

Irma's icy hands trembled.

"I can't believe Tara's dead." The words quivered as they came out of Wesley's mouth. His eyes rolled upward. It was easy to see he was fighting tears. His quivering hand rested on his forehead, as though keeping it from toppling off his neck.

"I am sorry for your loss." Sincerity reinforced Wyatt's words. He might suspect Wes but still had compassion; and he wanted Wes to relax so he would cooperate.

"Was Tara Bonner ill?" Wyatt's brow crumpled as he handed Carlton and Wes water bottles.

Wes stared at the floor as if dazed. "No. Not that I know of. She never said anything."

"I assume the two of you were close, traveling and working together as much as you do. How long was Tara with you?" The underlying question being, had they been lovers?

Irma held her breath, wondering why she cared at the time. She had no tie to Wesley . . . not anymore.

Wes's eyes rolled upward. He answered without looking at the sheriff, "About ten years, and yes. We were close."

"How close?"

43

Carlton put a hand on Wes's arm. "You don't have to answer that."

Wes snickered humorlessly. "Not that close. We weren't intimate. I'm much too old for her." He paused, but the sheriff didn't take over. "What happened to Tara?"

Irma stroked her arm through her shirtsleeves, warding off the cold blood rushing through her veins. Why did she care? This man was nothing to her. *No. Really?*

Wyatt met his gaze. "A maid discovered her in her bed when she went in to deliver a towel request. There was no sign of struggle. It appeared she died in her sleep." He paused, as if gauging Wes's reaction.

Wes pushed out some air. "Damn, I should've checked on her."

Wyatt shrugged. "The coroner will do an autopsy. There were signs her death was not from natural causes. Dr. Baker doesn't like to speculate until he has more information. We've cordoned off that section of the hotel. Your room is directly across from Tara's, but she was in your room in your bed." Knowing Wyatt, he was studying Wes for a response that might indicate more than his words.

Wes nodded calmly—more calmly than she would've been in this situation. "Yes, we switched rooms shortly after checking in. I wasn't sure how long we'd be in Sweetwater, but Tara intended to spend more time in the hotel than I did. Tara would work from her room. Mine turned out to be much larger with a better view. I ran into her in the hallway. She was heading to the front desk to request a change of room. She explained, and I asked her if mine would meet her needs. She looked it over and agreed. We exchanged rooms."

"You didn't notify the hotel staff."

Wes closed his eyes and shook his head. "No, I'm afraid we didn't. I didn't see the need . . . at the time."

"Why are you in Sweetwater?"

Wes explained his intention for the visit, how he and Irma had met and chatted, and up to when he and Irma arrived at the hotel.

Wyatt's head tilted slightly. "Why, after all this time, did you suddenly show up at Irma's door?"

Wes sighed and bit his lips. "Well, after a lot of soul searching and therapy, I've learned a few things about myself. If I wanted to get on with my life without remorse, I needed to see Irma in person and to apologize for what happened between us. I didn't call ahead, because she might have refused to see me."

"Your visit turned out well?"

Wes nodded. "Yes, better than expected."

"And you plan to renew your love affair with Irma?"

Wes chuckled. "Sheriff, you're buying a horse before building a barn. Let's not get ahead of ourselves. I'm just grateful Irma didn't shut the door in my face."

Wyatt placed his hands on the table. "Who all do you and Ms. Bonner know in Sweetwater."

"No one, except for Irma, and Tara doesn't . . . didn't know her. Tara only knew I wanted to meet up with an old friend." He paused for a loud inhale and then exhaled. "I met Irma's friend Dr. Baker today. I understand he's the coroner. I hope he's good at his job." He paused and blinked his eyes. "Far as I know, Tara knew no one here."

"She knew you." Wyatt's head jerked slightly toward Wes.

Wes closed his eyes, tilted his head back and down again to open them. "Since I'm the only person in town who knows her, that makes me your prime suspect. Right?"

Wyatt's head slowly nodded. "It appears so. That corridor of the hotel has been ruled a crime scene. That includes your and Ms. Bonner's rooms. This means you won't have access to your things until we rule out foul play."

"Foul play?" Carlton bristled. "You think someone killed her. Could this be suicide? Let's not put the cart before the horse. She may have had some unknown, underlying condition that resulted in her death."

Wyatt shrugged to the side with a shoulder rise. "Maybe. I hope that was it . . . for her family's sake. There was no sign of struggle. Evidence of poisoning was visible. We won't know for sure until the coroner determines cause of death."

Helplessness settled into Irma's bones. There wasn't much she could do for Wes, except be there for him.

Wyatt continued, "So, you can't stay at the hotel."

"What about my things?"

"We're keeping your things."

"For how long?"

He shrugged. "That depends on what we find."

Wes sighed. "I suppose I should call the hotel and see if they can arrange another room for me."

Wyatt's head rocked sideways. "I don't believe they will welcome you there—not at this time."

Carlton looked at his client. "Let's not worry about that now."

Wyatt's voice was stern, even with his southern twang. "You are a Person of Interest. Wherever you stay, do not leave town. I'm not charging you with anything currently. I expect to know where you are and how we can contact you, should we need more from you." Wyatt stood.

Carlton shoved his seat back and rose to his feet. Wesley followed the two out of the room. Jaiden and Irma left the observation area and met the three men in the hallway.

Irma grabbed Wesley's arm. "Don't worry. You can stay with me. Kyler's room is empty. He's away at school. There's a desk you can use if you need to work." She couldn't leave him hanging without a place to stay when she could provide perfectly good accommodation.

He huffed a sigh. "I don't want to be a bother."

She put hands on her hips. "Nonsense. You're staying. That's all there is to it."

He sighed again and smiled sadly. His lips closed. "You always were a little spitfire. I know better than to argue with you." He stood and put his hands on her shoulders. "Thank you, Irma. Thank you for everything."

"Not necessary. Haven't you heard of Southern Hospitality?" She winked.

Could she resist him if he stayed at her home? Would it end in disaster?

CHAPTER SIX

The following morning, they sat at the bar in Irma's great room. Wes hung his cellphone up. "That was Wyatt Gordon." His hands fell. "I'd best give Blakely a ring. Sage found her number in Tara's phone and notified her of her sister's death, but she'll want to hear from me."

"Why don't you go to Kyler's room? You can use privacy for your call. I want you to make yourself at home while you're here." She watched him stroll slowly toward her grandson's bedroom to make the call he clearly hated to make. "Just holler if you need anything."

Compartmentalizing her own sentiments about the situation, she busied herself getting some things together for Wes. This was about him. He needed her. She would not let him down.

The evening before had been such a muddled mess, they'd both fallen immediately into bed from exhaustion. Now she had time, she must be a good hostess. A good hostess was always prepared. Her urgent need to take care of the man over-rode any angst she had about protecting herself.

She collected a couple of fresh, fluffy towels, wash rags, a small tube of toothpaste, a new toothbrush, a bar of soap, a bottle of aspirin, and one of melatonin. Her houseguest would likely have trouble sleeping. She tossed everything but the towels into a gift bag and carried them down the hallway.

At Kyler's door, she listened. No voices. She rapped gently.

"Come in," a bleak tone answered.

He sat in the darkened room at the foot of the bed. Blinds were drawn, giving it a sense of doom.

Stepping inside, she flipped the light on. Her chest tightened.

His head slumped into his hands. Elbows rested on his knees. He looked up, a grave expression on his face. She handed him the bag.

He glanced inside. "Thank you. That was thoughtful."

She laid the towels on the dresser and slid the closet door open. Pulling out a pair of slippers, she sat them at the foot of the bed and fished around inside. She retrieved a bathrobe and laid it on the cover. "These are Kyler's. They'll fit you. He's a scrawny young man, but he's tall like you. He won't mind if you use them. We might need to take a run to the store for underwear and socks, though. I'm sure you'd prefer new ones."

"Yeah, I guess, and maybe a couple changes of clothing."

"Maybe. I can wash your laundry, but who knows how long they'll keep your things. It wouldn't hurt to buy an outfit or two."

With a grim twist of the mouth, he stared expressionlessly out the window. "I promised to call Blakely back after we hear what the coroner says." His voice broke with nearly every word.

"Makes sense. Hey, why don't you tell me what you want. I can run out and buy you some things." He didn't appear to have the energy to go shopping. She couldn't blame him. Poor thing looked pitiful. She resisted the urge to lie down beside him, cradle his sturdy shoulders in her arms, and hold him. No one wants to make that kind of call, and he obviously cared about Tara.

He nodded. "Thank you, Irma. Can you get me a couple of shirts, a pair of jeans, socks, and underwear?" He told her his sizes.

"Sure. That should tide you over until yours are freed up." She folded the cash he pulled from his wallet and tucked it into her jeans pocket. "Why don't you take a nap while I run out and get these for you?"

"Thank you, Irma. I'll do just that."

With a thick lump in her throat, she closed the door behind him and went to do what little she could for her grieving friend. Clearly, Wes slept no better than she had.

When she returned, his phone lay on the island top. Shoulders drooped as he nursed the coffee she placed in front of him. She ached with concern for her old friend.

That was who he was. *Right?*

She'd explained the situation to her granddaughter the evening before. Charli was understanding and welcomed Wes into their home, though she was leery. One couldn't blame her. She'd barely met the man.

Charli appeared dressed in her work duds. "Good morning, Gran, Wes."

Irma handed her the coffee mug and thermos she'd prepared. Charli kissed her cheek. "Thanks, Gran. You know how to reach me. Eli and I will be working at the house all day. Are you sure you're okay here . . . you and . . . Wes?"

With Irma's nod, "I'm certain, dear. Don't worry."

Charli stepped to their guest. "I'm so sorry for your loss, Wes. I'm sure Gran told you, but you're welcome here if you need a place to stay. If there's anything I can do, let me know."

Gratitude filled Irma that her granddaughter trusted her judgement completely. That dear child had grown into an incredible young woman.

If anyone did, Charli understood the loss of loved ones. Her and Kyler's parents had died when she was only sixteen. The boy was six. Luckily the folks in this town took over when Irma was unable to be there.

Still, losing someone so close changed a person's life forever. Charli became an adult and assumed responsibilities far beyond those of a normal teenager. It had also turned the young woman into a compassionate and understanding person that Irma was exceedingly proud of.

"Thank you, Charli. I appreciate it." His words were barely audible.

Charli said goodbyes and left them alone in the house. Irma walked to the island and laid a hand on Wes' cool one.

His phone buzzed against the hard surface of the countertop. He turned it over to pick it up. The screen showed a familiar local number, as he put it to his ear.

"Hello, Sheriff." He paused, lips but a thin, tight line. Eyes darted toward the floor. "Yes, sure. I'll be there shortly." He clicked off and stood. "Sheriff Gordon wants to talk with me. I need to go to the precinct."

She poured the remainder of her coffee down the drain and rinsed her cup. "I'll drive you."

There was no need for him to be alone at a time like this. The police had impounded his rental car until they could finish processing it, in the event there was a crime involved. Tara Bonner had done most of the driving—all of it since they'd arrived in Sweetwater.

Irma snatched her keys and purse. "Let's go."

Wes didn't argue. He appeared to be in a daze.

CHAPTER SEVEN

Wes's hands shook, so he kept them down at his side as they entered the bullpen off the precinct's lobby. Among the desks, some empty, a couple of familiar faces looked up from their work.

Jaiden Coldwater sat typing at one beside a tall, redheaded deputy Wes recognized from the event the evening before. He hadn't met the young man, but he'd caught Wes's eye because he reminded him of a grownup Opie Taylor from the *Andy Griffith* television show.

Redheaded Carlton Farmer sat on the corner of Leo Sander's desktop sipping a cup of something steamy. Irma didn't find most men with red hair attractive. Carlton had an aristocratic air and manner that women were drawn to. He wasn't much older than Charli and didn't seem to notice female stares in his direction. He preferred the other sex and acted loyal to his husband. He was the best attorney she knew, and she was glad he'd taken this case.

The young lawyer nodded a greeting, stood and strode their direction. Leo with a head nod. Jaiden finger-waved to them.

To the other side of the bullpen, Wyatt spotted their entrance through his glass walled cubical. He stepped out and motioned them toward him. "We can chat in my office."

They followed the imposing sheriff inside and took the guest chairs he indicated. Carlton sat beside Wes to one side and Irma to the other. The tall, imposing sheriff seated himself behind an ancient metal desk, the kind that weigh a ton, built like a tank to last an eternity. Its laminate top was scarred from years of use. It seemed appropriate for the man behind it.

Wyatt tented broad hands in front of his slim stomach. Fortyish and drop-dead handsome, Wyatt's coal black mop of thick hair prematurely turned silver in his twenties and only enhanced his commanding features. Irma had known him his whole life, and had been great friends with the previous sheriff, his father, now retired to Boca Rotan.

She could tell; Wes wanted to get this over with, and his nerves couldn't take much more. He fidgeted with his hands in his lap. "Thanks for asking us in, Wyatt. I assume you've heard something about the autopsy by now. I need to know what had happened to Tara."

Wyatt's head rocked up and down without changing his grim expression. He touched a machine in the office. "I will be recording this conversation."

Wes and Irma's gaze met. They turned to Carlton. He nodded, and they returned attention to the sheriff. "Coroner Baker confirmed Ms. Bonner suffered multi-system organ failure during her sleep."

"What does that mean?" Irma leaned forward in her seat.

Carlton interrupted. "Did she have an underlying condition that caused it?"

"No. She died of poisoning." Wyatt's expression remained stern.

That shocker jilted Wes in his seat. His brow furrowed. "I don't understand. How? Did she overdose on a drug? Sleeping pills? Was it an accident? I can't believe she would do something so horrible intentionally. Tara would never have committed suicide."

The sheriff's chin lifted slightly. "It appears she was murdered."

Wes's head shot back, and his eyes narrowed. "Murder? I don't get it. How? I thought they found her in bed. You said nothing about a struggle. She wouldn't go down easily. Tara was a gutsy female."

The stately sheriff kept a blank expression. "Ms. Bonner died of arsenic poisoning."

Wes hesitated as though letting the idea roll around in his brain. "That's ridiculous. How could such a thing happen? I thought the sale of arsenic was outlawed years ago. Isn't it an illegal substance?"

Sheriff Gordon leaned back in his chair. "There is nothing illegal about having arsenic in your possession, though the EPA rules it as Number 1 on its Priority List of Hazardous Substances and classifies it as a Group A carcinogen. All forms of arsenic pose a serious risk to humans."

Irma wrung her hands in her lap. "How? Did Tara ingest it? Are you sure she didn't poison herself? How does one get ahold of arsenic anyway?"

Wyatt wasn't forthcoming with details. He seemed to lead them in a particular direction, trying to draw information from them without asking. "It has wide-ranging uses in many forms and for diverse purposes. Some animal species, like chickens for instance, require trace quantities of arsenic in their diets."

Irma expired a heavy breath, and her head rocked back in disbelief. "Did Tara eat chicken feed?"

Wes exhaled a huff of air. "Sheriff, what are you getting at? Clearly someone dosed Tara's food or drink with arsenic. Just tell us what the hell happened." He shook and acted impatiently.

Irma stroked his arm to calm him, a tactic that used to work. It didn't appear to.

Wyatt stared silently for a few minutes, clearly a pressure tactic. Irma's frazzled nerves were starting to get the better of her. She took a deep breath and exhaled. She needed to remain calm to support Wes. Wes clutched his hands in his lap as though keeping them from trembling. Irma curled her fingers around his wrist and caressed it with her thumb.

Finally, the sheriff broke the hush. "Tara Bonner expired from absorption of a lethal dose of arsenic through her skin."

Irma frowned. "That doesn't make sense. Are you saying something she put on her skin was tainted with poison—lotion, shampoo, body wash?"

"No." One shake of the sheriff's head was all they got.

Carlton asked, "How then?"

Wes's last bit of endurance gave way, and he shook her hand loose. "Damn it, Sheriff, what the hell is going on?"

Carlton's hand touched Wes's arm. Wes must've recalled his attorney's warning not to lose his temper. He'd cautioned them, it could lead to saying something one didn't mean.

Wes's shoulders relaxed backward. "We probably should've alerted the front desk we'd changed rooms. It didn't seem important. Is it relevant now? Was I the intended victim?"

Irma leaned forward. "Was the room tainted or was it in Tara's personal care items she brought along?"

Wyatt gave no indication of his opinion or the facts. "Mr. Drake, how long had Ms. Bonner worked for you? Tell me again, what was your relationship with her?"

Wes blinked a couple of times as though taking in all he was learning. "Tara came to work for me about ten years ago as my professional assistant. She kept my working life in order, traveled with me, and was indispensable to my business. We were on friendly terms, good friends one might say."

Wyatt nodded slowly. "I see. The two of you toured considerably together over a long period of time. You must have an intimate relationship."

Wes's head bolted upright out of his slump. "Listen here. We were intimate only in that we were close friends. Sometimes we discussed our personal lives, but we were *not* lovers. Not now. Not ever." He stressed the negative.

He looked toward Irma. "Please, don't get the wrong idea about me and Tara."

Her brows squinched together. Why did he care?

His head rocked side-to-side. "Tara was like a younger sister, more than ten years my junior. She had no interest in me as anything other than a friend and business associate. Neither did I."

Wyatt's chin rose a hair.

Irma sat up straighter. "Wyatt, are Wes and I suspect in this murder?" She wasn't one to beat around the bush.

Wyatt let out a breath. "You are persons of interest. Mr. Drake, you must understand. You are the only one in town who knew Tara Bonner. You were on intimate terms with her. She was murdered. That naturally makes you the prime suspect."

So, now he was more than a person-of-interest. He was suspected of murdering Tara. Irma clutched his forearm and gazed at Wyatt. "What about me?"

"Irma, you are a Person of Interest as well. You claim to not know Ms. Bonner. You and Mr. Drake had a fiery past. If you had dreams of rekindling your love affair with him you could've seen Tara Bonner as a threat to that end, giving you motive. On the other hand, you claim the two of you were once lovers and had an emotional breakup. You had no way of knowing Tara Bonner and Wesley Drake switched rooms. I'm not saying you had the opportunity. If you held a grudge against Mr. Drake, you might've had motive. I don't claim any of these scenarios is fact. We're investigating this crime at this point. These are things we must determine. I've brought you both in today to get answers that might help determine what happened. I am not ready to book anyone for this crime.

Irma shot to her feet. "Bull! Wyatt, you know me. I'm certain in your heart, you realize I could never do such a thing—whatever it was that done to this poor woman. Wes and I haven't been together for decades. That's a lifetime ago."

Wyatt looked amused. "Sit down, Irma. I'm only stating what could be seen as motive. There's nothing yet to indicate you had means."

Carlton calmly motioned her down with both hands. "Irma, Wes, can't you see, Sheriff Gordon is doing his job. He is looking for facts, motive, and opportunity; and he's trying to rile you so you will lose your cool. He shot Wyatt a glare, and the sheriff looked amused.

Relieved, she settled into her chair beside Wes. He patted her hand and winked when he caught her gaze.

Carlton stared at the sheriff. "Let's get to the point. Sheriff Gordon, by what means did the victim ingest the poison?'

Wyatt's met the redheaded attorney's gaze. "The county's CSI team found traces of arsenic on bedding, towels, and on an open bar of soap. Blood stains in the room did not match that of the victim. We need a sample from your client, to determine if it is his blood."

Wes groaned and expelled a breath. "I can tell you right now. That is my blood. No need for a needle." He held his bandaged hand up. "I cut myself on a spur on my suitcase roller bar. I opened the soap and washed my hands. Then I pulled a bandage out of a zipper pocket on my bag and stopped the bleeding. That bar of soap was fine when I used it. So was the hand towel I dried my hand on. I didn't ingest any poison."

Wyatt nodded. "I see. So, you were in the room long enough to contaminate remaining towels, soap, and the bed before you swapped rooms with Tara."

Wes snorted. "Why on earth would I do such a thing? After I wrapped my hand, I left the room to go for ice. I had no idea Tara would be dissatisfied with her room, and we would need to swap. Someone else must've put the arsenic there after we exchanged rooms."

Wyatt glared. "Who made the reservations?"

"Tara arranged for everything."

"The vehicle was rented in your name, but the rooms were charged to each of you separately." Wyatt's brow rose.

Wes exhaled loudly. "Yes, the rental agency's standard policy requires an individual name on the agreement. Tara took care of it at the airport using my company credit card. We each have our own for travel expenses like when we check into hotels. It makes expense accounting easier."

Carlton laid a hand on the table. "It sounds logical and reasonable to me."

Wyatt's only answer was a nod. "Witnesses at the hotel and several guests observed you and Ms. Bonner in a heated argument in the dining room over breakfast. You see. You have opportunity, means and motive. That's what the prosecutor needs for a murder conviction."

"See here, Wyatt." Carlton sat up straighter. "Everything you have against my client is circumstantial."

Wyatt snickered. "But very convincing. You see my dilemma?'

Wes shoved to the edge of his seat. "I can explain. I'd just informed Tara of my plans to retire." He clarified why she was argumentative, about her new debts, and her assumption she would be out of a job. "She jumped to the wrong conclusion. Tara has a short fuse. She was angry, frustrated, and refused to give me the opportunity to explain."

Where did I hear that before? This time Wes was on the losing end of that type of situation. Irma shook the irony off to focus on the issue.

He shifted in his seat tensely. "I planned to ensure her continued employment. Or, if she preferred, to help her seek a suitable role elsewhere. I intended to compensate her extremely well whichever way she decided to move forward. Tara just needed some cooling down time. She would've been reasonable and would've let me explain had this not happened. We would've gotten past it, like we've gotten past many business obstacles together—if we'd been given the opportunity."

♥♥♥♥

Damn it all. Wes wasn't even able to properly mourn the loss of one of his closest friends.

Jaiden stepped into the cubical with a tray and started handing out steaming cups. "I thought y'all could use some hot coffee." She placed a handful of stirrers, creamer and sugar packets in the center of the table.

Irma looked up at the pretty deputy. "Thank you, Jaiden." Irma took a deep breath and reached for one of the cups.

Jaiden walked from the room, and as she turned a shiny pair of cuffs caught Wes's eye. Would he wear a pair of those on his wrists?

CHAPTER EIGHT

Wyatt's phone rang, and he strode toward the door. "Excuse me. I must take this call." He flipped the recorder off, left the room and disappeared down the short hallway. He was gone for several minutes.

Relief to have it nearly over helped Irma's shoulders begin to relax. She leaned back into her chair.

The redheaded lawyer stared at Wes. "Wyatt is merely doing his job. It's nothing personal. Keep your cool. Answer only what he asks. I will warn you if he pursues a line of questioning you shouldn't answer."

Wyatt returned carrying a folder. He took his seat with a stone-faced expression and met her gaze. "Do you know, or have you met anyone else in Mr. Drake's company?"

She thought back, wanting to make sure she didn't falsely answer. "I don't think so. When Wes was my agent, he only had a secretary who worked at his office and an accountant to help with the books. I mostly worked directly with him. That was long ago, before he and his current partner grew the agency to its current size."

One of Wyatt's brows rose. "So, you don't know Mr. Drake's partner, Greyson Corbin, or his assistant, Simone Claiborne?"

Where did that come from?

Wyatt had done extensive research if he already knew Wes's people by name.

"I do not." His thoroughness shouldn't surprise her.

Wyatt leaned his tall, broad frame against the chair that resembled a kid's seat with him occupying it. "There's been a new development." He gazed at Carlton. "I received a call from the N. Y. P. D. It seems they've been searching for the last few days erroneously in the Louisville area looking for you and your assistant. When they received the alert, we were investigating the murder of Tara Bonner, they realized you were in Sweetwater. They have a warrant for your arrest for the murder of Greyson Corbin."

Wes jolted and shot to his feet. His shoulders shook, and his eyes widened. "What happened to Greyson? I just saw him a couple days ago. What the f . . . ?"

Wyatt's wide hand came up and slowly motioned Wes into his chair. Wes followed the motion of Wyatt's big mitt, returning to his seat. He acted disheartened and confused— frantic.

She had to bite her lips to stop herself from jumping to his aide, to cradle him in her arms and kiss his quivering lips. All she could do was sit there and do deep breathing exercises to keep from losing it herself. Not one murder, but two.

"Sheriff," Carlton took control. "What is this—an N. Y. P. D. warrant for my client's arrest? This is the first I've heard of it."

Wyatt acted unshaken. "We've only learned of it ourselves. They want us to extradite Mr. Drake to be tried in New York for Greyson Corbin's murder. Witnesses state Wesley Drake was the last person to speak with Mr. Corbin during a heated argument. Mr. Corbin expired at the table they shared in the New York airport tavern mere minutes after Mr. Drake left the scene. Drake's fingerprints are on the murder weapon. Your client has been a busy man. Mr. Drake has had deadly altercations with more than one person over the last few days."

Carlton dug further. "So, Mr. Drake was not on scene when Mr. Corbin died. How can they assume he was the murderer, and what was the weapon used?"

Wyatt's thick, slow, Southern twang sounded unphased. "Corbin died from poisoning. His whiskey was laced with arsenic. Drake's fingerprints were all over the scene, including the tumbler of bourbon."

Wes's feverish eyes darted about, and his body jerked. "I can't just sit here and be accused of another murder I didn't commit. I don't deny I was in the airport lounge with Greyson. You haven't fingerprinted me. How do you know this? How could this be? Greyson can't be dead. Who would want to kill him? Certainly not me." His brow was tended, and his eyes moist.

Wyatt exhaled. "You have a passport. Your fingerprints are on file in the national database. N. Y. P. D. compared them. They match prints we've found in your and Tara Bonner's rooms."

Wes's eyes closed. His shoulders drooped. She didn't know what to do for him. He was obviously in shock. Who wouldn't be?

Carlton's shoulders straightened. "You invaded my client's privacy and searched his room. As you've stated, it was not the scene of the crime."

Wyatt sneered. "I have a warrant for Drake's arrest for the murder of Tara Bonner. Got it right after I took the call from New York. The district attorney agrees, there is enough evidence to convict your client of the crime in my jurisdiction. I'm not going to release Mr. Drake for trial in New York until he has been tried in Sweetwater for the case at hand. The CSI team is still searching Mr. Drake's room. They already opened the safe."

"My passport is in the room safe," Wes spurted. Irma gripped his hand harder, and he held it as though his life depended on it.

"Your passport and other belongings will be held in evidence. They are safe with us, Mr. Drake," Wyatt drawled. "You can see how the connection between choice of poisons in both cases would persuade a judge we have sufficient data for a search warrant." Wyatt turned to Irma. Clearly, their friendship would not interfere with the case. No first name basis today. "Ms. Owens, we're done with you. You're free to go."

Carlton gave Wesley a look that told him to keep his trap shut. Then he returned to the sheriff. "Is Irma still a person of interest?"

Wyatt nodded, blankly. "Yes. Ms. Owens, do no leave town."

Irma released Wes's hand and stood. The absence of her hold on him rattled his nerves, and his insides began to tremble. It was all he could do to hold it together. He avoided her gaze until she spoke.

"Wes, I'll wait for you in the bullpen. I'm sure Jaiden can find somewhere for me to be comfortable until the sheriff releases you." She glared at Wyatt, unintimidated by the powerful man. "Wyatt Gordon, you know full well that you must consider the possibility that someone wanted Greyson Corbin and Wesley Drake both dead. This could've been a business powerplay for someone who wanted control of their company or someone who had a grudge against it. Tara Bonner was sleeping in the room assigned to Wesley. She could've mistakenly been the victim in his place. Wes' life could be in danger. There is no way the Wesley Drake I know could've committed one of these crimes, let alone both."

Wyatt gave her a flat look. "As you said, it's been many a year since you and Mr. Drake were lovers. People change. Listen, Irma, you can wait; but we will not be releasing Mr. Drake today. He goes before a judge to be arraigned tomorrow. I'm confident there is enough evidence against him that the judge will rule for a trial."

Carlton's jaw looked clinched. "No worries. We'll get Wesley out on bond."

Wes sighed and rolled his eyes heavenward.

Wyatt turned toward Wes. "In the event Mr. Drake is granted bail and not considered a flight risk, he could possibly be released on bond. However, should that happen, he will not be leaving Sweetwater until after his trial."

She nodded grimly. "I see. I'll wait until you get Wes settled. Can I see him once he's in custody?"

Wyatt nodded without words, and she exited his glass-walled cubical.

Wes's back to the door, he couldn't see where Irma settled herself. He felt her watching over him from the larger room next door. Her presence eased his mind enough for him to pull himself together.

Who would want Greyson and Tara dead? Or did they want him and Greyson dead? This just did not make sense.

Wyatt retrieved a packet from his desk. " We need a DNA sample, Mr. Drake. You can do it now. Or I can get a warrant; and you can do it later."

Wes glanced at his attorney. Carlton nodded.

"Fine, Sheriff. I have nothing to hide. I'm willing to do whatever is necessary to prove my innocence."

"Good." Wyatt opened the package and handed him a plastic tube. "Remove the cotton tipped tool from the vial. Swab the inside of your mouth thoroughly. Replace it and seal the container."

Wes did as he was instructed and then handed the closed vial to Wyatt. The sheriff wrote his name and date on the paper label and laid it on his desk. He pulled out an inkpad and a form and pointed to the black sponge. "Place your fingers on this."

Wes followed the instructions. Wyatt carefully placed each of Wes's fingers onto indicated spots on the form. Once he finished, the sheriff handed Wes an alcohol wipe from a packet in the fingerprinting kit. "Clean up with this."

While Wes wiped his hands free of residue, Wyatt wrote pertinent data on the document. He waved it to dry and then sealed it and the vial in an envelope. Wyatt wrote the date and Wes's name on the outside. He sat back in his chair, flipped on the recording device, announced who was present in this interview, and why they were speaking.

Wes's stomach did a flip. He exhaled negative thoughts and thought of Irma watching him from behind the glass wall. His hand swiped the side of his nose.

"Mr. Drake, explain again what happened to your finger?" The Sheriff nodded toward Wes' bandaged hand.

Wes glanced at it and looked up at the sheriff. "When I checked into my room—the first one—I lifted my suitcase by the bottom and the handle, to place it on the luggage rack beside the bedside table. Something has been damaged in transit, apparently, because my finger caught on a spur on the bottom. It ripped the skin. You know how small cuts sometimes bleed like crazy. I grabbed a tissue from the dispenser in the bathroom and pressed it to the cut. When the bleeding stopped, I got a bandage from my suitcase, sat on the bed, and put it on. Damn thing tore off part of my fingernail. Guess that bag is junk. They go through hell, you know. Airlines are notoriously rough on luggage."

"Does it require stitches or further treatment?" Wyatt stared, showing no sympathy.

"I don't think so. It's nearly healed." Was Wyatt concerned for his welfare or their liability?

"Tell us how and why you were the last person to speak with your partner, Greyson Corbin."

Wes glanced at Carlton who nodded. "Greyson and I had been traveling at opposite ends of the world for some time. I wanted to discuss a couple of important things with him, so I asked him to join me for a drink when he arrived at the airport. We'd been unable to meet in person until then. I was scheduled to fly out shortly after our chat."

Wyatt frowned. "Why the airport instead of your New York headquarters?"

"I didn't want our conversation to be overheard by anyone in our office, and I was on my way to see a client in Nashville. Since I was headed in that direction, I decided to make this stop in Sweetwater to reconnect with my dear friend, Irma Owens. Irma was a past client, the former Starr Bright."

Wyatt's face was blank. "That sounds ominous. Why the secrecy about your discussion with Mr. Greyson."

Wes swallowed dread building in his mouth. "This is highly confidential. Any leak could destroy our business. I assume you will keep it as such."

Wyatt's brow furrowed. "It won't leak from my office. If this becomes pertinent information that comes out during a trial, you'll need to deal with any fallout then."

Wes nodded solemnly. "I had two things to discuss with Greyson. The first was that I plan to retire. I set the date to be no more than three months out. Given that, I'd spoken with our CFO concerning the financial state of our business, so I would know how to approach Greyson with my proposal. The CFO, Jonah Helm, is the only other person in our agency aware of my plans. During that investigation, Jonah and I uncovered anomalies in our books. He recommended I hire an expert to delve into it further. So, I hired a forensic accountant, Irvin Sands, to investigate it. Mr. Sands learned there were several bogus vendors regularly invoicing for services we could not identify. Payments to these phony merchants were deposited into a single bank that had been arranged to immediately transfer the funds into an untraceable, numbered account in an off-shore institution."

"So, you did not discover who is stealing from your firm?" Wyatt stared.

"No, not yet." Wes closed his eyes and shook his head.

"How much money are we talking about?"

That sinking feeling in Wes' torso dropped heavily into his gut. "Three-million dollars over the course of the last three years."

"That's a significant amount." Wyatt's lips pressed together. "Can you tell us more about that?"

Wes might as well explain. It would come out in the end anyway. "Greyson and I manage A level clients. Two agents under him manage B level performers. I have two reps that handle my B level celebrities. With the help of our assistants, Greyson and I are each responsible for our budgets and for those of our subordinates. All erroneous invoices were paid under Greyson's watch."

Wyatt kept an imposing stoneface. "How did Mr. Greyson react to this news? Did he have something to do with the money's disappearance? Were you under the impression Mr. Corbin was embezzling from your firm?"

Wes grimaced at the unpleasant recollection. "Absolutely not. Greyson would never steal from me. He owns . . . owned half of the company. Would that be theft or misappropriation?" He shrugged. "Anyway, Grey was angry and shocked. He became quite vocal. I'm sure that's what attracted attention of your '*witnesses*.' At first, he thought I was accusing him. I was not. When I could get a word in, I explained it was not the case. I wanted him to help figure out who was behind the larceny."

"How did he take the notion of your retirement?" Wyatt asked.

"He became irate that I planned to retire and accused me of leaving him in the lurch with a major load he could not possibly handle on his own. He accused me of deserting him. I told him he shouldn't be shocked. I'm a good ten years his senior and couldn't possibly keep up this pace forever. He had to understand, I would need to retire before he was old enough to. I figured it was better to leave during a boom time than to walk out when it was going downhill."

Wyatt's hands clasped across his flat belly. "It sounds like Mr. Corbin had a good point."

Wes bit his upper lip then relaxed. "I offered Greyson three opportunities. Buy me out—hence, my need to know the value of our company. Or we could hire an outside party to manage my clientele. I would become a silent partner and draw my portion of company profit as income. Another scenario is that we could sell my half of the company to another party Greyson agreed to. That person would become his new partner."

Wyatt asked, "Why not promote from within?"

Wes sneered. "None of our junior agents has potential to manage elite superstars. We need someone with finesse, strong negotiating skills, and a steel will. I offered a list of three potentials and asked Greyson to think it over so we could talk more next week when I return to the office. He unhappily agreed. I gave him Irvin Sands' contact information, and he said he would speak with him and our CFO, Jonah Helm, about the missing capital."

"That certainly explains his argumentative state when you met. You hit him with not one, but two major issues." Wyatt glared. "Explain how your fingerprints were on Greyson Corbin's whiskey glass."

With a nod from Carlton, Wes faced the sheriff. "I arrived in the airport tavern before Greyson and ordered Fire and Ice Bourbon on the rocks. The waitress delivered my drink as Greyson showed up. He asked for the same thing. She explained they were out of it. My glass was the last they had in stock. She offered a selection of other fine bourbons, so he chose one. I gave her my credit card to cover our drinks, which she returned when she delivered Greyson's bourbon soon after. He was disgruntled. Fire and Ice was his favorite brand. I didn't give a rat's ass and hadn't drunk from the glass. So, I offered to switch with him; and we did. We got into the heated discussion. Neither of us had time to taste our whiskeys. Once I'd told him what I had to offer, and he'd settled down to a reasonable state, I apologized for springing all of that on him. I chugged my whiskey—needed it by then, and left to join my assistant, Tara Bonner, at our departure gate. That was the last I saw or talked with Greyson. He was alive and well. Ms. Bonner and I flew to Louisville Airport where we rented a vehicle and drove to Sweetwater. We checked into the hotel. I explained how we managed the room switch. I already explained about the irate discussion with Tara in the dining room. Tara went to the hotel pool. I took a ride-share to Irma Owens' home. After our visit, Irma drove me back to the hotel. That's when we met you in the lobby."

The sheriff's head tilted. "Did you believe you would be welcome at Irma's house?"

Wes sighed. "It was a possibility she might turn me away. Ms. Owens and I did not part on the best of terms. It had been decades since we'd seen each other, but our last meeting had been casual and polite. If she didn't want to see me, I planned to call another car to pick me up."

"I see." The sheriff's lips pressed together. "According to eyewitnesses Mr. Greyson expired, and his head fell onto the table within a few minutes of your leaving. No one else had approached him between the time you walked out of the barroom and his death. The medical examiner confirmed Mr. Corbin died of arsenic poisoning which was found in his Fire and Ice bourbon—with your prints on the glass."

Wes thought he might choke on the lump building in his throat. His chest tightened by the second. "Look, I have no idea how arsenic got into that glass. I certainly didn't put it there. Someone else tampered with that bourbon and could have no idea Greyson and I would switch drinks. Apparently, it was meant for me. I have no motive to kill Greyson. He is a dear friend and successful business partner. With him dead, I can't possibly retire. Our agency will fold with his death. Can't you see, I had no motive to kill him."

Wyatt's face was blank. "It appears from our angle you suspected him of pilfering missing funds. Your company can survive his death and your absence. You could hire someone to manage your and Corbin's accounts. You said so yourself."

Holy crap. He was doomed.

CHAPTER NINE

Deputy Coldwater showed Irma to the lockup area, a short hallway with a barred window on one side and two small cells separating her from those arrested by thick iron bars on the other. She handed Irma a small item that resembled a phone. "Buzz me when you're ready to leave. I'll come get you."

She opened the cell door, allowing Irma to enter the concrete cubical, containing only a single bunk suspended from the back wall. A small sink was attached beside a stainless-steel toilet along the wall. It felt cold and dank, though the temperature was acceptable.

Wes stood as she entered, a dejected expression on his handsome face. He looked weary and exhausted. He gritted his teeth, pressing his lips tightly together, and slipped his hands along the hips of his newly donned prison clothing, as though looking for pocket to hide them in. The ill-fitting, orange sweatsuit draped his limbs, at least a full size or more too large.

Her heart sank at the sight, and her gut felt as though a cold wave swelled and crested within its confines. She was his only friend right now. He needed her. She couldn't let him down.

"Nice digs you've got here." She chuckled, hoping her expression and inflection didn't sound nearly as sorrowful as she felt. At least, not to him.

"Thanks, I'll give you my decorator's number." He grimaced.

When they were alone, she sat on his bunk. He slid into the spot beside her, covering his face with his hands.

Taking one of them and noting the flinch at her touch, she waited until their eyes met. "You're not alone, Wes. I'm going to do everything in my power to get you out of this."

His knees pulled together, and he sat as though speechless, looking down at his feet. He glanced about as though looking for an exit or means of escape—a caged animal.

When he finally spoke, his voice sounded weak to her ears, "I didn't do these things, Irma. I swear." Pleading ruled his expression, as he looked up to meet her eyes.

"I know but thank you for saying it." She stroked the top of his broad hand with her thumb.

His eyes widened, and he spoke slowly, "How can you have such faith in me after all I've done?" His smile appeared fake, and his chuckle sounded as though he was trying to laugh his predicament off, as though it was tough to fight off tears.

"What have you done that's so terrible?" She kept her voice steady and soft.

"I hurt you. You may've gotten over it quickly and moved on with your life, but it left a lasting scar on my soul. Now they're accusing me of . . . of murdering the two people I have been the closest to for many years. How could they believe I've done such horrific things? I'm not a monster . . . not a murderer."

Why had his past rejection of her touched him so deeply? It didn't make sense.

Had he cared as much as she had? He must've had more feelings for her at the time than he'd let on.

"Of course, you didn't murder these people. You could never kill anyone unless you were being attacked. You have a gentle, though possibly damaged soul; but you're not a killer at heart. As for the way you and I parted ways, you had your reasons. You had issues. We all have them. Who wouldn't? Your mother left you on the doorstep of the fire department. No wonder you had commitment issues. I don't blame you."

He smirked. "I was just an infant, but that single act made me feel worthless, like no one could love me for long. Like it was inevitable that all important relationships would end in tragedy. My therapist helped me realize I continually orchestrated situations in my life that either expected no real emotional intimacy from me or that I could end as I saw fit—before the person who meant something important to me did it."

Had she meant something important to him? "You need to stop blaming yourself. You must be strong and clear headed to fight the battle at hand."

He ignored her argument. "Even the building of my company, striving for more and more success, being totally engrossed in work, was my way of proving my worth." He bit his lip. "And for what? Look at it now. With Greyson . . . gone and me in prison, it's going to fall apart like a sandcastle in high tide."

Her palm went to his chin and held his gaze toward her. "Listen here, Wesley Drake. You've made mistakes. You've learned a lot and grown into the man you needed to be. You are so worthy. Do not put yourself down. You are worthy of love. This is no time to wallow in self-pity. If you've learned anything, it is to act and move forward."

He mocked. "Like you've done? I'm so proud of what you've achieved in your life . . . and a bit jealous. Not only did you excel at an extremely long career. You built a strong, independent, productive family of people who love and adore you. You've carved a place in this town for yourself as a part of a community, developed a circle of loyal friends; and you're enjoying your life."

"Thank you. You also have a circle of friends and associates who are loyal and care for you. You've had a fabulous career and an exciting life. Your marriages might not have worked out in the long haul, but you must admit they each gave you something you needed at the time. You've lived a good life. I have, too. Let's get on with the show and work toward the future. Besides, you've got bigger things to worry about." She patted his icy hand.

"Yeah, well. Two of those friends are in the morgue. As for loyalty, someone is stealing from my company. It's doubtful, but it could've even been one of them. It looks darned bleak from this cell. The future doesn't hold much promise from where I sit."

"Well, you won't be sitting here in this jailcell long. Tomorrow Carlton is going to spring you, and we're going to work on figuring out what really happened to your friends."

He glared at her as though she'd just escaped from a looney bin. "The police have damning evidence, enough to get a conviction in both cases. I'm sure they're not going to waste resources searching for the real killers when it seems clear to them I did them both. I had means and motive for killing Greyson, as far as they're concerned; and I had opportunity to kill Tara. I'm not sure they have settled on one specific motive for that, but they are convinced I did it."

Her back jerked up straight. "Well, you didn't. If they won't investigate further, we will. I understand they believe you killed Tara due to the room switch thing and since she didn't know anyone else in town. Why are they so certain you murdered Greyson? You said you and he were very close." She laid his hand on her thigh and stroked it.

He explained about his last meeting with Greyson, told her of the embezzlement issue within his company, and went on to share details of how his and Greyson's last meeting went.

"You didn't really think he was the thief. Did you?" She frowned, angling her head.

"Of course not. I wouldn't go into business with someone I didn't trust completely. It looks to me like he was set up to take the fall, should it be discovered the cash was missing. "

She winced. "I still don't understand why they think you killed him."

His brows furrowed, and he bit his lower lip. "Well, they say I was the last to see him alive. He and I met at an airport tavern before I flew to Louisville, and he and I exchanged drinks." He explained the switch. "Somehow, that drink became spiked with poison that killed him soon after I departed."

Her audible intake of air gave credence to her surprise. "But you didn't do it." It wasn't a question, but a statement of his innocence. "That bourbon was meant for you. You're in danger."

His sad smile showed how weary this day had been for him. "Thank you for that. No, I didn't do it. They say I was the last person at his table, and my prints are on the glass. There had to be someone else who stopped by and dosed his cocktail. Otherwise, it was like that when I received it. That would mean someone poisoned the glass or liquor. If it was the bottle, it could've been meant for me or for whomever the random person was who might've received it. Hell, it could've even been meant for someone at the tavern. Maybe it's a serial killer who didn't care who got poisoned. Who knows? The police don't believe I'm in danger."

She closed her eyes, shook her head, and then exhaled. "That's pretty compelling evidence against you." She looked him in the eyes. "I understand you had access to Tara's room so you could plant the poison that killed her, but why on earth would you do such a thing?"

He shook his head, dejectedly. "Not sure. They believe I was lying about having an affair with her. Maybe they assume I thought she was in on the embezzlement, but that's crazy. Tara was the final watchdog over all company finances. She went over budgets monthly with a scrutinizing eye before they were handed over to the CFO. It's part of why she and Greyson didn't get along."

He sighed then explained, "Tara called Greyson out on his overspending of travel funds last year. Greyson and his assistant got into an altercation with Tara about it. Tara ultimately won the argument. She had to cover Grey's deficit with money from other company resources. His travel budget for this year was reduced drastically to make up for the previous year's movement of funds. It forced Grey to be more discerning about travel plans and to fly

Business Class instead of First Class. The three of them were never comfortable working together since that incident. It's a shame really. They all want . . . wanted what's best for the agency."

"Are you sure of that, Wesley?" Irma had listened quietly to the whole story. "That is unfortunate; but it sounds like Tara had more cause to murder Greyson than you did." She let out a sad snicker.

He sneered. "Thank you, Irma. Yes, I'm sure. The three of them are . . . were as loyal to the bone. None of them would've considered stealing from the company. You're really something you know, . . . but you look exhausted. You need some rest. You should go."

She nodded her head, stood with shoulders back, and pushed the button on the device Jaiden had given her. "You don't look so spry yourself, my friend. I'll get out of your hair, so you can enjoy this luxurious accommodation. We'll figure this thing out. No worries."

He might've been swindled and not feel these people had been disloyal, but clearly someone had been. She was determined to be here for Wes and help him find out what was really going on.

She hadn't quietly loved this man in the background all these years to sit by and let him inappropriately spend his life in a cell. That wasn't happening on her watch—not in her town.

Jaiden arrived and unlocked the cell.

Irma gave Wes what she hoped was a hopeful smile. She winked. "See ya tomorrow, Handsome."

He chuckled, despite his desperate situation. Unfortunately, they'd meet next in a courtroom.

CHAPTER TEN

Irma returned home exhausted and had turned in early, before Charli had come home from work. In the morning, she'd remained in her room until she'd heard Charli leave for her job. She didn't want to talk with her granddaughter about Wes—not yet anyway.

Irma drove to the Sweetwater Hotel and found Ralph Bacon, the owner-manager, talking with a young desk clerk at the check-in counter. Ralph smiled when he looked up. "Irma, it's so good to see you. How have you been? I'm so sorry about your friend being arrested." He stepped to her and put hands on her shoulders before pecking her cheek.

"Thank you. I'm good, Ralph. How about you?" A glance around the empty room said more than words.

He frowned. "Let's just say, recent events have taken a toll on my business. Rentals are down. People are checking out earlier than planned, and restaurant sales are non-existent. Why? Are you planning a stay with us?" He winked.

"No, sorry. I'm wondering if you have surveillance tapes of the night of the murder, and if so, might I look at them? Specifically, the hallway where Tara Bonner's room was located and the lobby, from the time she and Wesley Drake and Ms. Bonner checked in."

With a sigh, he shook his head sorrowfully. "I was afraid you'd get involved more than you already are in this . . . terrible incident."

"Ralph, Wesley is a close friend. I can't sit idly by and do nothing. I've got to at least try to find some way to help him."

"You need to be careful, Irma. You could be putting yourself in danger. Who knows what is really going on here?" He put a hand to her back and nudged her toward the security office.

"I mean to find out." She was adamant.

"If you're sure, I don't see why you can't look at the videos. It's all done digitally. Sheriff Gordon copied the files, but I still have the runs in my computer system. You might be wasting your time. The cops didn't seem to find anything unusual about them." He opened the door, and she entered.

Computer monitors mounted along one wall of the long, slim room. A countertop beneath them held a laptop computer and was flanked by two chairs.

Ralph took one and indicated the other. She sat beside him while he clicked a few things on to the laptop. It came to life, and finally he indicated the date parameters she wanted him to pull up. The screen showed the hallway in question.

"Here you go, sweetie. All you need to do is watch. If you want to move faster, click here." He pointed from one button to another. "To slow down click here and here to stop the screen. If you need to print anything, hit this button. He pointed to a printer at the other end of the counter. "It will spit out there." He pushed the laptop in her direction and stood. "You hungry?"

"I could eat." Smiling, she assumed control of the keyboard. She hit the faster button to speed up the feed and kept her eyes glued to the monitor.

He strode to the door. "Great. I haven't had breakfast. I'm going to go see what they've got cooking in the kitchen, and you can have some privacy."

He left her alone and shut the door behind him. She continued watching the screen. A couple of units were vacated by guests who dragged or carried their luggage from the accommodations. A maid pushed a housekeeping cart into the hallway. The short, Hispanic, middle-aged woman took a bundle of fresh sheets and towels into the murder room. She propped the door open while she worked.

Irma pulled a pen and pad from her purse and noted the time of her entry into Tara's room, evidently to clean. Moving about inside, the woman eventually returned to the cart with an armload of dirty sheets and towels. She dropped them into the laundry section of the cart. Returning to the room, she was visible as she disappeared into the bathroom area for a while, then sped on the fast-moving screen about the room cleaning it. Lastly, she ran the sweeper and returned to the cart before moving on to the next room—the one directly across the hallway—the one Wes had occupied.

Irma maneuvered the video until she located the clearest visual of the housekeeper. She hit *STOP* and then *PRINT*. Irma observed as the woman cleaned Wes's room and then moved on down the hallway continuing to do the same in other rental units.

Guests came or went. No one moved into or out of either of Wes's or Tara's rooms until the twosome arrived at 12:45 p.m. Irma noted the time on her pad. Ten minutes later, Wes stepped out of his door at the same time Tara dragged her suitcase from hers. Irma wrote the time down. *12:55 p.m. First Exit*. They talked then went into Tara's room. Irma noted, *12:57 p.m. Into Tara's Room*. They returned to the hallway. Irma noted, *1:00 p.m. Exchanged Rooms*. Tara went into Wes's room, and Wes disappeared down the hallway carrying a small plastic bag. He returned five minutes later with that same bag filled with ice and took it into his new room. She noted the time.

As Irma watched them leave together soon afterward, she noted the time as having been when Tara left with Wes to drive him to her house. A half an hour later, Tara returned to her room. Irma noted every entrance or exit by each of them. Tara had obviously returned to her lodgings to work while Wes visited with Irma and her family.

Later, a uniformed man from Room Service entered Tara's room when she opened the door to him. He exited minutes later, leaving the food cart inside.

Irma hit *PRINT* to capture the stilled figure of the Room Service delivery person. Awhile later, Tara pushed the cart outside and left it in the hallway. Later that evening, Wes returned to his room, after Eli had driven him home after dinner.

The next morning, Tara left a few minutes before Wes did. This must've been when he went to the hotel restaurant to have coffee with Tara while she ate breakfast—when Irma had found them having the heated discussion before Tara sped out of the hotel. She made a mental note to confirm this when she viewed the lobby video.

Much later, after having breakfast with Irma, Wes returned to his room. This was after he and Irma had eaten at The Royal Diner, and the town driving tour she'd taken him on.

A different housekeeper with short blonde hair entered the room carrying a bundle of towels over her arm. She was only inside a couple of minutes before leaving Tara's room. This one didn't push a cart, so Irma assumed Tara must've requested extra towels.

Irma printed a visual of this cleaning lady, and it spit out of the printer. A little while later, Tara returned to her room.

Early that evening, Room service delivered a meal, entered and left shortly after. There was no activity in or out of either rental unit during this span of time.

Wes left his room shortly before he arrived at Irma's house. They'd spent that day together—enjoying each other's company—before tragedy struck. Irma sighed. If only they could go back to that period—that hopeful time—blissfully ignorant of what the future would bring.

The Hispanic maid returned that morning. She cleaned Wes's chamber first, following the same procedure as the previous day. Then she entered Tara's apartment. She flew out of the room, hands flapping about in the air, terror on her face, and screaming something. She headed toward the lobby, Irma assumed, to let Ralph know there was a dead woman in that room.

Ralph returned to the Security Room. "How's it going?" He sat the tray of delicious smelling food on the counter beside the laptop.

"Slow, but sure. I'm keeping track of all the activity in that hallway. I guess I've got all I need off this reel. Can I review the lobby visuals during this time?"

"Sure." He sat down beside her and took control of the laptop. "I'll need to sit with you for that. No photos of anyone may be printed, not pertaining to Mr. Drake and Ms. Bonner. Privacy is important to some guests."

"Understood." She nodded. "What have you got there? It smells delightful."

He smiled, pushing the savory tray toward her. "I hope you like chicken Cascadia. It's the special today." The tray held two plates covered with stainless steel domes, utensils and two glasses of soda.

She helped herself to the food and drinks. "Love it. I didn't come here today to invite myself to lunch, but this was exceptionally thoughtful of you. Thanks."

"Well, it appears the closest I can get to taking you on a lunch date—at least for now." He winked and joined her at the table. They ate the delicious meal and chatted casually, staying as far away from the issue at hand as possible.

Once they'd finished eating, Irma returned to the surveillance videos. Soon she had noted comings and goings through the lobby, of anyone she considered might be important to the murder case. Having expired all hope of finding anything unusual going on there, she closed her notebook. "Ralph, you've been so helpful. I don't know how to thank you."

"Simple. Have dinner with me. I've been meaning to ask you out. Every time I run into you, you're with Dr. Baker. Are the two of you an item?" He stood and stepped to the printer and removed the sheets she had printed.

Accepting the papers he handed her, she smiled. "I'd love to have another meal with you, Ralph; and no. Sam and I are just dear friends."

Sam wanted more from her, but she couldn't give it. He'd chosen to accept that, and they'd enjoyed a lovely friends-with-benefits relationship for the past few years. Their off-and-on connection as nothing steady or serious—at least not for her. She'd been clear with Sam up front. They were free to see other people.

"Right now, my life is a bit complicated. Why don't you call me in a couple of weeks, and we'll set a date."

Who knew what would happen to her household? No need to get Ralph any more involved in her fiasco than he already was. She gave him her cell number and then flipped through the photos she'd printed.

Ralph's hand shot over to stop her at one picture. "Let's look at the timestamp on this. That's the bartender I hired last week. See here. She's got a tattoo on her neck. What the hell was she doing, entering Tara Bonner's room?"

Her forehead crinkled, and she inspected the photograph closely. "I didn't think much of this one, just assumed Tara had requested more towels, and this 'maid' delivered them."

Ralph shook his head. "First of all, she's wearing our housekeeper's uniform, not her own. That's strange. If she was simply filling in, there was no need for her to change clothing for that simple chore. Possibly she figured we would expect her to if she was assuming the cleaning staff's duties. She could've borrowed the smock from the locker room. There are usually a few older ones hanging from a hook, in case one of the gals soils her uniform and needs a spare to change into." He looked at the picture closely.

He pulled the media run for that time. The video played on the laptop of the blonde female, sporting a handful of towels over one arm.

Ralph zoomed in to her neck. "I've been terribly understaffed. My best bartender took off to Arizona with her boyfriend without notice. Last week this gal came in with a good resume and a glowing letter of recommendation from an airport lounge in New York. I hired her on the spot, and she was good at her job. She worked in the restaurant bar—not housekeeping." His finger pointed to the screen. "This mark on her neck looks like a winged 'V' with an upside-down V through it. I don't normally like hiring people with visible body ink. Some guests find it distasteful, so I shy away from skin art. Hers wasn't blatantly obvious or obnoxious, so I let it slide." He hit PRINT on the visual of her tattoo and handed the photograph to Irma.

"How would she get a room key or even know Tara had requested extra towels?"

"The keycard could only come from the desk clerk, unless she took one from a housekeeper." He flipped videos back to the lobby. "Let's take a look at that day before that particular time and see if we can figure that out."

He scanned the video at high speed. The feed showed barkeep in the lobby. He slowed the frame. The gal entered the lobby wearing her bartender uniform. She stood at the desk, chatting with the clerk in a flirtatious manner. He acted taken with the woman. Finally, he nodded and stepped away from the lobby. The clerk was only away for a couple of minutes, according to the time counter at the bottom right of the screen.

During that short period, the tattooed female clicked a few keys on his registration computer monitor. She moved toward the machine that programmed keys, stuck a plastic key card into it, then withdrew that key. By the time the man on duty returned, the spikey-haired blonde had pocketed the programmed room key.

Ralph turned to Irma. "Well, now we know how she gained access to the room. I'll ask Simon at the front desk about it. We're very understaffed. She could've seen his request for extra towels on the monitor and decided to help."

Irma nodded, not buying it. "Maybe, but why would she bother putting a housekeeper uniform on for one simple request? It seems a waste of time and energy."

"You've got a good point there, Irma. I have no idea. She's new and maybe she thought that would make a better impression. She was probably just trying to help, knowing how bad our staffing situation is."

"You need to find out, Ralph."

He winced. "I can't approach her about it. Unfortunately for both of us she up and quit. Can't say as I blame her. She was brand new on the job, and she was a keeper. Her first week a guest gets murdered. I'd probably have quit too, in her shoes. I have a hard enough time maintaining good staff lately, and now this—"

"Oh? When did she leave?" Irma frowned.

He shrugged. "Who knows? She just didn't come in again after that day. I guess she heard about the dead body discovered in the hotel and didn't want to work here anymore. Probably frightened her. All my people were shaken up about it. I had to hire a psychologist to be on call for any of them who want to talk about it." That wasn't unusual for workers in a location connected with tragedy.

"I can see how that might freak a person out, but I'm still suspicious." She scowled. "Can you give me her name and contact information? I'll look her up and ask. She might know something that could help Wes."

"You're really reaching there, Irma. It's an unusual request, but this is a murder case. I don't think it would be inappropriate to share." He pulled up another screen and typed a few things until he got to employee records. "Here you go. Her name is Sue March. Her references were from a tavern at LaGuardia Airport called Sip On The Fly. Her reference was from the manager, Ray Sanders. Here's a copy of the letter. Her name is on it. I'm not sure what you can do about this. If she hasn't left town yet, maybe you can find her and ask whatever questions you have. She's not staying here though. Must've had an apartment or boarding room somewhere else."

"Thank you, Ralph. You've been a big help." She took the paper and leaned to peck a friendly kiss on his cheek. She stuck the photos and information into an envelope Ralph gave her and readied to go.

Ralph walked her to the lobby. "Before you leave, I must ask something I've put off for too long."

"Oh, what would that be?" She studied his face.

"I'd love to spend more time with you. Why don't I buy you dinner sometime soon." His smile was sweet and non-threatening.

"Ralph, I would enjoy dining with you. Right now, my life is so complicated. Maybe in a couple of weeks, after things settle down a bit. Give me a call, and we can figure something out."

He waved. "Sure thing."
She turned to go.
Will things ever settle down again?

CHAPTER ELEVEN

Gran and a tall, well-built man about her age walked into the house. She'd warned Charli she would be late getting home, and she was bringing a house guest. She failed to say he was a looker.

The house smelled delightful, full of savory scents. Charli and Eil met them at the door. "Welcome to our home. I'm Irma's granddaughter, Charli Owens." Charli pushed a hand toward their guest. "And this is my fiancé, Eli Lange."

The man accepted the offered shake. "Wesley Drake, thank you for having me. I don't know what I would've done without your and Irma's hospitality."

Charli waved Eli. "Any friend of Gran's is a friend of ours. She hasn't told us much about you, only that you're old friends from her singing career."

Wes's brows furrowed as he gazed at Gran questioningly and then back to Charli. He shook Eli's hand. "Yes, I was her agent and promoter when she was Starr Bright. I managed Irma and The Terrestrials. We go way back."

Irma chuckled. "No sense beating around the bush, Wes. They're grownups. Charli, Eli, Wes and I were lovers for a couple of years before we parted ways." She went to the oven. "What's cooking? It smells wonderful."

"Salmon, baked potatoes, broccoli and fresh bread," Eli beamed.

Charli laughed. "My man is a darned good cook. I hope you're hungry, Wesley."

Wes smiled. "Absolutely, and please call me Wes."

Gran took Wes's hand. "Come, I'll show you to Kyler's room where you'll be staying. You can freshen up while the youngsters put the food out."

Eli pulled the cork on a bottle of wine and poured four goblets. Charli checked the bread. "It's golden brown. I'll get the food from the oven."

Eli placed the wine goblets around the table they'd already set for dinner. By the time they'd plated the food and put it at the table, Gran and her friend returned to the great room.

Gran indicated where he should sit, and they all took their place. The food was delicious, as she'd suspected. During dinner they chatted about Wes's company, and he answered their questions about his travels and famous clientele.

As dinner wound down, Wes put his fork down, wiped his mouth, and pushed back a bit from the table. "Wow, that was a fabulous meal." He gasped. "I'm just glad to get out from behind bars. You didn't need to go to all this trouble but thank you for welcoming me into your home."

Brows rose, and Charli glared at a loss for words. Eli broke the silence. "Bars?"

Wes stared at Gran. "Irma, you didn't tell them?"

She sighed heavily. "I'm sorry. I wanted to break the news as easily as possible. I guess there's no good time." She heaved. "Charli, Eli, Wes is in town to visit me. He was traveling with a companion—his assistant. The woman was killed in the hotel. Wyatt arrested Wes on murder charges just because he was the only one in town, they know of who knew Tara."

Eli gasped. "We heard about that on the news. Good grief, Irma how did you get involved in that?"

Wes intervened, "Irma was kind enough to give me a lift back to the hotel. When we arrived, the sheriff was there with a lot of police. We had no idea what had happened."

Between the two of them, they outlined the situation. During their explanation, Charli went from happy to meet Gran's old friend, to shocked, and then to terrorized that her grandmother might be involved with a killer—one staying in their house.

"Irma," Eli stared. "Are you sure this is a good idea?" He glared at Wes. "Look, I'm not saying you're guilty; but Wyatt Gordon is an incredible lawman. I trust his judgement." He glowered at Gran. "Don't you, Irma?"

Irma nodded. "Yes, you're correct. However, I know Wesley Drake. Wes is innocent. He doesn't have the stomach for murder. The man wouldn't even let me use normal mousetraps in my apartment when we were together. We had to have the humane type of catch and release. I'm telling you, something else is going on here. Either the killer meant to kill Wesley, or someone is framing him."

Wes interjected, "Someone has been embezzling from my company over the last couple of years. My CFO and I only recently uncovered the crime. We don't know who the mastermind is yet, but I have experts working on it. They alerted me this morning. They've brought in the Feds since it involved a banking institution and funds being shifted offshore. Maybe whoever is stealing from my company saw me, Greyson or Tara as threats."

Irma nodded. "Yes, or it could be someone in the industry who wants to ruin your agency and wanted you and Greyson out of the way, so they could steal your clients or take over the agency." She turned to Charli and Eli. "Whatever is going on, Wes is not the problem. He's the target or the scapegoat."

Eli groaned and slid an arm around Charli to hug her close. "Still, I'm not comfortable with Charli staying here. Wes's presence could put you all in danger."

Irma glowered "Fine, you're welcome to stay too, Eli. I'm sure Charli can accommodate you in her bed."

Charli frowned. "Stay if you wish, Eli. I'm not leaving Gran alone with a suspected murderer." She stared at Wes. "No offense, Wes. Gran is usually right about people. You're likely innocent; but as Eli said, Wyatt is good at his job. If he arrested you, he must have enough damning evidence to take you to trial. The man doesn't waste his time."

Irma glowered. "Whatever. You're both right; but Wes is staying. Go or stay as you wish."

Charli glared at Eli and then back at the frustrating older folks across the table. "Welcome, home, Wes.'

He choked on his words. "I don't know what to say. Thank you, I guess."

Charli helped her grandmother clear the table. "I'm sure jail food didn't measure up to Eli's cooking. Just wait. Gran's the real chef around here."

Eli picked up his plate. Wes followed the younger man's lead. They cleaned plates and put them in the dishwasher.

Ei motioned Wes toward the couch. "Let's get out of the way so these ladies can do their thing. Tell me, Wes, just how long will you be staying?" He sat at one end of the sofa, motioning to a side chair for Wes.

"I have no idea. I suppose until the trial or until evidence of my innocence is uncovered."

The women sped about the kitchen putting leftovers away. Eventually, after some stilted conversation, they joined the men. Irma carried a tray of fragrant coffee mugs to the living room area to join the fellas.

Irma sat next to the one Wes occupied. Charli cuddled close to Eli on the couch.

Wes shook his head dubiously. "I'm so sorry to intrude on your hospitality this way. I had nowhere else to turn. Irma offered, and I accepted. I apologize. I hadn't considered how it might make you two feel. I couldn't believe it when the judge agreed to Carlton Farmer's proposal to reduce bail and release me into Irma's custody. Of course, they kept my passport. Guess they need to ensure I don't skip out of the country."

Irma sat down to his side. "Yes, but you're not a flight risk. Everything you have would be lost if you skipped out of the country."

"The cops don't see it that way. They probably figured I stole from my company and moved it to an island financial institution."

Irma gasped. "Ridiculous. You are the one heading up the search for that theft." She turned to her granddaughter. "Wes isn't allowed to leave town. The Sweetwater Hotel was the scene of the crime. There's no other viable rental option in the area. The boarding house has started renovations. Motels out on the highway are not decent options for more than an overnight stay at best. It just wouldn't be comfortable. Of course, Wes could look for an apartment, but why bother when he can stay with us?" She didn't seem to care how this would affect the whole family.

She grinned at Wes. "Besides, you'll love my home cooking. Tomorrow I'm making Kentucky Burgoo."

Eli moaned. "The Owens women sure do know how to feed a man. You're going to gain weight while you live here." He rubbed his belly.

Charli chortled. "I'm the baker. Gran's the real cook around here."

Irma patted his hand across the space between their seats. "No worries. We'll sneak a salad or two into the menu every now and again. Of course, you might want to keep up your exercise program."

Wes snickered. "I have no idea what burgoo is, but I'm sure it will be fantastic."

Charlie laughed. "It's a kind of stew, with a variety of meats and veggies. You're in for a treat. I'm going to make my famous cheesy jalapeno cornbread muffins to go with it."

Wes leaned forward, elbows on his knees. "Charli, I am so sorry to put you out. I should go to a motel. I just feel awful about this."

Gran swatted his arm. "You absolutely will not. You're our guest in this house."

The more they talked the more Charli realized Gran was probably right about Wes. Gran was the best judge of character Charli had ever met. She would never do anything to endanger Charli or Eli. If she had even an inkling of distrust in this man, she never would've offered their home up to him.

She might as well give in and go with the flow. Otherwise, she'd feel like a tidal wave had mowed her down. "Wes, I admit, I've been apprehensive about this. I know Gran though. If she says you're trustworthy, you are. You're our guest and Gran's friend. We take care of family and friends. She says you need help—you'll get it from us. This isn't the first mess we've found ourselves tangled in. No need to apologize."

Eli snickered. "Wes, I've found it's useless to argue with these two. Things are better all-around if you just concede to their will."

Wes sat up straight. "Well, if you're not going to let me leave, would you mind if I go shower the jail stink off myself? I've been looking forward to hot water."

Irma stood as he did. "That's a good idea. I'll bring you some fresh towels. Make yourself at home."

He nodded. "Sounds perfect."

Eli stood and pulled his cell phone out. "I need to answer a few business calls." He looked at Charli. "Babe, mind if I take them in your room, for a little quiet?"

"Sure. Go ahead."

CHAPTER TWELVE

Wesley Drake was suspected of two murders. Charli trusted Gran, but something wasn't right. This whole thing just didn't sit well with her. There was something going on, and Gran needed to fess up.

She might be a tiny imp, but Charli was no pushover. Wes acted enamored of Gran, and Gran was acted like a teenager with a crush. This guy was more than a distant old friend.

She and Eli had given him an apprehensive once-over, though they greeted the man with the expected southern hospitality. She remained suspicious about the sudden appearance of Gran's long-lost '*friend*.' She would see what she could learn about the man during dinner.

As Wes showered, he recounted the evening. Charli Owens' copper colored curly ponytail swayed behind her head. Cut-off jeans frayed above her petite but firm legs tucked into thick socks and manly work boots. The orange tee shirt matched her mood as she stood beside tall, dark-haired Eli Lange.

Charli fidgeted with her short nails devoid of polish. Her calloused hands shook Wes's hand firmly to greet him.

Relief seeped through Wes at the surprised but welcoming greeting of Irma's family. He could hardly believe she'd invited him to stay with them. It gave him hope he might have an opportunity to start fresh with the woman who had haunted him for decades.

There had been no hint that Irma had bad-mouthed him to her family. She'd apparently never mentioned him before. Why would she?

It wouldn't be kosher for a grandmother to discuss her love life with family, especially one as long ago and short-lived as his romance with the stunning rock-in-roll singer who still held his heart in her hands.

That must mean she'd gotten over their breakup years ago, as she claimed. Good. He had a clean slate to work from—if you don't count his current predicament with the law.

Wes must've exaggerated what their affair had meant—at least to her. He'd only been a momentary fling to Starr Bright, or Irma, as she was known as here. She'd been everything he had wanted but couldn't have.

Whatever it *had* been, it was up to him to make it what it *would* be. Irma didn't seem to harbor a negative opinion of Wes. She'd invited him into her home. It was a start. He'd take it.

Wes was done screwing up his life. He'd messed up more than four times with the opposite sex before finally realized that substituting other females for the woman he longed for was a useless endeavor. The expensive lesson—financially and emotionally—left him running out of time. Life was an hourglass. One only had so much sand to work with.

He had a long way to go and needed to tread carefully if he wanted to convince Irma he could make her happy for the rest of her life. No matter what it took, she was worth the cost. Wes wasn't leaving Sweetwater until he gave it his best shot. Not that the police would let him leave anyway. He might as well make the most of the time he had here.

During dinner Irma mused about her grandson, Kyler. "I'm used to cooking with a teenaged boy in the house. We always have plenty of meat at the table. The boy eats like his stomach is a bottomless pit. I sure do miss that young rascal." She was exceedingly proud of the young man, her absentee grandson.

Wes joked, "How can I resist a woman who blatantly seduces me with meat?"

Irma chuckled. "I have been praised for my powers of seduction. It's good to see I've still got what it takes." A wicked twinkle in her eyes showed she meant the innuendo.

Wes teased Irma about her many conquests, hoping she would reveal who the father of her son was. Quickly after their breakup photos in industry publications showed her at the party of one of the world's most famous painters known for throwing lavish affairs with lots of celebrities attending. "I understand you've had many a famous conquest during your career."

When the four of them were sated, he shoved back his chair. "Charli and Eli, thank you for a delightful meal. It was delicious."

Charli smiled. "You're very welcome, Wes."

The women stood and began clearing plates. He joined in, taking his to the dishwasher. "I'll help clear the table."

She spoke behind him, "I like a man who works for it. Hop to, Wesley Drake."

He laughed and turned his head to salute her, loving that she'd maintained her wacky personality. "Yes, Ma'am. Before you became a mother, you sure played the field with a lot of famous men."

She went along with his jibes with humor and no hint of embarrassment. The woman had remained a good sport after all the years. "What do you mean by conquests? Are you turning into a gossipmonger?" Her scolding was an obvious tease.

With a snort he grinned. "I read industry rags, too. I've told you I botched my love life. How about you spill a bit about yours? A few months after our split, photos of you and a famous crooner with his whole gang were splashed all over the pages. You sure keep good company."

Her head rocked back, and her mouth went open. "Ah, yes. Esi and I went to one of those elaborate New York parties. She insisted, to cheer me up . . . after you tossed me to the curb. I met Frankie there before he married that cute actress. He was so charming and urbane. I couldn't resist when he asked me out. He and the '*pack*' were a blast. We hit every elegant nightclub in the city. He knew everyone who was anyone and ran in some notorious circles. It was thrilling and at the same time a little scary. Some of his buddies questionable—he was close with some powerful people.

He'd heard the same thing but didn't know personally. "I understand he was buddy-buddy with the President at the time. Is that who you mean?"

"Oh, no. That was way after the assassinations and after that glamourous, blonde actress's death. They were all tied together, you know. The ones I was leery of were mobsters, so I kept my distance. I wanted no part of that. God, forbid I hear or see something I shouldn't. I could've ended up like that sweet girl." She hesitated. "They weren't all goons though. The regulars we hung out with were so much fun." She stopped and shrugged. "That time was fun and games. Nothing serious."

Ignoring his insinuation, she didn't mention her baby daddy. If not one of those ballad singers, who had she been with during that time?

"Let's see." He put a finger to his nose and thought a second. "I read you dated The Pelvis. Any poop you want to share about that affair?"

Her head rocked up and down, and her mouth screwed to the side for a second. "Now there was a southern gentleman. The best of 'em. I've never been out with anyone who treated me more like a queen." She didn't act offended or secretive.

His brow rose. "How did you meet?"

"I was playing a gig in a Memphis nightclub. He and his crew came for the show. In fact, he bought the whole club out that night, so he wouldn't have to put up with groupies tearing his clothes off."

He chuckled at the image but said nothing.

Irma glared. "Don't laugh. It's how it was with him . . . everywhere he went people followed in droves. They were brutal. He feared for his life sometimes." She paused. "Anyway, after the show we talked and talked for hours. The next day, he took me to his home for breakfast. His mama made a huge country spread—biscuits and gravy, sausage, bacon, ham, eggs, and pancakes. That place was like a three-ringed circus. His large troupe ran wild like a bunch of kids. His ma didn't complain. I think she liked all that craziness. She doted on her boy, and he was devoted to her."

"I wondered if he'd taken you to his Memphis mansion." He took a stack of plates from her and slid them into a dishwasher compartment.

"Oh, yeah. We even flew in one of his personal airplanes to San Diego and stayed the weekend at his beach house, swimming, scuba diving, snorkeling, we even skied behind his boat. One day we drove his motorcycle up the coast. It was so fun. I felt alive and free." Her hand rested on her chest.

The glow of her smile made him envious. Someone else caused that elated look. If only Wes could put that expression on her face.

She chuckled and went on, "We stopped at a roadside amusement park. He rented the place for a couple of hours. We rode go-carts and bumper cars without fans swamping him. We dined on hot dogs and milk shakes, and then flew back to Memphis. We parted friends. I caught my tour bus for the next town. Nothing big could've come from our little fling. I would never have lived the way that poor man was forced to. Not many people would. Damned shame. Anyway, he never got over love for his ex-wife. Our fling was fun while it lasted. I never regretted being with him, even for a short while."

The green-eyed monster rose up from down under. Jealousy was a damning emotion. Wes, of all people, had no right to envy men Irma turned to after he'd pushed her out of his life. He fought the devil down and shoved it into the cubical where it belonged.

Who was the father of her son? Lucky son-of-a-bitch, whoever he was. One of the many famous men she'd dated. Or some other guy who had meant something important to her? The dude was long gone from her life.

Wes may never know. It wasn't his right to ask. If she wanted him to know, she'd tell him.

Irma's family was polite, friendly, smart, and enjoyable. She was a lucky gal. She had a loving family and wonderful home.

The woman seemed content in her world. Did he dare throw a wrench in her happiness? It would be selfish of him. "Irma, how will your fella feel about me staying here? Won't Sam be upset?"

Charli had been quietly helping clear the table within earshot of their conversation. Her occasional gasp at one of Irma's revelations was her only remark. She snickered and eyed Irma as she answered.

Irma's chin dipped, and she met his stare. "Wes, where Sam is concerned, it's not really a date. Sam's a special friend. We go out sometimes and spend time together, but there's nothing serious between us. In fact, I would love to introduce you to folks in our sweet, little town."

Good to know. The question was, did Sam know? "That sounds great, but maybe after this trial is over with. Your friends are going to be leery enough knowing you are harboring a potential killer."

Charli cleared her throat but didn't say anything.

Irma did something she was not known for. A slight blush of pink colored her smooth cheeks. Stunning beauty of her classic face had remained devoid of wrinkles one expected of a sixtyish female. Her style had changed . . . for the better, much classier. Thigh-length, raven hair had hung like a thick blanket down her straight back. It had been cut to a shoulder-length bob that framed her face in silky silver that shined in the light.

"You're probably right about waiting to meet the townspeople. It could be uncomfortable for you. As for me, I don't give a rat's patootie what people think of me. The ones who know me well and care about me all know I wouldn't endanger them."

Her eyes and mind had remained bright and alert. Her wit and tongue were sharper than ever. A woman worth fighting for.

Wes had come to accept deep ridges that formed along his chin line, above his nose and at outside edges of his eyes. He faced them daily in the mirror as he shaved. They'd shocked him at first. Evidence of his aging body more so than the way he felt—energetic and vital.

Avoiding his reflection and unwillingness to face the inevitability of aging had passed. In time, he'd grown to appreciate his maturing appearance. He enjoyed increasing respect his age had garnered from some and tolerated those who disregarded the wisdom those years had earned him.

Wrinkles were warning signs of time's value, bringing attention to the manner the dwindling, priceless asset was used. The abundance of minutes he'd once taken for granted was now in limited supply. An urgency had settled in his being, to put affairs in order; and to step forward with some plan for how he would spend the remainder of his existence. He smiled at the rare creature before him, satisfied with today's usage of his allotted moments.

Wes patted his bulging tummy. "Damn, I can't remember the last time I've had a homecooked meal. That was delicious. Thank you." He gazed at Charli and Irma.

One of Charli's cheeks perked up. "You're welcome."

Irma winked. "I'm glad you enjoyed it. I won't sport you around town if it makes you uncomfortable. You can't sit in this house doing nothing and waiting for the police fix this mess. You are a free man and should go about your life however you want."

"Long as I don't leave town."

Irma spit out a breath with a head roll. "This whole thing is ridiculous. You are an innocent man. You have nothing to be embarrassed about. Neither do I. If I cared what people thought of me, I never could've had a successful rock n' roll career." The woman was fearless.

Irma had done everything in her power to make Wes instantly at ease. Charli's welcome had stilted, once she realized why Wes was staying with them.

He placed a hand on Irma's forearm. "I'll at least need to go shopping. The sheriff confiscated my luggage. Hopefully, he will release it soon. Until that happened, I need to purchase a few things."

Her chuckle had a musical lilt to it that sent his heart into double-time. "Of course."

When they were finished, Eli sauntered over and put his arms around Charlie. He nuzzled her ear and gave her a long, sweet kiss. "It's getting late." The tall man, about Wes's size, peeled himself away from the beaming beauty. "Thank you for the meal and company." He looked at Irma and Wes and then turned to his fiancé. "Charli, can we have a word in private?"

Irma beamed. "Of course, Eli. You are family now. Our door is always open."

So, Charli didn't live with Eli. Not what he'd suspected. Charli lived here with Irma. Wes enjoyed the younger woman but was anxious for alone time with Irma . . . as much as she'd give him.

Other things crowded his mind, each begging for priority, but he'd come for Irma. She held the top spot on his radar. His insides were on fire at seeing her again. He hadn't felt this giddy since he was a teenaged boy who asked the prom queen to go out, and she'd accepted.

CHAPTER THIRTEEN

Eli and Charli went to her bedroom. She shut the door, and they sat at the foot of her bed. Eli took her hand and looked into her eyes. "Okay, I understand Irma's obsession to help this man. He clearly means a lot to her, even though they haven't been together for a long time."

Charli pursed her lips. "Yeah, I can see how crazy she still is about Wes. She might not admit it, and he doesn't seem to get it, but she never got over Wesley Drake. It appears he's the one who slipped through her manicured fingers."

Eli's head rocked back. "That aside, Wes acts like a decent fella. It's hard to picture him killing someone. Still, I'm not comfortable with you and Irma alone in the house with this man. He's virtually a stranger to you, and she hasn't seen him in years."

Charli's head tilted to the side. "So, what are you getting at?"

"I don't want to leave you alone here with him. I get it that you don't want to set a bad example for Kyler, but I'm just not okay with this situation."

"Eli, Gran has invited you to move in many times. I hear what you're saying. If you'd like to stay here while Wes is our guest, it's fine. Kyler is away at school. I just won't mention it to him . . . unless he asks. I would never lie to my brother."

"I understand. Well then. I'm your new roommate, my adorable fiancé. Damn, I can't wait until December when you're going to be my wife."

She stroked his square jaw and slid her fingers into his shaggy, blonde locks to pull him close into a sweet kiss. "Me either, but no worries. Time flies." She stood. "Let's go tell Gran."

Eli followed her toward the great room. "Oh, Lordy."

Charli giggled. Eli was right. Gran was sure to have a hilarious response to the news.

Gran and Wes sat chatting on the sofa facing each other. Her knee propped sideways on the cushion and am arm draped along the back. Spying their return, she snickered. "Well, it's about time the two of you joined us. Have a nice little chat?" Her tone was filled with innuendo.

Charli chuckled. "Of course. By the way, Eli will be staying with me for a while."

Eli's head rocked back. "Yes, the project house we're working on is a bit drafty. Charli thought I might be more comfortable here."

Irma's brow wagged. "I'm sure you will. Charli will see to it."

Their evening was pleasant and much less awkward than Charli had thought it might be. Wes was a great conversationalist, and he was interested in their lives and what the town had to offer. He talked about retirement, and said he would like to find a nice, friendly community where he might fit in. "I've never really had a home. I grew up in foster care going from one house to another, sometimes group homes."

"But you were married." Eli scowled, looking confused. "Surely, you had a home then."

Wes's smile showed understanding. "I was—several times. I bought houses. My wives lived in them, but I traveled so much it never felt like home."

The more they talked, the easier it was to see Gran's view of Wesley Drake. He was an open book and never avoided a subject, regardless of how personal it might be.

By the time they all retired to their three bedrooms, Charli had gained a strong liking of the man. Once they were alone, Eli confessed, "I really like Wes. It's easy to see why Irma adores him."

♥♥♥♥

The following morning, Charli joined Gran in the kitchen space and poured them cups of coffee Gran had prepared. The woman was stunning, dressed as usual as if she was attending a photo shoot. Her long legs were concealed by baby blue linen worn with a matching cashmere sweater. Only pearls graced her ears. Hair and makeup were perfection.

Eli entered the room. "Good morning, Irma."

"Ditto, you handsome devil. I trust you slept well." She winked from across the room.

Eli approached the front door with Charli at his side. "You bet 'cha." He glinted at the feisty older woman. Turning to envelop Charli in his arms, his head bent to kiss her soft lips. "I'll see you soon."

"Sure thing." Melted into his arms, she beamed up at him.

Eli released Charli and left through the front door. She turned to Gran. "He's got to meet the electrician for an early appointment. I want to talk with you, so I'm driving separately."

Charli sat on a tall stool at the island beside Gran. She took a sip as she contemplated how to broach the subject. With an exhale she met her gaze. "Gran, I'm concerned about this Wesley Drake thing. Eli and I both really like the man, but he's going to trial, hopefully soon, for killing two people. I realize you care for him as a friend, but it's been a long time since you two have known each other. People change."

Gran nodded and put her cup down. "You're absolutely right, Charli. They do, and Wes changed for the better."

Charli palmed her grandmother's delicate hand. "But you don't even know him now."

Gran stared as though tolerating an errant toddler. "My dear, I know Wesley Drake better than he knows himself."

"How can you say that . . . after all these years?"

"I've been with him long enough. We've talked about important things . . . things that show character. Wes has been through hell in his life. He's grown from his experiences and delved into the devil that was holding him back—the one that drove us apart in the first place."

"Gran, he tossed you aside like a used towel."

Gran shrugged. "He had his reasons. There had been tension between us before the breakup. I saw he was pulling back. His past was eating at him. His mother dropped him off as an infant at a fire station. He believed he wasn't worthy of being loved. He had nothing. Wesley was driven to prove his worth by creating a successful business. It was his sole focus. The more we fell in love, the more terrified he became. I could tell he was looking for an out, and he took the first opportunity to bail."

"But you trust him now?" She grimaced.

"With all my heart." Irma's glare said it all.

"You're still in love with him. Aren't you?" Charli's exhale huffed out.

Gran shrugged a shoulder. "That's my problem—not his." Her pointed look told Charli the confession was confidential. "He's not ready to know that—maybe never will be."

Charli mulled that over for a couple of minutes that felt like an eternity. Since she'd seen the glint in Gran's eyes, she'd wondered. She met Gran's gaze. "Is Wesley Drake my grandfather?"

Irma's grimace looked like she was trying to put a smile on but couldn't. "I'm afraid he is. How do you feel about that?"

Scrunching her eyes closed, Charli considered the idea. The more she learned, the more questions she had. "Did Daddy know?"

Gran gave a solitary nod. "He did. I told him when he was eighteen, but Tucker didn't want to meet Wes. He figured if Wes didn't want me, he wouldn't want him either. Tucker said he didn't need him. He had me, Mama, and Pop. That was before he met your mother in college."

Charli blew out a breath. "Does Wes know?"

Gran's eyes squeezed together and opened. "He doesn't, and he can't know—not yet. Maybe someday. Wes has enough on his plate right now. He's innocent of these crimes. I'm going to do everything in my power to prove it."

She'd always assumed her grandfather had died. Never had she comprehended he was alive, and her father didn't want to know him. That had been his choice. Charli felt differently. Wes seemed to be a good man, and she agreed with Gran. He was innocent.

Charli laid a hand on her grandma's. "Gran. I understand. You're not alone in this. I'll help you, and I'm sure Eli will feel the same."

Gran beamed at her. "Thank you, Sweetheart. I'm sorry I hid this from you, but not sorry I hid it from Wes. He was singularly focused on work and terrified of a relationship that might've required intimacy from him. I didn't want that to affect my son. I wanted a good life for Tucker surrounded by people who loved him unconditionally. With Mama and Pop's help, I gave him that."

Charli frowned. "What about Kyler and me?"

Gran's eyes tented together. "I couldn't tell you and Kyler when your dad was alive. Once he and your mother passed on, you kids had enough shock to deal with. As time went on, it just seemed to not be important. You and Kyler are building wonderful lives. Why would I throw a wrench into them?"

Everything she said made sense. There was logic in it. She had come to trust Gran with her life. No reason to doubt her now. "Okay, Gran. I promise. Your secret is safe with me. . . for now; but at some point, we've got to tell Wes."

"I'm leaving that to your discretion. Just be sure to swear him to secrecy."

Charli nodded. "When this is over, we tell him. Agreed?"

"Agreed." Gran was clearly nervous about that, but she didn't argue.

Stirrings from Kyler's bedroom alerted them Wes had awoken. His muffled voice channeled from the hallway, probably talking on his phone.

"Wes must be checking on his job. He had to neglect it while incarcerated. Let's not disturb his focus." Instead, she made omelets and placed Wes's in the warmer.

Charli and Gran ate in silence. Each had lots on their minds. Charli left for work, feeling more confident that Gran was safe at home with Wes.

♥♥♥♥

Late morning Wes emerged with a grin on his face. "Good morning, Sunshine."

Her heart soared. He hadn't called her that for many years. His nickname for her filled her with joy. "Good morning, Wes. You certainly look upbeat on this bright, fall day. What have you been up to?"

He accepted the cup of Joe and sat at the bar. She pulled his omelet out of the warm oven and placed it beside him where she'd set a place for him earlier. "Eat while you fill me in on your morning."

"Thanks. This was thoughtful." He bit into the savory eggs then released a delighted sigh. "You've become a fantastic cook."

She took the stool beside him and sipped her coffee. "I never had time for it while I was on the road. Constant travel, hotel rooms, and buses. Music took all I had." She sat her cup down. "So, spill."

"Well, I checked in with my CFO. He and the forensic accountant traced the missing money. We now know where it is. They plugged the leak so the thief can't drain more funds. None of us has a clue how to get the money back. We have no idea who did this. Without an arrest, we can't prosecute the embezzler."

She frowned. "Do you think whoever stole the funds killed Tara and Greyson? One or the other might've caught onto the scam. They could've been ready to expose him. That would be motive for murder."

He sighed. "Could be. No way of knowing, until we find out who the culprit is."

She studied his disillusioned expression. "It's a good theory. Who else might want Greyson dead? An unhappy client? Business associate? An employee? His assistant? A family member? His son? You said they'd been estranged since Greyson's wife died five years ago and that Taylor blamed Grey."

His head waivered. "Who knows for sure? Grey loved his boy. He paid for private schools and college, though Taylor put little effort into any of it other than partying. Still yet, Grey funded startup of the kid's business. He didn't blame Taylor for hating him. He might not have been around all that much while the boy was growing up, but he always wanted the best for his son."

"What type of business is Taylor in?"

"I don't know for sure. Some sort of manufacturing enterprise nearby that services businesses in New York City."

"Why did Taylor blame Greyson for his mother's death? It was an accident. Right?"

Wes gave a heavy sigh. "Greyson claimed the kid had a right to be angry. It was a car wreck. Grey was driving. He blamed himself for his wife's death. The man was devastated. Far as I know, Grey and Taylor had no contact at all since then." His hands cupped around his mug, and he stared into it as though in a daze.

"That's really sad." She needed to change the tone of their discussion. "I have been busy myself this morning. I called my friend, Sage Gordon."

He frowned. "Isn't Gordon the sheriff's last name?"

She smiled. "Yes, Sage is married to Wyatt. She has an organic farm not far from here, Parsley, Sage, Rose, Mary & Wine. That keeps her busy most of the time, but Wyatt appointed her as the sheriff's department liaison to the Kentucky Cyber Crime Unit in Louisville. It's a part-time position, and she steps in when needed. Sage grew up in New York State and worked for the FDA when she was married to her first husband. She's no novice when it comes to crime fighting. Someday I'll have to tell you all about the predicaments she's got herself into. Anyway, she gave me the number of a New York expert in tracking internet scams."

His brows furrowed. "So, a lawman of sorts?"

She shrugged. "Not really, but he has worked with law enforcement before."

His eyes widened. "A hacker?"

"I guess so. She said he should be able to find the person who stole your money." She slid a piece of paper toward him with the man's contact information on it.

Wes picked up the sheet. "Wow. Well, I guess that's exactly what the situation requires." He gave her a grateful smile. "Thank you for this and for everything you and your family are doing."

She patted his hand casually and then refilled their mugs. "Learn anything else this morning? I heard muffled sounds from your room and assumed you were catching up on calls."

"I spoke with Simone Claiborne, Grey's assistant. With Grey gone, she has decided to retire. She's getting up there in her late fifties and has worked with Grey since he and I started the partnership. She doesn't feel up to working with a new boss. I convinced her to stick around long enough for me to hire his replacement and hers, so she can train them."

"That's good news." She took her seat to his side; increasingly sure it was where she belonged. Too bad, he didn't realize it.

"It is. I don't need to lose anymore key people in the company—not now." He sighed. His closed lips turned up slightly. "On the bright side, I spoke with a couple of Grey's clients. They heard of his passing and were starting to panic. I convinced them to stick around for a while longer. The good thing is they're busy under current touring contracts. Grey was in the process of booking future events for them. They'd be crazy to bail out—if I can save those events for them."

She gave him her most ambitious smile. "You will. You're great at what you do. Those powerful in the industry know you well enough to have faith in you."

His eyes were moist as he gazed into hers. "I appreciate you, Irma. That means a great deal to me. In fact, the top candidate I pinpointed to Grey as my replacement left me a message. She's interested in buying him out. I need to call her and get more details. I'm not sure how to go about that. I have another message from Grey's lawyer I need to respond to. He can probably handle details. He should be working on Grey's estate. I should call Taylor myself, but I'm afraid he won't speak with me. After all, I'm accused of murdering his father. I'm assuming he's Grey's sole heir. It may be what the attorney wants to discuss. I doubt Taylor wants to manage the company. He might want to be a silent partner or have me or someone else buy him out."

"I suppose so, and you're right. The estate attorney will likely need to handle any transfer. The only thing you have in common is your shares in the corporation. Right?"

He pushed his empty plate aside and took the last sip of his drink. "Yes. I'll follow up with the attorney now I've had some nourishment. That was a great breakfast. I appreciate it."

She stood to clean up. Her phone buzzed. "What now?"

CHAPTER FOURTEEN

That evening the foursome sat at the table enjoying a glass of wine. Gran pulled out a manila envelope. "Wes, you know I'm beside you in this trial thing. I did a bit of snooping myself. The owner of The Sweetwater Hotel is a friend. I asked him if I could look at his security footage, to see who all entered Tara's . . . your room."

Charli gasped. "Gran, aren't the police supposed to be checking that?"

Gran nodded. "They did, and they have a copy of it all themselves. I thought I might see something they missed, since I'd look at it from another point of view."

Eli sat his goblet down. "What did you find, Irma." He didn't act the least bit surprised at her sleuthing.

"Here are some printouts of things we found interesting. I don't know if they mean anything, but these were somewhat suspicious." She pulled a stack of printed sheets from the package and laid them out. They all leaned forward to inspect the photos. Gran pointed to one. "This is the woman who serviced the room prior to your check in. She's a new employee. In fact, they have several new people and are still understaffed. No one entered either room after that until you did."

They got a good look at the maid. Gran pointed to the date and timestamp on the bottom right. "Here's the time stamp." There was a similar mark on each page.

"Here's when you and Tara first entered your registered rooms." She pointed to one and then another sheet. "And this is when you came out."

Charli reached behind her to a desk to secure a pen and pad. Gran chuckled. "No need, Charli. I wrote the times and events down in a log." She patted the envelope indicating its thickness, enough to hold a small booklet. Charli returned her focus to the pages.

"Here, you and Tara went into your room together." The shot showed only a few seconds difference from the last one.

Wes nodded. "Yes, I wanted her to see if it would suit her needs." He pointed to the next photograph. "See, we were only in there about a minute." The image showed Tara going to her room alone. She returned momentarily with her suitcase. "She knocked, and I let her in. Then I rolled my bag to her room and entered." He pointed to the next photo.

Gran gave a nod. "You came out a couple of minutes carrying a small plastic bag."

He smiled. "Yes, I was going to get ice when I found Tara ready to go to the front desk to change rooms. Once she settled in my room and I in hers, I did that." He indicated the next in the sequence, showing his return to the room.

Gran sat up straight. "Room service came and went, but other than that, no one entered or left either room until the next morning. She pulled out a shot of him leaving his room with the newspaper he picked up off the floor at his unit's door.

"That's when I knocked on her door." He picked up another photo. "She was packing her bag; I suppose with what she needed at the pool. Anyway, I told her to meet me in the café; and I left." He pointed to the next page. A few minutes later, she met me at the breakfast table, carrying a large tote." He pointed to the date and timestamp.

Gran selected another photograph showing Tara leaving her room.

Charli scowled. "Eli and I were dining there that morning. We didn't pay you any attention until Tara became so loud. We couldn't ignore it. She caused a heck of a scene."

Eli took her hand in his. "Tara was really riled up. You had to be embarrassed."

Wes shrugged. "Listen, I stopped being embarrassed by the actions of others a long time ago. Some of the pampered celebrities I work with every day are so high strung nothing they do surprises me. All I can control is my own actions. I wasn't angry at Tara. She had a right to be frustrated. Tara has . . ." His head bent a second. "She had a short fuse, and she'd been under pressure lately. Recently she took on a lot of debt—a car loan and mortgage on her home. Her mother is ill. Without giving me time to finish outlining my plans, she jumped to the wrong conclusion. I intended to ensure her continued employment, if that's what she wanted. If she chose to leave the company, I would've compensated her well. She would've had no need to worry about money and would've had plenty of time to find other employment. In fact, I intended to help her with that, if it's the way she chose to go."

Charli grimaced. "That might be the case. To onlookers—and there were many of them—it appeared to be World War III." Hopefully her exaggeration would help him realize the ferocity of their argument.

Wes's brows rose and fell. "I suppose so. Anyway, she stormed from the restaurant saying she was going to the pool. I figured she needed cooling off time, so I went on with my plans. If she'd made it through the night, everything would've been fine. Unfortunately, I never got the chance to fully hash it out with her."

Gran glanced at the two of them. "At some point, she must've told a staff member to bring extra towels to her room. We couldn't find that on the recordings. It could've been while she was in the pool room. Or she could've run into a maid in the hallway."

"If that's the case, she might've simply gotten the towels from the maid at the time." Eli ruled that out.

Charli squirreled her mouth to one side. "Yeah, it must've been someone who serviced the pool area. She probably told them to stop by while she was swimming."

Ima gave a shoulder shrug. "Sounds right. She must've intended to shower and wash her hair after her swim. Extra towels could've been in case she chose to shower again in the morning."

Gran went on through the stack of papers. "This maid delivered towels at twelve-thirty. She knocks several times and then enters with her passkey. She's in the room less than five minutes, steps out and leaves. At three-thirty-five Tara returned with wet hair. Room Service delivered a meal at four o'clock. The server was in her room for about five minutes, enough time for him to set the table and for her to find him a tip. She was alone for a few hours after that."

Eli's face was stonelike. "She probably decided to take a nap, because she was found a little while later in her bed."

Charli scowled. "Let me see that shot of the maid with the towels." She picked it up and studied the visual closely. "I recognize this woman. You can't see her face in this photo, but she was behind the dining room bar when we ate breakfast."

Eli took the picture she handed him. "Yes, she does look like the same woman. She's in a different uniform. You can barely see her tattoo sticking out of the color of her dress. Yes." He laid it on the table. "It's the bartender."

Gran pointed to a shot of her leaning on the checkout desk talking to the new fella manning it. "Yes, that's what Ralph said. We found this of her flirting with the desk clerk. Something drew him away from his station. She waited at the desk for him and fiddled on the desktop—probably seeing the towel request come through. Then she went down the hall toward the service area. She must've gone there to change into the maid's uniform and to pick up towels, which she then delivered to Tara's room. Ralph said employees are doing everything they can to help, back each other up, and maintain hotel quality standards. The flirty bartender must've seen the request come up on the front desk computer screen and figured if she was seen delivering something to a guest's quarters, it would look strange if she didn't have suitable attire on." Gran sighed. "Next is the maid who did the pre-check-in cleaning knocking. She then entered, and here she is running from the room with panic on her face."

CHAPTER FIFTEEN

Gran's elbow leaned on the table so she could meet Wesley eye-to-eye. "No one entered that room except for you, Tara, the room service deliverer, the maid who cleaned the room originally, and the bartender who delivered Tara's towels. I assume you don't believe Tara poisoned herself."

Wes's eyes widened, and his mouth flew open. "Absolutely not."

Eli blinked. "I should hope not. I looked arsenic up. I won't go into gory details, but it's a horrible way to die."

Heat sizzled down Charli's spine. She shuddered.

Gran somberly nodded. "Well, then, there's those three folks—or you."

Wes proclaimed, "Well, I didn't do it."

Gran placed a manicured hand on his. "I know that, Wes. That leaves those three. The maid has been at the hotel for a month. She's a local resident. I don't know her, but she should be easy to check out. The guy from room service has worked there for years. Ralph vouches for him, but he should be easy to check out as well. I think he lives somewhere between here and Bonnyville."

Eli squinted. "What about the bartender? I trust she's new at the hotel."

Irma nodded with a sigh. "She is. Ralph hired her a few days before Wes and Tara arrived. She was very good at her job and was highly recommended by her previous employer." She laid the woman's employee record and letter of recommendation on the table.

Wes stared at the woman's face and homed in on the tattoo. "What is this?"

Eli glared. "It looks like a capital V. Why would someone have that tattooed on their body?"

Charli winced. "Lots of reasons. Involvement in human trafficking. The letter symbolizes a person's initial."

Gran's nose snarled up. "Wouldn't they have both initials?"

Charli shrugged. "Who knows. Let me do an internet search." She pulled a screen up on her phone and typed in the request. Several things popped up, mostly with different designs of the same letter. An explanation showed what it symbolized. "This says V is for Vengeance. That's weird."

Eli's head leaned back. "Wow, that woman must've had something awful against Tara, if she was the reason for that odd tat."

Gran wiggled her eyebrows. "Or it could have another whole meaning for that woman. If it meant vengeance to that gal, the person she wanted vengeance from was likely not some stranger. Odds are she and Tara didn't even know each other. Wes, you said yourself that you and Tara didn't know anyone in town, except me; and she and I weren't acquainted."

His vague head rock was almost imperceptible. "Right, not to my knowledge."

Gran bit her lower lip, something she rarely did. "Okay, this is our only clue. Any one of us can investigate the two hotel workers who are Sweetwater residents. This gal was from out of town. She also quit when the body was discovered. Ralph said she wasn't the only one to up and quit. A murder in house must've scared the workers shitless."

Charli groaned. "We need to track all three of them down and question them. Either one of them is involved, or they might know something we don't."

Eli squeezed her hand, and her shoulders relaxed.

Gran grimaced. "We don't know where she stayed while in town. It wasn't the hotel. That means she rented an apartment, a room at one of the motels out on the highway, or at the boarding house. It's closed now, but this happened before they started renovations. We can easily find the ones who are from here. The bartender is another story. She may still be living in town, or she could've moved on. She was recommended by the owner of the tavern where she last worked in New York City. It's called Sip On The Fly—catchy name. This is probably a lark, but someone must check it out. The sheriff isn't going to."

Wes's face went white. "Where the hell is this joint?"

She shot him the recommendation letter. He looked closer. "Oh, hell, unless this franchise has another bar in the city, this is the airport tavern where I met Grey before flying to Louisville."

It wasn't but felt like several minutes, the only sound in the room came from their breathing hard. Charli's chest ached with dread and tension, as she gazed at her grandmother. "What do you propose we do?"

Gran squirreled her mouth up. "I'm going to New York to see if she returned to work there. If not, I'll talk to the owner. Maybe he can tell me where she lived when he employed her. If so, I'll go see her. I just want to see what she knows and how she reacts."

Charli half stood. Her hands slammed on the table. "You are doing nothing of the sort. For one thing, Wes is in your custody. He doesn't know anyone else in town. You are his only ally. You need to be here for him. Stay and investigate the maid and room service deliverer. Check out locations where the bartender might've lived and find out if she's still in town. I'll go to New York and explore this barkeep lead."

Eli glared at her for a minute before speaking. "I'm going too. She's right, Irma. I see you're determined to do this. It would be best if you remain in Sweetwater with Eli and let us handle this."

She gave him her biggest smile, leaned over, and pecked his bristling cheek. It didn't surprise her that he would have her back. He always did. She leaned toward Wes. "Wes, do you recognize that woman?"

He studied the spiky-haired blonde's image. "The face is vaguely familiar, but I can't place her. There's something just not right about it. The tattoo isn't fully visible, but it is an odd one. I've seen that somewhere before. I'm sorry, but I don't. Damn, this is going to haunt me."

Gran's brows went up. "Not as much as going to jail for life . . . or worse."

Wes winced and went quiet. Meeting their gazes again, he acted on the verge of tears. "I don't know what to say. Irma, what you've already done for me goes way beyond friendship. Charli, Eli, we've only just met, and here you are dropping everything to run off on a wild goose chase to help prove me innocent."

Eli's brows went up. "Yes, Wes, we're doing this partly for you; but the truth is, Charli, like Irma, is convinced of your innocence. Wyatt and his people are busy building a case against you. They won't be looking elsewhere. Irma and Charli are adamant about helping you. I would do anything for these women. I'm not letting the love of my life go to New York to look up some strange female without me at her side. If she's doing this, so am I."

Irma stood and picked up her phone. "It's settled. I'm making reservations for the two of you for a flight tomorrow morning. I'll also make hotel arrangements."

Wes stood, fumbled in his pocket and pulled out a wallet. He selected a card and pushed it toward Irma. "Use my card. I'm paying for this little adventure." She took it and moved away to find silence to make her call. He drew out a fistful of bills and pushed it toward Eli. "Here's some cash to cover food and transportation once you're in the city."

Eli's hand went up. "No, thanks. I've got it; but if you wish, you can reimburse me once we return."

Wes flinched. "Listen, if you sense any danger at all . . . anywhere . . . anytime . . . you drop it all and head immediately back to Sweetwater. I don't want to risk you putting yourselves in harm's way. Understand?"

Charli nodded, unclear how she would react if something shady came up. Eli didn't sound as unsure as she was. "Absolutely, we'll be on the next flight home."

Wes put the money back and pocketed his wallet. "Listen, while you're in town, would you mind checking in personally at my agency headquarters? It would be good for my people to hear from a real, live person, that I'm on top of this thing and have their best interests at heart. Also, maybe you can meet with the CFO and forensic accountant, possibly the FBI agents working on the case, and see if they've learned anything more about the embezzlement. Who knows? Maybe a set of fresh eyes on the data will help."

Eli nodded. "Sure, it can't hurt."

Charli chuckled. "We might even stumble on some new evidence to clear your name." She could only hope. This plan would likely come up a big fat zero but doing something . . . anything felt like they were moving forward.

CHAPTER SIXTEEN

Eli opened the door to Sip On The Fly tavern. Charli stepped inside. The quaint barroom-restaurant was occupied with a dozen or more travelers accompanied by various backpacks, computer bags and luggage. Most focused on their phones, drinks, food, or conversations with companions, ignoring the newcomers' entrance.

Charli stepped to the empty end of the bar and took a seat on a tall chair. She slipped her backpack off and laid it between her feet on the riser. Eli accepted the chair beside hers and did the same.

A green-haired waitress with a spikey, short hairdo and four earrings to one ear walked toward them. Dressed in black, even to the lips, the woman appeared to be in her early twenties. Her tee shirt's short sleeves displayed multiple tattoos on firm forearms. The goth looking gal wiped the bar in front of them off with a damp cloth. "What's your poison?"

Charli smiled casually. "I'll have the BLT, a spicy Bloody Mary and a tall ice water."

Eli perused bottles displayed in front of the well-lit, green and yellow back wall. "I'll have a Fire and Ice Bourbon on the rocks, a cheeseburger with everything and fries." The Gen Y female disappeared without further word, behind what looked like the kitchen door.

Charli snickered. "Either she isn't aware of the tragedy that had occurred here, or she has a sick sense of humor.

It's difficult to say which, from her stone-faced expression."

Eli snorted. "I'd guess the latter."

The millennial gal returned, busied herself at the bar for a few minutes the stepped toward them with their drinks. "Food will be right up."

Charli smiled and cupped her drink in two hands. "Thank you." She paused while the woman placed napkins in front of them. "This looks like a nice place to work. You been here long?"

A shoulder shrug as the other woman eyed her. "It's decent. Not long." Clearly, she was a person of few words.

Charli laid a photo on the countertop. "Do you know this woman?"

Without a glance at the picture, the gal cocked a brow. "Nope."

Eli propped the photo up. "We're looking for this woman and understand she used to work here. Do you recognize her?" His tone was matter of fact, and the bartender reacted to its insistence by glancing at the photograph.

"Never seen her before. I ain't been here long—only a couple a weeks." She glared stone-faced.

Charli stirred her icy drink. "Is Ray Sanders in? I understand he's the manager."

The waitress's head tilted. "Ray is in the back office."

Eli smiled congenially. "Would you mind terribly, asking Mr. Bacon if we could have a word with him? It's important."

With a shrug of shoulders, the barmaid disappeared through the kitchen doors again.

"Friendly—that one." Charli snickered.

Eli chuckled. "Typical New Yorker."

They sipped their cocktails and waited, quietly discussing their next moves. A few minutes later, the bartender returned with a tray. She sat plates of their food in front of them. "Ray will be out in a few." Then she sped toward customers at the far end of the bar.

They were nearly finished with their meals when the pudgy, balding man with a sparse ring of greying black hair entered from the kitchen. He spoke quietly over the bartender's shoulder to her then turned and strode his short legs toward them.

His accent was thick Jersey, and his glare indicated he had little patience for his busy day being interrupted. "What can I do you fer?"

Charli extended a hand and a smile "Ray Bacon?" He nodded acknowledgement. "I'm Charli Owens, and this is Eli Lange. We've flown into town in search of a woman, and we believe you might be able to help us locate her."

Eli pushed the photo toward the man. "Mr. Bacon, do you recognize this woman?"

Bacon picked the photograph up and stared. His face screwed up. "Looks familiar, but something's off. I don't know."

Eli pushed the picture of Sue March, the alias the woman had taken the job at the Sweetwater Hotel under toward him. "What about now?"

Ray stared at the second photo. "Yeah, I recognize her. That's Dana Sue March. She tended bar here for a while, but I ain't seen her for a couple a weeks."

Charli smiled at their progress. "How did her employment end?"

Ray raised a shoulder. "Same as most. Just didn't come in one day. It's a hazard of the biz."

Eli pushed. "It's okay, man. We know about the murder here. Did that have anything to do with Ms. March's quitting?"

Ray eyed them critically. "That why you're here? I told the fuzz everything I know. I'm just a businessman. Never seen them guys before in my life. Ain't got nothing to do with me."

Charli laid a hand flat on the bar. "We realize that. We just need to ask some questions and need to find Dana Sue March."

Eli took another tactic. "I'm the attorney for her deceased aunt's estate, and I need to locate Ms. March. She has an inheritance coming. We learned she'd worked here, and we hoped you'd be able to provide us her forwarding address."

Without a word, the man disappeared into the kitchen again. Charli's eyes met Eli's. "Guess he's not going to be much help."

Eli frowned. "Maybe not." He finished his bourbon and pushed the remainder of his food away.

Charli took her last bite, as Mr. Bacon returned carrying a folder. Ray walked to them and flopped the file on the countertop. "Dana Sue was a good bartender. Dependable. Quiet girl. I figured she got spooked when that dude offed that fella in here. Some folks are leery of working where a person croaked. You know?" When Eli's head rocked indicating agreement, Bacon went on. "She didn't leave a forwarding address. You sure she left town?"

Charli smiled. "Relatively sure. She worked in Sweetwater, Kentucky for a few days after she left here.

We hoped you could point us in the right direction to locate her." She laid the copy of his glowing recommendation letter for Sue March.

"Kentucky?" Ray grimaced. "What the fuck?" He picked up the letter, glanced down at it with a chubby finger then met Charli's look. "Son of a bitch! Pardon my French. I didn't write this piece of shit. I gave her a good reference, but she never bothered to ask. Didn't have to steal my stationery and write it herself. That bitch forged my signature. Did pretty good, too. I ain't never heard of no Sue March though. Why did she use that name?"

Eli tried to get things back on track. "No clue. Regardless of what name she used in Kentucky or how she came about that recommendation, this is Dana Sue March we're talking about. Can you help us find her?"

The puffy-faced man snickered. "Who knows? You might be able to track her down with her previous address. I wouldn't normally share such private information, but that bitch clearly doesn't deserve my loyalty." He laid her employment record sheet in front of them. An image of Dana Sue with a mousey brown ponytail and the company shirt on took up the top right corner.

Eli took a photo of the paper with his phone. "Thank you, Mr. Bacon."

Charli smiled innocently. "What exactly happened in here that day?"

Ray grimaced. "Not real sure." He wiped a sweaty looking hand across his balding head. "Far as I can tell from what the fuzz said, some traveler spiked a drink and switched it with the other dude at his table. I think it was rat poisoning or something like that. He hightailed it out of here, and his buddy croaked right there on the table." He shook his head wearily. "It was a bad scene after that. Cops all over the joint. People in and outta here. It was twelve hours before I could close and head home, two days before I could clean up the mess they left and reopen. I'm still trying to recover lost revenue." His mouth quirked to the side. "Damn shame. At least, it's a transient clientele. Folks come and go . . . traveling, you know. Not like we've got a regular customer base. It's a good thing."

Eli shoved a fifty-dollar-bill in front of Bacon. "Thanks. You've been helpful, and we appreciate it." The man pocketed the bill, snatched the file, and disappeared through the doors he'd come from without further ado.

Charli took one last sip of water, stood, and slipped her backpack on. "The folks from Wes's office are expecting us. We'd best get going. After that, we need to visit Dana Sue March's last known New York City address."

Eli laid another fifty on the bar, sat his empty highball glass on it, and followed Charli out. "Hopefully someone in her old neighborhood can tell us where she moved to."

CHAPTER SEVENTEEN

CFO Jonah Helm met Charli and Eli in the lobby and took them to his office. They asked every question they could think of about Wes, Greyson, Tara Bonner, and the missing company money. After a half hour with Helm, he walked them across a hallway to a temporary office space set up in a conference room where they spent time with the forensic accountant. Wes had hired Irvin Sands to inspect company finances in preparation for his retirement, with hopes Greyson would buy Wes out of the firm. When they exhausted their questioning of him, Sands escorted them to Wes's office suite and turned them over to Simone Claiborne, Greyson's assistant.

The fifty-something, stately, urbane female in a form-fitting two-piece suit, greeted them with an ingenuous smile and off-putting expression. She showed them to leather, wine-colored guest chairs facing her mahogany desk, backed by a burgundy wall that contrasted the taupe room. A sizable, ornate, wood-framed, modern art painting depicted rolling waves and a beach scene. The desktop's only adornments were a closed white laptop computer and two framed photos. Thick claret carpeting gave the small space an elegant air.

With a wave, Simone instructed them to sit, then smoothed her pencil skirt as she took the executive chair across from them. She folded her hands on the desk and met their eyes matter-of-factly. "How may I help you?"

Eli took the lead. "As I'm sure Wesley Drake has told you, we're investigating the deaths of Tara Bonner and Greyson Corbin, as well as the company's mis-appropriated funds. Wes assured us you would be cooperative."

Noting Eli's choice of words, she doubted how much cooperation they could expect from the standoffish female.

The woman's head barely nodded. "Of course, but I'm not sure how I can be of assistance."

Charli gave her a cordial smile. "We understand you knew Greyson better than most. Can you tell us about him?"

Simone's shoulders rocked slightly back. Her eyes went to the side and down, and her lips barely smiled. "Greyson was a wonderful man, dedicated to his work and clients, and as honest as they come. His integrity was without question. He was handsome and well-liked." Moisture filled her eyes, and a hand dabbed corner tears away. She sighed heavily. "He will be missed."

Eli cleared his throat during the pause. "What was your relationship with him like?"

She met his eyes with a dignified stare. "If you're asking if we had a romantic or sexual connection, that is out of the question. Grey was not my type." She turned the photographs on her desk toward them. "This is our wedding day. My wife and I were married on a beach in Rarotonga and spent our honeymoon there ten years ago."

Emotion wasn't something Charli had anticipated, given Simone's attitude as they'd arrived. "What a lovely wedding! The setting is gorgeous. Do you like the beach? I've never heard of Rarotonga. Is it nice?"

"Yes, it's beautiful there. It's in the Cook Islands, in the South Pacific. We love it and plan to retire to the island and have since purchased a small oceanfront cottage. We try to get there as often as work allows."

Charli let her interest show, given the opportunity to establish a personal rapport with Simone. "Eli and I are trying to figure out where to go on our honeymoon. Since you're a beach fan, what would you suggest?"

Simone warmed a bit toward her. "Well, there are hundreds of thousands of fabulous beaches in the world. My wife and I prefer the South Pacific for its laid-back atmosphere. Our bungalow is on the larger island of Rarotonga. With about seventeen-thousand people, it is more densely populated than the other Cook Islands. We love its lush green and it is ringed by white-sand beaches. stunning coral. and s blue lagoon. We've traveled the world, but the beauty of the Cook Islands and the entire Polynesian group can't be beat."

Charli chuckled. "Seventeen-thousand? That's only about twice the size of our little town in Kentucky."

Simone finally smiled. "Yes, it's small, but being the most populated allows for conveniences the smaller islands don't have."

Eli pretended to be interested in the idea of honeymooning on the distant island. "My only concern about going to such an exotic location is banking. We are self-employed and may need to manage financial transactions for our business while we're away. I fear we'd have limited access from such a remote, distant location."

Simone's facial expression turned reassuring. "Not a problem. That's one of those conveniences I mentioned. The Cook Islands' financial system comprises about thirty financial entities to manage any financial transaction you need between businesses, individuals, governments, or other public entities in the island nation, as well as the rest of the world. In fact, Aria and I do our banking through a private trust she and I set up when we married there. Their new asset protection vehicle is attractive compared to other offshore banking jurisdictions."

He glanced at Charli then back to Simone. "That is reassuring. Aren't the Cook Islands part of Australia?"

Simone's head shook. "That's a misconception. They are a self-governing island nation in free association with New Zealand."

"New Zealand . . . that sounds exotic and interesting," Charli cooed.

Simone gave her a condescending smile. "You should go sometime."

Charli nodded agreement. "Aria, that's an unusual name. Did she take your last name, or did you take hers? I hope you don't mind my prying." It was the reason for their visit, after all.

Simone smiled. "Yes, it is. My wife's name is Aria Clemmons. We chose not to change given names due to the nature of our businesses."

Charli noted the name on her phone, assuming Simone would think she was making note of a fabulous honeymoon spot. "Well, we've wasted enough of your time on our upcoming nuptials. Let's get to the reasons we're seeking your help. Do you know anything about Greyson's private or love life?"

Simone returned to her unmoving business manner. "Grey didn't have a love life. Elana Corbin died five years ago in a car accident. Grey was driving. They hit an icy patch. The vehicle skidded out of control. He was injured, but she died at the scene. As far as I know, he hasn't dated since. He was very much in love with his wife. Her death broke his heart."

When the woman hesitated to go on, Charli picked up the thread. "What about family and friends?"

"As I said, Grey was well-liked. He didn't have much time for personal friendships, though he and Wesley have been close since they first met. Grey had no family I know of, except for his son Taylor."

Eli prompted, "Tell us about Taylor Corbin."

She swallowed visibly. "They were not close. The boy resented his father's extensive travel while he was growing up. Grey was gone most of the time during the boy's youth, leaving his upbringing to Elana. Grey gave Taylor every advantage money could buy—expensive private schools, ivy-league college. He even financed Taylor's business startup. Naturally, the boy was close to his mother. He blamed his father for her death—understandably. Grey never forgave himself for the accident. Why should his son? The rift between them grew wider after that. Far as I know, they have had no contact since."

Charli made notes on her phone as they talked. "What kind of business is Taylor in."

Simone's lips pursed. "Some sort of printing facility in Jersey City. They mostly serve companies in the New York City area. Grey mentioned they were successful. He was proud of his son and loved Taylor, though the boy didn't reciprocate. I believe the facility is on one of those low numbered streets. I don't know the exact location."

"What's business name?" Charli frowned.

"I'm sorry. I recall it was something simple, maybe including Taylor's name."

Eli changed the subject. "Tell us about your interactions with Tara Bonner."

She went stone-faced. "We had a professional relationship. Ms. Bonner managed Wesley's team workload and budget. I managed Greyson's business. Tara Bonner and I barely interacted, only when it came time to reconcile budgets. I reported Grey's financial results to Tara. She merged it with Wes's. Quarterly, she reported the combined moneys to the CFO who then created corporate reports."

Not satisfied, Charli prodded. "I understand there was friction between the two of you."

Simone stared down her nose at Charli. "Our interaction was work-related. We may've disagreed from time to time on how to administer accounts. It was purely business. I know nothing of her personal affairs."

Did she choose the word 'affairs' for some specific reason? The woman seemed deliberate in everything she said and did. Charli kept digging. "Wes said Greyson disliked Tara. What can you tell us about that?"

"Wesley is correct, though I resent his . . . or you, trying to shift attention from Wes toward myself and Greyson. Grey would never do anything to harm Tara. Neither would I, for that matter. Besides, what does that have to do with anything? Grey was gone before Tara died." A slight choking fringed her voice. "Grey was bitter about Tara's implication he and I mismanaged company funds. He took it personal and did not care for her attitude. Grey would never do anything underhanded." The woman certainly sounded loyal to Greyson.

Eli played the peacemaker. "Wesley never indicated he distrusted Greyson. Nor did he mention Tara having any notion Greyson might be responsible for missing company capital."

He didn't mention Simone's part in it.

Simone's shoulders straightened more than her normal prim posture. "That's an entirely different subject. I have no idea how that theft happened. I'm sure the experts will get to the bottom of it. It isn't my responsibility or area of expertise."

Charli tried to keep the peace. "Your wife is lovely. Does Aria work here in the city?"

Simone smiled with her lips closed. "She's an investment broker on Wall Street."

Charli wanted more. "Wes said you're considering retiring, now Greyson is out of the picture."

Simone's eyes closed as she nodded. "I am. I'm too old to adjust to working with a new manager. I promised Wesley to stick around long enough to train Grey's replacement and his assistant."

Charli smiled. "Retirement sounds nice, especially since you have that little place on the beach. What a life. I envy you that. So, will Aria retire also?"

Simone's expression didn't change. "She will. In fact, we just listed our condo for sale yesterday."

"Well, it shouldn't take long to sell. I hear a nice home is hard to find in New York City."

"We're in no hurry."

Charli laid her phone in her lap. "Do you know anyone who might've meant Greyson or Tara harm?"

Simone met her gaze. "No one. The only person I know of who didn't like Grey was his son. Grey and Tara butted heads, and he didn't like her. She couldn't have killed him. Could she?" She paused and changed gears. "I believe Tara had a sister. Wes mentioned her mother was ill. Maybe one of them can give you more information about Tara."

Charli made a note on her phone. "That's a good idea. We'll talk with them."

Simone smiled with lips closed. "A man used to send Tara flowers on a regular basis, so she must've had a boyfriend. I don't know what else I can tell you that would be of help." Simone's hands clenched together on the desktop. "From what the police tell me, they're positive Wesley killed Grey. He's been arraigned to stand trial for Tara's murder. They must have ample evidence to convict him, or he wouldn't be in that situation." Clearly, Simone believed Wesley to be guilty. Or she was pointing fingers in his direction for another reason.

Charli stood and spoke in a non-confrontation manner. "They have not looked past Wesley to find the complete truth. That's why we're here—to get a comprehensive picture of the situation. We don't believe Wes is guilty."

Eli got to his feet. "We've taken up enough of your time. Thank you. You've been a great help. Unless you have something to add, we'll let you get back to work."

Simone smiled sadly. "I hope you're right about Wesley." She walked them to the exit. "You don't believe Wesley and I are in danger. Do you?" They and the CFO were the only top executives left alive in the company.

Eli shook her hand. "Let's hope not." It was a possibility.

Charli extended hers. Simone's hand was icy as she shook it. "Thank you, Simone. We'll get back to you if we have further questions."

CHAPTER EIGHTTEEN

Charli stepped out of the hotel bathroom after a long, hot shower, feeling refreshed and hopeful. Wearing only a towel, she sauntered into the bedroom, finding Eli flipping through news channels on the television.

He stood and winked. She stepped into his arms and laid her head against his hard, flat stomach, her short stature meeting him only that height. He stroked her hair, and one strong hand slid along her bare back. Her chest tightened, and a lump blocked her air. Tears racked her body, and she allowed them to flow while he held her tight against his hard frame.

"You're obviously committed to proving Wesley's innocence. He's a nice enough guy. I like him, and I understand your wanting to support Irma in this. I figure you're doing it mostly to prevent her from putting herself into a potentially dangerous situation. What I don't get is, why are you so emotionally vested in proving his innocence?" Eli had accompanied Charli to New York to protect and support her, but she couldn't expect the man she loved to not question her when she totally lost it with a fit of blubbering in his arms.

"He's got to be innocent. I can't believe anything else." She sniffed the end to her tear-fest and looked up into those incredible eyes she always got lost in.

One brow rose, and he gave a single nod. "Care to share why that is?"

She swallowed hard. "Because he is my grandfather." Relief came with the admission, and her steadiness was somewhat restored by saying the words aloud.

Eli held her by the shoulders and moved away just enough to create a gap. "Seriously?" She nodded solemnly. "Wow. He doesn't know. Does he?" Her head gently shook once. "Damn." He paused. She remained quiet, giving him time to let the idea settle. "Are you going to tell him?"

She heaved a sigh. "I wasn't sure before. Now I am. Yes, but not now. Not with all this going on. His life is hanging in the balance. He's got too much else to worry about. It's not a good time."

Eli's head rocked up and down slowly a couple of times. "Okay. When is a good time?"

She pursed her lips and exhaled. "When he's proven innocent."

His head pressed back. "What if he isn't . . . proven innocent?"

The deliberate clarification caused a heaviness to settle into her chest, weighing heavily against her lungs, and making it hard to breath. "He is, you know . . . innocent."

"Okay."

She knew Eli well enough to realize it wasn't a question. "If he goes to jail, we'll tell him then. It will give him something to cling to . . . to live for." *Would Wes serve life in prison?*

Eli's head lolled to a tilt. "I don't get it. Why did Irma keep this from him all these years? Did your dad know? When did you find out?"

She nodded. "Daddy knew. Gran told him when he was a teenager. He never wanted to contact Wesley. Gran said Wes didn't love her. He didn't want her and wouldn't have wanted her child. I'm not sure that's true, but it's what she believed . . . at least at the time. She didn't want to interfere with the life Wes wanted for himself. He kind of proved her right—never had other children."

His brows rose and fell. "Yeah, but that could be due to the women he chose. I can see how raising a family might not have been in the cards for him. He traveled a lot in his work."

She winced. "Yeah, well, if he'd have known, maybe their relationship would've turned into something like Greyson's and Taylors. Dad could've ended up hating him. As it was, he just didn't care. At least, he didn't seem to care. It's not worth speculating. That's all water under the bridge. Nothing anyone can do about it now."

Eli pulled out two cold beers the mini-bar, snapped tops off and handed her one. He took a long draw on his. "You're right. All we can do is make the best of what is now and do what we can to make the best future possible." He held his bottle toward her.

She clanked hers against it in a toast. "To building a future."

"A future . . . with a grandfather in your life, and an upcoming wedding. We really should set a date." His voice took on a wistful sound.

"We will, soon as this trial thing is settled." She took a hefty sip of her beer, hoping to end the train of conversation.

Eli flipped the computer screen around so she could view the company's website. "While you were in the shower, I searched online and found what I believe is Taylor Corbin's business address."

A photo of a good-looking, blonde Taylor Corbin was strategically placed among company information and his bio. Blonde, like his mother, Greyson's late-thirties son was the owner and manager of Taylor Printing Company on Fourth Street in Bayonne, New Jersey.

Eli pointed to the screen. "This is our first destination tomorrow. Then we can go to the address Bacon gave us for the bartender."

She stroked Eli's smooth, square jaw. "It's a good plan. Thank you, Eli. I appreciate that you came on this trip with me. We make a great team. Like always, we're better together."

The next morning Charli and Eli arrived at Taylor Printing Company. A flighty acting blonde receptionist told them to wait in a row of stiff-looking chairs. She took a call, diverted it to another party, then buzzed another line and announced, "You've got visitors," with a thick Jersey accent.

A few minutes later, a large, burly man in a pale blue work shirt with 'Buzz' embroidered on a breast pocket entered through a door and toward them. "Yeah, what can I do for yous?" His inflection was nearly as Jersey-thick as the woman's.

Eli and Charli stood, and Eli shook the meaty mitt the man offered. "We're here to see Taylor Corbin."

"The boss ain't in."

Charli spoke calmly, as firmly as her soft voice allowed. "When do you expect him back?"

"Not a clue, Sista'. Something I can help ya wit'?"

Eli kept a businesslike tone. "How can we reach Taylor?"

The brawny guy smiled down at Charli. "Listen, babe, I'll take care a ya, if you want." His eyebrows wagged.

She smiled without revealing her disgust. "No thank you. I need to speak personally with your boss. I understand Taylor owns this company."

The big man's eyes rolled, clearly thinking she was one of his boss's romantic conquests. "Yeah, so. What 'cha need lady?"

She sighed. "I . . . we need to speak with Taylor."

His lips tightened. "T ain't in. Listen, I've got real work to do."

Charli gave him her sweetest smile. "When will Mr. Corbin be back? We can wait."

Buzz chuckled. "You're in for a long wait. The boss is out of the office indefinitely. I'm in charge while he's away."

Eli frowned. "I don't understand."

Buzz pushed out air. "T is on hiatus. I'm holding down the fort in his absence. I can handle whatever the two of you need."

Eli scowled. "When was Mr. Corbin last in the office?"

The guy's brows scrunched together. "Last week. I believe it was Tuesday. Why?"

Charli kept her smile casual. "We're not here to place an order or anything. I'm afraid this is a personal matter. It's rather urgent, and we really need to speak with him directly."

Buzz's head eased back. "Well, get in line. Good luck with that."

"What do you mean?" Eli scowled.

"Awh, nothin' much. Some lawyer's been calling every day, wanting to know when the boss will return."

Eli nodded. "I would assume that's his father's attorney. Yes, he's in dire need of speaking with Taylor as quickly as possible. We're here on a similar matter. Where is Mr. Corbin if you don't mind me asking?"

Buzz shrugged. "Not sure. He came in one day, tossed his phone in a desk drawer, took a wad of dough from his safe, and told me to take care of things here until he got back. Said he'd be out a while and didn't want to be disturbed."

Charli eyed the big man. "Is that something he does? Disappear like that without leaving a way to reach him?" It seemed a strange way to conduct business.

Buzz's shoulders rocked up and down as though it was inconsequential. "Nah, but he's the boss. You know? I just do as I'm told. I figured he was on a bender or something. Maybe he just needed a vacation. Not mine to question."

Eli handed him a card with his name, email address and phone number on it. "When he returns, please ask him to contact me. It's extremely important."

Charli beamed. "Yes, please; and be sure to tell him to call his dad's attorney. He has some urgent news for Taylor."

Eli handed the man a large, folded bill. "Thanks for your help. If you would, please call me if you hear from Taylor."

The guy took the money, unfolded it, smiled, and shoved it into his pants pocket. "Yeah, I'll let T know." He spun and disappeared back through the door behind the receptionist's desk. The female didn't look up to watch them go, as she continued talking with another party on the phone that had continually rang while they'd chatted with Buzz.

As they walked out to the street, Charli moaned. "Well, that was a bust."

Eli took her hand, as they ambled toward the bus stop. "I don't know. We found out Taylor Corbin was out of pocket while both murders occurred. That leaves him open to suspicion. He's probably the sole heir to whatever estate Greyson's death leaves. Combined with his unknown whereabouts and motive, sure makes him a likely candidate."

She mulled it over for a few seconds. "I suppose so, for Greyson anyway; but it's doubtful he had anything to do with Tara's death. There's nothing to indicate they even knew each other."

Eli brought up something she hadn't considered. "We're not certain they were both killed by the same person. They could be two totally unrelated cases."

"Wow." She groaned. "If that's the case, it's going to be even harder to find the guilty party and prove Wes' innocence."

"Could be." Eli didn't argue her point. "Either way, we need to go check out Dana Sue March's last known address."

They took a bus and then a subway to the address Mr. Bacon had given them.

CHAPTER NINETEEN

Irma complained of going stir crazy being locked up in the house. She told Wes, "Get your duds on, Stud. We're going out to lunch. It's high time you see some of this little town and meet some of the people." She had hesitated and then snickered. "I mean other than those you met at the hotel and police station."

He tried arguing; but she'd insisted, claiming she was not embarrassed to be seen with him even if he was an accused murderer. In the end, he gave up. Wes had always had trouble saying no to the fiery woman. So, they drove to the heart of town.

He got out and opened the door for her and fed the antique meter with a handful of coins. She inserted an arm through his and directed him to the diner next door. He felt like a king escorting his queen to a royal event.

The eatery resided in a well-kept, ancient, three-story, brick structure with wide display windows to either side of the tall, wood-carved door with a leaded glass panel in the middle. He held the massive door open for her to enter and they stepped back in time.

He exhaled and whispered in her ear. "This restaurant could've been the set of a movie scene anywhere from the 1920s to the 1950s. I almost expect to see Fonzie sitting at a booth wearing his black leathers and haughty attitude."

She laughed and searched the room with her eyes for an empty table. "Yes, it's the way Sadie prefers it. Wait until you see her get up."

Vintage black and white ceramic tile checkered the floor. The tall ceiling was ornamentally designed metal circa an early period. It was painted black, so it wouldn't draw attention upward. Long pedestals hung low enough, so light fixtures and ceiling fans attached to them efficiently lit and cooled the space.

White ceramic topped tables trimmed with chrome strips sat in the middle of red and white vinyl booths. A counter along the back wall housed a row of round, shiny, chrome stools for customers to sit at with a direct view of the stainless-steel area behind it housing a drink station. A juke box along the back side wall crooned a soft country tune.

Wes laughed. "I haven't seen juke boxes like this for years. Each table has its own music selector box." Customers didn't need to get up to choose what they wanted to hear.

The room was filled all but one table, where a couple left as the newcomers arrived. Everyone looked up to check out who had entered. They eyed him critically. Some appeared on the verge of hostility.

Maybe this was a bad idea. It didn't matter what they thought of him. He didn't want his appearance to cause friction between Irma and her friends.

Several patrons spoke to Irma as they walked to claim the newly vacated spot. She chatted casually to each of them and waved to others. It appeared Wes's Starr Bright, known locally and born as Irma Owens, was popular among her neighbors. Wes attributed the hostile once-over a few gave him as their way of letting him know that she was also their girl, and they had her back.

It was good. She seemed well liked and comfortable in her chosen surroundings—as comfortable as she had once been performing on stage for hundreds of thousands of fans. Wes wanted that for her.

Hell. He wanted that for him. He yearned to be a part of this new life she'd built.

As they started to sit, a back metal door with a porthole window in it swung wide. A waitress looked as though she'd stepped straight out of a scene from an episode of that ancient television show about happy days of teens during the fifties. She wore white nursing shoes. Her pink polyester dress sported a white collar and was accompanied by a frilly apron.

Atop the puffy mountain of flaming red hair teased to death into a French twist, a white, starched waitress's crown rested. Her eyes went wide as she spotted them.

She quickly served the tray of food she had carried from the kitchen. Then the redheaded icon sped to where they stood. Arms outstretched; her sixtyish but still attractive face grinned broadly. "Well, I'll be durned if it ain't my dear friend, Irma."

Her accent was so thickly Southern, Wes had to focus to understand her words. Irma stepped into the gal's embrace for a hug and then moved backward.

The spicy female grinned broadly and blatantly inspected Wes up and down. "Just who is this delicious, tasty treat of a man you brought me?" Her thickly made-up brows waggled.

"Don't get your panties in a bunch. You'll scare this man right out of town." Irma giggled like a young girl.

"And don't go getting ideas about Wes. I saw him first, and you're a married woman."

The gal stuck a hand his way. He gently shook it.

Irma smiled. "This is my dear friend, Wes Drake. Wes and I know each other from the music business. He's here for a visit. I couldn't let him come to town and not sample your food." To him she explained, "Sadie Carson is an institution in Sweetwater and a lousy poker player. I'm still trying to spend all that dough I won off her in last week's game."

Sadie joined her in a chuckle. "Now shut your trap, you scoundrel. You know I beat the drawers off a you most times. Don't go bragging to this here feller." Sadie winked at Wes. "Don't let this one fool you."

Hopefully, he wasn't being a fool. It had happened before. Only time would tell.

The twosome slid into the booth.

Sadie squinted. "Ain't you the feller Sheriff Gordon arrested for those murders?"

Irma rolled her eyes and touched Sandie's hand gently. "Now, Sadie, arrested but not tried and convicted. Wesley Drake did not commit those crimes. Those people were his friends. He has barely had the opportunity to grieve their loss with all this confusion. Wes will be proven innocent. I guarantee it."

Wes's nape burned from stares by the other patrons. Whether they stared or not, it was clear from their fidgeting that they were hanging on every word.

Sadie adjusted her stance from leaning on one hip to the other as she glared at him. "Well, I admire and trust Irma's judgement. However, I'll tell you right now. You had best not hurt this little woman. One hair on her head shows up out of place, you've got this whole town to answer for."

Wes exhaled and glanced down before meeting her stare head on. "Sadie, I'm thrilled that Irma has loyal friends like you and the others in Sweetwater who are willing to go to bat for her. I appreciate that. I swear. I have no intention of harming Irma, or anyone else for that matter."

Sadie cleared her throat. "Well, then, long as we've got that straight, any friend of Irma's is welcome around here. I'm very sorry for your loss, Wes. I trust Sheriff Gordon to uphold the law, but I believe in innocent until proven guilty." She withdrew an order pad and ink pen from her white apron pocket. "Now what will you lovebirds have?"

Irma slid into her bench seat and rolled her eyes. "Oh, Sadie. Get a grip. We're just friends. Wes and I haven't seen each other in decades."

Sadie wiggled her eyebrows. "Yeah, yeah, tell yourself what cha want. Ain't no breathing female who could resist them soulful eyes." She rested a hand on Wesley's shoulder as he adjusted into his seat across from Irma's. "This one is gonna woo you right into the sack before he leaves town. Mark my words." She winked at Wes without guile.

Irma's eyes rolled. She sighed heavily, shaking her head. "Wes, I apologize for my profane friend. She can't help her sassy ways. Ignore everything she says." Her mouth snaked to the side, and she stared at Sadie. "Damn it, Sadie. Is nothing sacred? You're going to ruin my immaculate reputation."

Sadie chuckled, making it clear what she thought of Irma's, or was it Starr Bright's reputation. Her voice was low as a whisper. "Let's face it, Irma. Everyone knows this feller is living at your place." Clearly, these two females were extremely compatible.

It seemed time for a change of topic, though he had no objection to what Sadie had suggested. In fact, he would relish the opportunity to take Irma to bed.

Time to get off that thought train. First things first. He still had to convince the woman he was worth keeping around. "I'm not sure what to order. Why don't you choose for me, Irma?"

She nodded and then ordered three eggs over easy, sausage, goetta, biscuits and gravy and a pot of coffee with honey for them to share. For herself she selected goetta and dry toast.

"All righty, then. It'll be out in a shake of a mare's tale." Sadie spun, strode to the small, eye-level window over the drink station in the rear and stuck their order onto a spinning wheel for the cook.

"What—?" He frowned.

"She means breakfast will be ready soon." Irma chuckled. "Sadie's southern drawl takes a little getting used to."

"Good thing I've got an interpreter. What is goetta? I've never heard of it." He pointed to it on the menu that sat on the table beside his place setting.

"Oh, that's right. Goetta isn't found just anywhere. It's a German specialty that is widely popular in Northern Kentucky and the Greater Cincinnati Area, where lots of German folks settled. Many of them were builders, craftsmen, and brew meisters. They are meticulous craftsmen and built some of the most gorgeous homes that are still in great shape today. That's also why there are so many beer breweries in the vicinity. It's also where the best goetta made is produced in Covington, Kentucky. I can't wait to find out how you like it."

"So, why aren't you joining me in this breakfast feast. You ordered me enough to feed an army. Only goetta and toast for you?" His head cocked to the side.

She snickered. "You deserve a man-sized breakfast. A girl must watch her figure, or no one else will."

He laughed. "No problem of that with you. You're incredibly watchable. I can hardly keep my eyes off you."

Her head tilted slightly with a smile. "Well, thank you, sir. I do try to keep in shape. Yoga, water aerobics, and the occasional horseback ride help."

"A solid plan," he agreed. "This aging thing sucks. It's not easy."

Her shoulders rocked up and down. "Nobody said it would be. It's surely not for pussies. Besides, I can't recall life ever being easy."

With a chuckle, he blinked. "Good to see you haven't changed, sweetheart."

The spread of delicacies was shortly served, and they ate while catching up on things that had happened in their work, personal lives, with friends in common, and the music industry. She told him more about the town and people in it, and about growing up there as a child.

"I believe the last time I saw you was when you brought one of your wives' backstage to introduce us after my show in London. I barely remember her. I recall that she left us alone in my dressing room rather quickly. She acted anxious to get you out of there . . . so you wouldn't be late for your late dinner reservation with friends." She pushed her plate aside, empty of all but a piece of crust.

He folded his hands over his empty platter. "Yes, that was Paulette, number three. I owe you an apology for our rudeness. Paulette had told me how she was a fan, and she wanted to meet you. So, I bought tickets to see you and then brought her backstage after your show. I couldn't believe she took off so suddenly to check on our guests. There is no excuse for her behavior. It was nice to find you doing so well, though. You looked amazing, even after putting on a long stage concert. Your career was in full swing, and your performance was phenomenal."

"Thank you. I appreciate that. It means a lot coming from you, being an expert. No worries about Paulette. I completely understand. I suppose she must've known we'd once been an item. I figured she was just checking out what, she presumed, might've been her past competition. Clearly and rightfully so, she wasn't all that concerned." She shrugged.

Paulette might not have been worried, but it wasn't rightfully so. She'd probably sensed he'd never gotten over his passion for this woman. His wife had nothing to fear. He never would've violated his wedding vows, however. "Anyway, I'm glad to have this opportunity to apologize for our rudeness."

"I did notice one thing about your wives that surprised me. They all looked similar. Each was a well-educated, smart woman, beautiful, and cultured. Every one of them had black hair. Funny—even I had black hair when I was performing."

They had resembled her—the one he'd let slip through his fingers. He wagged his brows. "I recall it well. Who could forget you, with that silky, raven mane blanketing your shapely backside and hanging below that sweet, little, heart-shaped tush of yours?"

She waved a hand to dismiss his flirty praise. "Men! It seems you have a type."

"Guess so." He couldn't argue. He'd come to realize during therapy, that he'd been unsuccessfully choosing women who resembled Starr Bright, to substitute them and drive the flame that burned brightly from his heart. "Did it ever occur to you my wives might've been surrogates for the real thing?" Did she think she was just another brunette to him?

Her brows shot up, and she met his gaze. "And the real thing would be?"

He shrugged his shoulder. "Maybe it was you."

"Doubtful." She chuckled with a shrug. "Well, I certainly don't fit that description any longer. I let my hair go naturally as I aged, and I've grown used to the silver. I kind of like it."

His lips pursed in a prolonged release of air. "Oh, you're still the fabulous female who stole my heart when we were young. You are rocking the silver."

CHAPTER TWENTY

Standing on the street corner across from the house Ray Sanders identified as the last known New York address for Dana Sue March, Charli and Eli gazed at each other. "Now what do we do? *That's an understatement.*

Eli bit the side of his mouth. "Well, we try the house first. If that doesn't work, we chat with neighbors. You'd be surprised how much people around you know about what's going on in your life."

"Okay, but we can't bombard whoever lives there now by both of us butting into their business." As if on cue, a middle-aged female with a broom in hand stepped out the front door of the house sitting uncomfortably close to Dana Sue's past residence. "Here's a thought. I'll check with the current resident. You charm that neighbor lady into spilling whatever she might know . . . since you're such a good-looking dude, and you have a way with the ladies." She winked conspiratorially.

He eyed her down his nose, head back. "Okay, but don't go inside, especially if whomever lives there is a male. If so, I'll be right by your side before you can step over the threshold."

He had come to New York with her to provide protection, should she need it. The poor guy would've worried himself sick had she come alone on this exploration adventure. "You've got it." She saluted, then marched across the street to the narrow front porch of the disheveled house.

Unlike those around it, this one had been neglected. Peeling paint shards decorated the aging siding of the two-story, shotgun style building sitting barely apart enough from its neighbors to allow for narrow walkways to their rear entrances. Old roofing was worn to the point of possible leakage. Had curtains not been drawn tight, it would've been impossible for sunlight to penetrate layers of grime coating the single front window. A discarded, broken screen door propped against the building's side wall, possibly from storm damage.

Compared to its next-door neighbor, the cottage to the right had been properly maintained, its similar window glistened in the afternoon sunlight. Eli approached the woman wielding the broom, as she attempted to reach a lone cobweb in a corner of the porch ceiling. As Charli knocked on the grimy, dented, steel door of their target residence, his smooth, approachable voice reached her ears. "Can I help you reach that, Ma'am? You seem to be struggling." No woman in her right mind could resist him when he turned on the charm.

No answer came from inside, so Charli knocked again. This time a light thud sounded. She rapped a third time, resulting in a series of bumping noises on the other side of the dirt-stained barrier. Her fourth rap brought an approaching shuffling. Then a series of clangs and snaps as someone released several of the four locks lined above the doorknob. The entrance creaked open about four inches.

An aging female face peeked below the single chain barrier protecting her from intruders. "Yeah, what do you want?"

Charli put on her friendliest smile. "Hi. I'm sorry to bother you, but could you help me with something?"

The snarling woman didn't appear to be influenced by Charli's perky attitude. "What the hell do you want?" Her sagging jaw went into a slow yawn.

"I'm looking for someone who used to live here. I was wondering if you knew how I might reach her. Her name is Dana Sue March."

Her wrinkled face scowled. "You a cop? Creditor?"

Charli giggled. "Heavens no. Do I look intimidating enough to be either? No. I'm a friend of hers. We worked together at the airport bar, Sip On the Fly. I know she used to live here, and I'm just trying to get in touch with her."

The older woman spit a breath. "News to me. Didn't know the bitch had any friends. Dumb Shit should a kept that job. It was the longest she ever held onto one."

She'd hit pay dirt. "So, you do know her? Any idea where she lives now?"

The old gal scrunched her lips and winced her eyes. "Guess she still lives here . . . when it suits her. Comes and goes as she damned well pleases, no regard for how it affects her old ma. Why do you want her anyhow?"

Hope filled Charli's lungs with ammo to push forward. She was getting somewhere. "Oh, great. Did she move back home with you? You're her mother. Right?"

The chain slid loose, and the gap widened to about a foot revealing her hostess wearing stained, mis-matched sweats. The oversized, red top rippled across saggy breasts and met purple pants mid-thigh. Messy steel-grey curls didn't appear to have been combed in the near past. "Guess you could say that. Unfortunately, yes. She ripped her way outta my hoo-ha. What's it to you?"

Lovely woman. "Wonderful. I'm pleased to meet you . . . Charli Owens. Is Dana Sue home? I'd like to speak to her."

"Nah, the bitch is out somewhere. Best be lookin' for a job. She ain't freeloading off me anymore. I done my time, feeding, and raising the ungrateful cow."

A piece of work. That explains the strange tattoo on Dana Sue's neck.

"That's too bad. I've come clear across town hoping to find her home. She left me a message when she quit work at the tavern saying she'd found my earring and would keep it until I could retrieve it. It's sentimentally important—the only thing I have left from my grandma."

A sneer formed on her face. "Sorry 'bout your luck. She ain't here."

Through the opening, past the disheveled living room and past a kitchen the building split into two bedrooms. A purple polka dotted suitcase stood guard between their open entryways.

She needed to get a look around. "Well, at least Dana Sue's back in town. She said she'd leave it here in case I missed her." Charli was betting on a longshot. A desk appeared to be sitting against the back wall of one rear room.

The woman's mouth squinched up. "I ain't got time for this nonsense." Oh yeah. It was clear she was super busy. Busy boozing it up from stench oozing its way from her breath to abuse Charli's nose.

Reluctantly Charli forced a friendly attitude, smiled, and shoved a hand toward the woman. "I'm pleased to meet you, Mrs. March."

The female stared at the offering for a moment. The age-spotted, thin-skinned hand gripped it quickly and released Charli's hand. "It's Jodi, Jodi March." Clearly, Jodi March was hungover, the way she winced at the sunlight invading her dismal space.

Could Charli use that to help gain entrance? "Any chance I could take a quick look-see? If it's okay with you, we could check her room and see if she left it on her desk for me, like she said she would."

"Eh, what the hell?" Jodi stepped back, her rear against the door, widening the opening. "Take a run at it. Don't know nothing 'bout no earring. Don't expect me to help ya. Just make it quick. I got shit to do."

Charli stepped forward before she changed her mind. Two empty liquor bottles lay on the coffee table and one on the floor explaining what exactly Jodi 'had to do.' Half-eaten pizza lay drying in its open, crusty cardboard box. To say the house was messy would've been a compliment.

Clearly, Charli had disturbed Jodi's siesta, probably sleeping off the gin. She quickly made her way through the room, past the kitchen with its rusty metal cabinets and sink full of dishes with dried food sticking to them toward the back rooms. Oddly, Jodi didn't follow her.

"It's too bad I missed her." Charli kept the conversation rolling, afraid of being caught in her little white lie.

Over her shoulder Charli spotted the old woman settling herself into the age-worn sofa. "Stopped in long enough to eat my grub, then high-tailed it outta here. She'd best be job hunting if she knows what's good for her. She ain't a gonna live here Scott free." Dana Sue had returned here from her short residence in Sweetwater. How much about that did the old gal know, and how best to get the info from her? It seemed a good idea to keep the conversation going.

The polka-dotted roller-bag propped beside an open doorway. Charli's voice was loud enough to be heard from the living room, as she inspected what must have been Dana Sue's chaotic bedroom. "I'm sure she'll find work soon. Ray said Dana Sue was a good worker."

Jodi's voice echoed from the front of the house. "Who the hell is Ray?"

"Oh, sorry, Ray Sanders, our boss at the bar." Obviously, mother and daughter didn't share information.

"Humph, whatever."

"You going somewhere? I love to travel." Charli nodded toward the suitcase.

"Shit no. That piece of junk is my no-account daughter's. Too lazy to unpack, I guess. Either that or she's planning to skip out on me again. Probably just dirty laundry she'll add to the pile of crap in her room. I told that gal I ain't a cleanin' up after her. Bitch is a slob."

Like mother, like daughter.

Alone in the bedroom, Charli snapped a photo of the desktop with her phone then rifled through a pile of makeup. She photographed the large yellow mailer that lay open with sheets of filmy paper sticking out of its lip. Crushed sheets of shiny paper were in and falling out of the overstuffed trash bin beside the desk. Three ruffled sheets on the desktop appeared to have been wet and dried.

What the hell had she been doing?

Shooting photos of the curious disarray bolstered hope they might learn something of value here. *What* was uncertain. Snapping pictures felt like Charli was going in the right direction. At least, it gave her a sense of being productive.

A large mixing bowl with a crusty ring inside its rim sat atop the desk. Something had dried from evaporation, leaving the residue. After shooting images of everything, Charli pulled a pair of rubber gloves from her backpack, slid them on, and lifted the glass bowl to retrieve the envelope. A piece of wrinkled flypaper lay beside the bowl. It looked rippled, as though it had been wet and dried. An overflowing trashcan stood beside the desk. Stuffed among its rubbish were several sheets of crinkled fly paper appearing to have dried and lacking coloring of the ones that hadn't been used yet. It appeared Dana had soaked those sheets.

Why?

Charli snapped a shot of the Amazon label addressed to this house and Dana Sue March. Pulling zip-lock bags from her backpack, she inserted one of the new sheets, a ruffled one and a crushed one from the trash, sealed it and stuffed it into her backpack.

Choosing a metal nail file from the cosmetic assortment, she scraped a sample of the bowl scum into the bag, sealed it and shoved it into her backpack. Charli took a white envelope from the opened lap drawer. She removed the gloves and added them to the knapsack's contents.

"You about done in there?" The rough voice followed by a choking cough nailed the woman as a heavy smoker, as did thick cigarette odor throughout the house and a brown nicotine film coating wallpaper and paint.

Charli turned toward the front room and paused beside the luggage, the envelop in one hand. Her backpack rested in place on her shoulders. The cellphone held in the other, still set on the camera, discretely pointed toward the suitcase. She snapped a couple of shots without being able to see the display. Hopefully they were aimed properly.

She waved the white envelope. "Oh, yeah. Thanks so much. I found it right where Dana Sue said it would be. Did she go on a vacation?" She pointed to the baggage.

"Hell, she don't tell me nothing. Not sure how she could afford a vacation. Probably shacked up with some slick talker with a little dough, who will knock her up and screw her life up like mine."

Dana Sue, a bastard child? Interesting.

Clearly, there was more to this story. "When does Dana Sue get home? I'd love to see her."

The words spat out of her mother's mouth. "Showed up a couple days ago. Been out and about ever since. Listen, I got no idea when that little bitch will show up again, and I got no idea where she's been."

Charli bent and flipped the airline's label over, hoping the woman couldn't see from the distance she'd snapped a photo. "Says here she flew back to New York from Louisville, Kentucky."

A gruff tone spouted, "Huh, what the hell was she doing in Kentucky? She don't know no one there. Like I said, probably been on a bender with some dude who wielded his way into her pants with some shiny object or a roll of cash. Her sleezy rendezvous didn't last long. Makes sense he'd tire of her soon. She ain't no prize pig, you know."

Charli had gotten enough out of this callous gal. She couldn't take much more of her attitude. She strode to the front door, gazing around as she went at the clutter and filth the March women lived in.

Resisting the inclination to shudder, she put a polite smile on her face as she grabbed the grimy doorknob with one hand and took Jodi's with the one holding a folded twenty-dollar bill and a card. "Thanks a ton. My name and number are on this card. Please, call me if your daughter returns. It's vital I speak with her."

Jodi smirked. "Vital? Well, la-de-da." She looked at the card and cash in her hand as Charli released it. Then Jodi shrugged. "Guess it won't do no harm." She toasted Charli with a half-full glass of gin as her visitor left and shut the door shut behind her.

Charli stepped outside and took a deep breath of fresh air, as fresh as New York City could provide. Shallow breathing in the stank March household had left her a bit lightheaded.

She met Eli's eye as he stood speaking with the elderly woman next door. "Well, got to be going. It was nice chatting with you." He rushed to Charli's side, swung an arm around her shoulders, and they strolled toward the bus stop on the next corner. "Man, talk about the nosey neighbor. That one could chew one's ear off. She sees everything going on around here, like the neighborhood watchdog. I take it she doesn't get much opportunity to share what she knows, a bit over-eager if you know what I mean."

"Yeah? What did you learn?" Charli took a thick gulp of city fresh air. At least it wasn't nicotine filled.

With Eli once again by her side and her hand in his, a sense of wellbeing and assurance was renewed. Listening to the horrid woman had come with a foreboding uneasiness. Jodi wasn't sinister exactly, but an ominous air had saturated her environment. Charli was glad to shake it off.

They reached the corner as the bus arrived, boarded, and Eli fed the meter. Once they were seated, he took Charli's hand, their thighs together on the worn, vinyl bench. "That old gal loves to gossip. Alice Corrigan said she's lived next door to Jodi and Dana March since Dana was about twelve. Jodi stays drunk most of the time. She used to hang at local barrooms and bring home scary-looking men for the night. Never had a steady fella. Neither did Dana, as far as she could tell. Said Jodi liked to slap the kid around. Dana tried hiding it, wearing long sleeves in summer and all; but it was easy to tell she was hiding bruises. She'd hear Jodi shouting, banging around inside, and Dana crying a lot."

Charli's mouth fell open, appalled but after spending time with Jodi, she didn't doubt the truth of it. "She didn't report it?"

He shook his head. "You know how New Yorkers can be. They like to stay out of things not directly concerning themselves. She never called the cops or did anything about it. Eventually, Dana grew up and stood up to her mother. Alice overheard them brawling one night when the kid was a teenager. The next day Jodi sported a black eye when she came out to get her mail. After that, Alice didn't hear physical fighting, only shouting and cussing coming from the March house. Jodi called Dana a 'no-good tramp,' a 'good-for-nothing piece of shit.' Alice overheard Jodi saying she hated Dana's guts because she was a mistake. Reminded her too much of the 'slug of a jock who knocked her up and then disappeared.' She said something about her 'baby daddy might have brains enough to win a scholarship. Too bad Dana didn't inherit his smarts instead of his looks."

"Jodi shared similar information about her daughter, while I was snooping around inside. So, Dana looks like her father. I wondered about that. In the photos, she sure doesn't look like her mom. That Jodi March is a piece of work. No wonder her daughter wears a '*vengeance*' tat."

Charli told Eli what she'd learned. They discussed the weird use of fly paper and decided to research that curious finding later.

Finally, Charli leaned against his shoulder and fell into a much-needed nap.

CHAPTER TWENTY-ONE

Charli made a note in her phone to remind her to research uses for fly paper when she had time. Then she dialed and smiled at her grandmother's cheerful, "Hey, Babe. How's it going? I've got you on speaker, so Wes can hear you also."

"We're good. Exhausted from the day of running around. We've talked with the tavern owner, Ray Sanders, and followed up at the address where Dana Sue March last lived, here in New York. Her mother lives there, and she said Dana Sue returned after being gone for a while, during the time the murders occurred. Her baggage was still sitting unpacked by her bedroom door, but her mother didn't know when or if she'd return. Those two must really hate each other. Let's just say that after meeting Jodi, I understand the meaning of her weird tattoo."

Wes's strong tenor sounded. "Jodi March? Hum . . . that name sounds vaguely familiar."

Charli snickered. "Wes, if you'd met this gal, you could never forget her."

Eli stepped closer to the phone to be heard. "I chatted with the neighbor lady who says they fight all the time. Jodi stays drunk. She thinks the old gal beat Dana Sue when she was a kid."

Irma sounded sympathetic. "Takes all kinds, I guess. We've been busy here, too. I checked all possibilities but came up with the location where Ms. March stayed when she was in Sweetwater. She checked into that old strip motel out on I65 under Sue March, the name she gave the Sweetwater Hotel. Paid with cash, but they had her license plate number. It was a rental from the Louisville Airport facility. She rented it under her own name and credit card. You know, to rent a vehicle these days, you must present a government issued picture ID, like a driver's license and a credit card with the same address and name on it for payment. They won't accept cash to rent a car nowadays."

Charli moaned. "I'd still like to talk with her, but doubtful that will happen. I gave her mom my name and number, and a little cash, hoping she'd let me know if Dana Sue returns while we're in New York City. Dana Sue might still have information that would point us in the right direction, though it's a longshot."

Eli took the lead. "We went to your office, Wes, and talked with the CFO, your forensic accountant, and Greyson's assistant. Nothing came of that to help build a case for you. We dropped in at Taylor Corbin's printing facility. He's been suspiciously out of town for a couple of weeks. His facility manager had no clue where he went, why or when he'd return. Considering Taylor hated his dad, it smells bad to me that he was out of pocket during the murders."

Wes chimed in. "Sure is, but I don't think Taylor even knew my assistant. He'd have no reason to kill her."

Irma had an opinion. "You all know, there's nothing to confirm both of those murders were perpetrated by the

184

same killer. It could've been two separate murderers and have nothing to do with each other."

Charlie groaned. "Yeah, but given the poison was arsenic in both cases, I just figured—"

Irma cut her off. "Yes, dear, but Sam Baker, the coroner," she must've explained for Wes's benefit, since he and Sam were barely acquainted, "tells me they were two totally different methods of murder. Tara was poisoned with a powder arsenic that absorbed through her skin. Greyson was poisoned orally in his bourbon. That doesn't sound like a serial killer to me."

Wes also had a notion about that. "Whoa, I hadn't even considered it could be someone who didn't even know either of them. Would a serial killer have poisoned Wes in New York and followed Tara and I here because we had some link to his last killing?"

Irma chirped, "Anything is possible. He could've watched you and Wes talking and decided to follow up with you. Maybe his next victim is someone he saw Tara talking to here in Sweetwater."

"Damn, woman. You're scaring the be-Jesus out of me." Wes chuckled.

Charli took the reins. "Wes, I wouldn't worry too much. It's probably not even a serial killer. For heaven's sake. Can you imagine a serial killer coming all the way to Sweetwater, Kentucky to chase after a victim?" She wanted to laugh but didn't have it in her. They really couldn't rule it out.

Eli snorted. "Doubtful, but who really knows? Doesn't someone have to kill three victims before it's officially a serial killer? Anyway, the best use of our time is to chase down facts about leads we know. For instance, Taylor.

Hopefully, his manager will let me know when Taylor returns to work."

Wes added, "Actually, I got an offer on his dad's part of the agency. I didn't figure he'd want to talk with me, since I'm suspected of killing his dad. I called Greyson's attorney. He said he's been trying to reach Taylor about the reading of the will and has not been able to catch him. He's not returning his calls."

Eli explained, "Yes, Taylor left his phone, telling his manager he didn't want to be disturbed on his vacation, and to handle anything that came up. I told the guy it's important and not Greyson just trying to reach his son. I didn't tell him about Greyson's death. Figured that would be best coming from him. With his mysterious absence, Taylor might not even know about it yet."

Charli sneered. "Yeah, or he's responsible for it."

Wes had more info. "The attorney said he needed me for the reading of the will also. Apparently, Grey left me some small token to remember him with. I explained I can't leave Sweetwater, so I'll join the meeting virtually on my computer from here."

Irma added, "It sounds likely that Taylor is the sole beneficiary of Greyson's estate. He didn't have any other family, according to what Wes shared with me. That, his hatred for his father, and his mysterious absence makes him a prime suspect."

Charli had more on that. "Yes, that's what Simone said as well."

Irma added another thought. "We need to share this information with Carlton, so he can talk through it with Wyatt. This shades the possibility of your guilt and might help on your case."

Wes's voice was lined with hope. "I'll do that as soon as we hang up. Carlton hired a private detective with links to the NYPD and FBI to work with the forensic accountant, hacker, and my CFO to track down the culprit who stole from the agency. Maybe he can track down Taylor and find out where he's been all this time."

Charli added, "Ask him to try to locate Dana Sue March. We still need to find out what she knows. Likelihood of her returning home while Eli and I are in New York is slim."

Wes's voice sounded tentative. "I'll do that."

Eli brought up another suggestion. "Maybe ask Carlton to have the PI check out Simone's life. She acted awfully proprietary where Greyson was concerned."

Irma asked, "Why, Eli, do you believe they were lovers? Maybe she killed Grey out of jealousy or some lovers' spat?"

Eli, Charli, and Wes laughed simultaneously. Wes broke the short bout with an explanation. "No way. Simone's gay. She's married to a woman. Greyson wasn't her type."

"Oh," was all Irma added.

Wes added, "You two have been so helpful. I hate to even ask, but is there any way you can stay over another day and go visit Tara's sister? I can text you her address and contact information. She might know more about Tara's personal life and provide clues that could help us figure out who killed Tara. I'm sure she wouldn't talk with me, now I've been arrested for killing her sister."

Charli met Eli's gaze. He shrugged. "I suppose so, and it's a good idea. Simone mentioned Tara had a boyfriend who sent her flowers. She didn't know anything else about

Tara's private life." She paused, trying to read Eli's expression, and finding support there. "Eli talked with the inspector. It's going to be a couple more days before he can get around to our house. It wouldn't do any harm to chat with Tara's sister."

Eli added, "She won't talk with us if she knows we're working for you. Maybe we just imply we're working on her sister's case with the Sweetwater police. We won't directly lie, but a little implication might go a long ways toward getting her to open up to us."

Charli brought up another idea. "Wes, is there any chance Tara's sister could be involved? Will her ailing mother leave a large estate she might not have wanted to split with her sister Tara? After all, Tara was free to travel and live her life, while the sister was stuck home nursing their dementia suffering mother. She could resent Tara's freedom and feel she should be the sole heir."

Wes's answer didn't dissuade Charli's apprehension about the sister. "I doubt it. Those two gals seemed thick as thieves. They talked frequently, and Tara supported her sister by paying for home nursing care whenever her sister needed or wanted a break. From what I gather, it was a regular thing. I don't think Tara and her mother had the same type of relationship her sister and mother had, so I assumed they'd decided together the arrangement for their mom's care was best for all of them."

Eli supported Charli's opinion, and his words fortified her. "I don't know. Sounds too easy to me. I'd bet there's more to that situation than meets the eye. It bears keeping in mind. We'll go see her tomorrow."

Wes's heavy sigh came through the phone. "That would be amazing. Thank you so much. You two be careful up there, you hear?"

Irma demanded. "You take good care of my granddaughter, Eli. I'll have to treat you all to a special meal when you get home. You've gone way beyond our expectations with your help."

"You're welcome." Charli hung up the phone to a choral of 'goodbyes' and wondering what twist or turn the next day would turn up.

CHAPTER TWENTY-TWO

Wes had texted them the address the evening before, after their phone conversation. Mid-morning, they arrived at the twelfth-floor door of Blakely Bonner's home that she shared with her mother, Rita Bonner. Eli took Charli's hand, and it was swallowed up by his massive warmth, giving her confidence they could face this next challenge together. By his side, she felt invincible. No matter what they ran into, Eli would let no harm come to her. She was sure of it.

A lovely chime sounded inside the condo door, and after a series of lock clicking sounds. The door opened, revealing a shorter, older version of Tara Bonner, only this one wore a long, brown ponytail swinging behind her. Dressed in jeans and a fashionable blue sweater, she smiled.

Her unadorned face sported only a coat of mascara and a friendly grin. "May I help you?"

Charli took the lead. "Hi, I'm Charli Owens, investigating the case of your sister's murder. First, let me say how sorry I am for your loss."

"Can I bring Tara home for burial? Is that why you're here?"

A crotchety voice sounded from somewhere deep in the background of the apartment. "Is that Tara? I want to speak with her."

"No, Mom. It's not." Blakey answered in a loud enough voice to be heard from a distance, even from a person who might be hard of hearing, but soft enough to sound patient.

Either she hadn't told the mother Tara was dead, or the woman had forgotten it. Probably that. Wes had mentioned she was suffering from dementia, and her memory came and went.

Charli kept her voice soft and sympathetic. "No, not yet. The coroner will be in touch when he's ready to release the body."

Blakely gave a disappointed sounding sigh. "Okay. Thanks. Then why are you here?"

Eli took that one. "We've got a few more questions, if you are free to talk."

She stepped back and widened the entrance. "I guess so."

Eli pushed a friendly hand forward. "Ms. Bonner? Blakely Bonner?"

She tilted her head, and her brows moved together, appearing to study his face. "Are you from the NYPD?"

He shook his head. "No, Ms. Bonner. We're from Sweetwater, Kentucky. Charli Owens and Eli Lange. We're working on the Sweetwater Sheriff's Office's case concerning your sister's death. We were in town on the investigation and thought we might learn a bit more about her from you, to help make a solid case."

Blakely waved them in. They didn't hesitate but followed; and she shut the door behind them. With a few clicks, she turned toward them, stepped past, and led them into a living room. "I'm happy to help in any way you think I can. We can talk here." She pointed to the cushy sofa facing a wide, solid window.

"Wow, you have a fabulous city view from here." Charli made herself comfortable on the couch, and Eli sat beside her.

Standing across a modern, mahogany coffee table from them, a stack of conversational photograph books stacked neatly beneath a lovely candle, Blakely smiled at her guests. "Could I get you something to drink, perhaps some tea?"

"No but thank you." Eli smiled. "We just had breakfast, and I couldn't swallow a thing."

Charli followed his lead. "Me either."

Blakely took the accent chair across from them and straightened her shirt. "Well, then, how can I help you? I was under the impression Sheriff Gordon had an open and shut case against Tara's boss, Wesley Drake."

Charli tried not to wince. "They're confident but need to ensure no stone is unturned and to build a solid case. So, here we are."

Eli started the ball rolling. "Can you tell us about your sister, and her relationship with you and your mother?" Open-ended questions were the best tactic to get someone talking.

Blakely studied a moment, rubbing her hands together. "Well, we've always been very close, and of course with Mother also, though I'm closer to her than Tara ever was. I'm the first. You know how it is. Our father died when we were in high school. He was a professor at NYU. Mother was quite a successful fashion model until I came along. Then she became a stay-at-home mother. We never wanted for anything, and Mother saw we had a good education. Tara had a wanderlust, but I was a home body—never hankered for travel other than the rare vacation at the beach. I do enjoy the Caribbean occasionally."

Charli painted her tone with genuine sincerity. "We understand your mother is ill, suffering from dementia."

Blakely nodded. "Yes, Alzheimer's. It's a horrific disease. Mom's memory comes and goes. Sometimes she doesn't know me, or even who she is. Some days she's normal—as normal as it gets."

Eli's voice expressed sympathy. "It's heartbreaking, as much for the caregivers as for the victim."

The woman's head rocked up and down. "It's difficult, but I love Mother. She left her career to see I had the proper upbringing. It's not a burden for me to see to her care now. I'll do it in-home as long as I can, until or unless she needs special care I can't provide. Tara and I talked about that and decided if that time came, we'd hire a full-time nurse to take care of Mother at home."

Charli looked up from taking notes on her phone. "Did Tara uphold her share of your mother's care, in your opinion?"

Blakely smiled, seeming forthcoming. "From the outside, it may not appear she does. In all honesty, I'm the driving force behind our arrangement. Tara went along with it and bore the financial cost of extra help as I see fit to use it or need it. She's been wonderful that way. I have a standing date with some friends every other week, and I bring them in whenever I have an appointment outside of home. They take turns staying with Mom when I take a vacation, about once a year. I'm not sure how I'll manage that now. Tara had more disposable income than I do. She traveled so much, most of her expenses where covered by a company expense report. She made a good living and put much of that money toward helping me out."

Eli bit his lower lip. "Didn't your mother have money of her own? Did your father leave an estate?"

Blakely smiled sadly. "He did, and it was substantial. Also, Mother had socked away her modeling earnings after they married, so she has a hefty nest egg. Dementia care isn't cheap. Neither are medications. Medicare doesn't cover all of it, so some of it comes from her funds. The condo is paid for. That's a blessing. Tara and I decided not to touch Mother's money for more than what she seriously needs. I make enough to cover our living expenses here and put some away. We figured keeping her money intact would help when she progresses and needs it more."

Charli asked the loaded question. "Who inherits her money and the condo, should she pass on before it's depleted?"

Blakely rolled her eyes at the ceiling, cleared her throat, and met Charli's stare. "Mother put the condo in my name long ago. I pay taxes on it, and it is mine either way. Tara was agreeable, given I'm living here and caring for Mother. The money was to be split evenly between Tara and me, in the event of Mother's death."

Eli tapped a finger against his knee, where his hand had been resting. "I assume, you will inherit it now."

Blakely's eyelids shut for a second. Without changing expressions, she looked him in the eyes. "Yes, Tara's attorney contacted me about transferring Tara's assets into my account. I'm sure you're going to ask anyway. It's a good deal of money—well over a half-a-million dollars. Mother's account at present is just over a million. It's not enough for me to kill my sister for it, though. I'm a simple woman with simple needs. Money, if there's enough to support Mother's and my needs, isn't important."

Charli swallowed a lump in her throat. "Please, don't take offense. We must have clarity on these things, so the prosecutor can address them properly in court. They will come up. The attorneys just need to know everything so they can handle anything the defense throws at them. They will try to bring doubt."

Blakely blinked and wrung her hands in her lap. "It's fine. I understand. At least, if I must testify, it won't be the first time it's been asked of me."

Eli's voice was soft and kind. "Thank you for understanding. We appreciate your assistance. What do you do for a living?"

Blakely smiled sadly. "I'm a computer programmer. I mostly write programs for small businesses systems, so they can manage their operations. I work for a company, and they sometimes have me write code for larger corporations, as well."

Charli and Eli's eyes met. His stare told her he shared her thoughts without showing it on his face. She tried to keep her expression steady.

Eli returned to Blakely. "We heard from her co-workers Tara had a boyfriend, but their relationship ended awhile back. What can you tell us about her love life?"

Blakely appeared relieved to move to a topic away from herself. "Tara traveled too much to have much of a New York social life outside of her work. She had tried at first, but the career was more important to her than anyone she met. "I don't think she was seeing anyone special. She went to dinner with people on the road now and then, but nothing serious. I don't believe she'd had a steady fella since she broke up with some guy named Tee."

Charli made a note on her phone and glanced at her hostess. "Is that T-e-e or T, as in the initial standing for some name?"

Blakely's brows went up. "Don't have a clue. She just called him Tee, so I assumed that was his name. Or it could've been Terry, maybe. I really don't know. It didn't last long, so I wasn't too interested. Never mentioned his last name."

Eli's head leaned to the side. "Why'd they break up?"

Blakely put a finger to her chin and looked up. "Tara said he was needy, and she couldn't handle that. He resented her constant travel. It didn't last more than a couple of months before she broke it off. She mentioned something about him trying to get back with her, but she had no interest. He wasn't too happy about it. The poor thing pursued her to the point where she dropped her personal phone coverage and only kept her work phone. We had to contact her that way, and it was fine. She hadn't given the Tee guy her work number."

Charli noted this new information on her phone. "What do you mean pursued? Did he stalk her?"

Blakely's face screwed up. "I don't know that I'd use that word. She didn't return his calls. It was frustrating enough for her to change her phone situation. Her Super told her the guy stopped by her place a few times, but she wasn't home. He sent roses to her home every week, whether she was in or out of town. The Super put them in her condo, but they just sat there and dried up. She told the Super to refuse deliveries from the man and not to admit him in the building. I understand he started sending them to her office after that."

Eli's chin went up. "That must be why Simone was aware Tara had a boyfriend."

Charli and Eli's locked eyes. She could tell he was thinking along the same line as her. "Do you know how they met, what he did for a living, anything that might help us track him down?"

"I'm sorry, I don't. Tara never said much, but she mentioned he owned a printing company in New Jersey. Taylor Printing, I believe. I can't recall exactly where; either Fourth or Fifth Street."

Blakely's attention turned toward a thumping and knocking from a short hallway ending in a door and flanked by two closed ones. The center one opened, and a short, frail, hunched older woman plodded her way out of what appeared to be a restroom.

White, curly hair was short cropped in a fashionable style. Her pale, wrinkled face bore stylish makeup, even lipstick. Short nails on delicate hands gripped the sides of a walker. Her clothing had been stylish a couple of decades back, but the well-made garments, linen pants, and silk blouse, had held up well under no-doubt attentive care. She wore black designer flats with skin-colored stockings. The only thing amiss was her underpants secured atop the trousers.

The impressive woman seemed oblivious to this err in judgement.

Blakely jumped to her feet and strode to her mother's side. Her cheeks flushed. "Mother, why didn't you call me? I could've helped you in the restroom." She cringed as her eyes turned toward their visitors, and her shoulders rocked upward in distress.

The old woman shooed her daughter's helping hand away with a light swat. "Nonsense, I didn't need help."

"Mother, we have guests." She walked patiently beside, as though standing guard in case she needed to snatch her mom from a sudden fall and escorted her to the second chair across from the couch.

"Please, excuse us, Mother was not aware you would be dropping by. If we'd had some notice, I could've helped her be more presentable." Blakely stood beside her mom's chair. Arms tucked to her sides, she shoved hands into her pants pockets with a deep inhale and exhalation.

The old gal swiped her daughter's watchful hand as she sat, shooing her toward her own seat. "Nonsense, I'm always ready and eager to receive visitors. Shame on you, young woman, you failed to serve our callers tea. I've taught you better than that."

Blakely flinched at her mother's swat, rubbed the back of her own neck, and emitted a small cough into her fist. Looking at Eli and Charli, her shoulders rocked up and down, and she winced.

Charli smiled at the older woman. "You look lovely. Thank you for welcoming us into your home. Blakely offered refreshments, but we declined. Too much breakfast, you know." Her chuckle brought a smile to the woman's furrowed face.

Blakely waved a hand toward her. "Mother, these lovely folks are Eli Lange and Charli Owens, investigators from Kentucky. They've come to learn what they can about Tara."

A glint filled the old gal's eye. "Well, my Tara is quite the woman. She's very skilled, well-educated and has an impressive career. Don't tell me you're sweet on my daughter, Mr. . . ."

Eli filled in the blanks. "No, Ma'am. I'm just here to ask a few questions." He stood. "I believe your daughter, Blakely, has given us everything we need, for now, at least. We should be going."

Charli followed his lead. "Yes, we have tons more to do while we're in town. It was good of you to have us, and your help is greatly appreciated. We plan to do everything in our power to see the person who committed the crime is caught and brought to justice." She kept words vague, given Tara's mother was in a state at the present where she didn't appear to realize Tara was not among the living.

When someone was suffering from her horrific disease, it was generally best to humor them—no matter what they were thinking at the time. As unaware Rita Bonner was that she'd put her underpants on over her clothing, she was just as oblivious her daughter had been murdered—at least at the present.

Charli had dealt with the ailment before. What she was aware of would change from time to time, depending on her mood of the day. It did no good arguing or trying to straighten the victim out on a situation. It would merely frustrate Rita, Blakely, and them more. Best to go along with her delusion.

Rita glowed. "I'm sorry you must leave. Please, come again when you can stay longer."

"Thank you. That would be lovely." Charli spoke as she took the boney, pale hand and shook it gently, noting the coolness of her thin skin.

Strolling toward the door, footfalls from Eli and Blakely followed her. Blakely took the lead and unlocked the door.

Charli spoke quietly so as not to be heard by Rita in the living room. "Thank you, Blakely. I'm so sorry for your loss. We appreciate your help."

Eli shook Blakely's hand and gave her a card that Charli knew only had his name, email address and phone number printed on it. "Yes, you've been very helpful. We will follow up on the lead you provided and be in touch, should we have further questions. If you think of anything at all that might be pertinent, please call. It doesn't matter how insignificant it might seem to you. It could be important."

Blakely took it, glanced at it briefly and shoved it into her pants pocket. "Please, find the bastard who took my sister."

CHAPTER TWENTY-THREE

Eli took Charli's hand. It was strong and reassuring. Her man had her back, not the only thing she admired about him. He wore his sandy blonde hair in the same chin-length shaggy style she had grown to adore. The thin black knit sweater clung to his broad shoulders and rippled across his tight abs. His six-six frame towered above her barely over five-foot stature, even as they sat nuzzled closely together on the subway train, heading toward Wesley's office building.

She glanced into his dark chocolate-colored eyes. "I'm glad we decided to return to Wesley's office. I'm sure Simone hasn't told us everything she knows."

He smiled. "She does give the impression she knows everything that goes on around her and suppresses information. I suppose it's important for someone in her position to maintain confidences."

She heaved a sigh. "Yes, of course, about business matters; but this is a murder investigation."

He shot her a tolerant grin. "Yeah, but, Charli, we're not cops. We have no official authority here with any of these people."

Charli frowned. "Sure. I know that. Only, we're working for her only boss now. She knows that." She released an exhale through lips forming an 'o.' "I guess I just don't like her."

He snickered and squeezed her hand supportively. "To be fair, she's a formidable female. I don't care for her sort either, but I'm sure she's a prize employee and devoted to Greyson. She may be trying to protect his memory."

"I suppose you're right." Charli bit the side of her lip. "She's probably worried about being displaced before she's ready to retire, though Wesley said he'd stressed to her how much he valued her and begged her to stick around at least long enough to train some of the newcomers he's going to need to bring on to keep the agency running."

Eli stroked her hand with his thumb. "Yes, he knows her intention is to retire now Greyson is gone. Her loyalty lies with Greyson, even in death. She probably believes, like the police do, Wesley is responsible for his murder. I just hope she's not hiding something that could help us find the real killer."

Something had been niggling at the fringes of an idea since they'd left Blakely's condominium. "You do realize, Blakely has the training necessary to pull off embezzling from her sister's company. She could be the thief."

Eli's brows lifted. "Yes. If she'd ever had access to her sister's computer, someone with her skills might find a way into their secured system to set herself up with whatever access she might need to pull it off. Why would she, though? Blakely stands to inherit close to three-million dollars between Tara's estate and her mother's. The old gal can't be long for this world. At some point Alzheimer's patient bodies systematically forget to operate properly. The heart simply forgets to beat."

Charli's head rocked up and down. "Sure, but who knows how much her care will drain out of that stash of cash before the end comes. We don't know Blakely well.

Perhaps she has a gambling or drug habit and needs the money now. Weird things can motivate people to kill. She might turn around and put her mother down '*because it's the humane thing to do.*' You know, put her out of her suffering, once this deal is all settled about Tara's demise." She sighed. "Some people are just greedy."

He frowned. "Yeah, but Blakely didn't strike me as a greedy person."

She exhaled loudly. "Me either, but good actors hide their true nature."

He snickered with a boyish grin. "What we need is a killer who is a bad actor."

She chuckled quietly. "Yeah, for sure. Is T or Tee, Taylor Corbin, Greyson's estranged son? How did Greyson feel about Tara dating his kid? Did he even know? It seems strange no one mentioned Tara having a relationship with Taylor Corbin. At least, it sounds like that's who this mysterious Tee is. T or Tee could be someone completely different."

Eli's eyes shot sideways, a sure sign he was mulling that over. "Odd, if Greyson knew, did that add to or was it the cause of his dislike for Tara? Was Simone aware? I get the feeling she knows everything going on around her."

She snorted. "Yeah, but she's shady about sharing. Wesley would've told us, had he known."

He nodded in agreement. "Did someone want them both out of the way? Who would've been jealous of their affair, or responsible for their breakup?"

Charli rolled her eyes. "So many questions. This puzzle gets more confusing with each clue we uncover."

Eli snorted. "Tee, or possibly Taylor, sounds a little stalkerish."

Charli couldn't dispute that. "For sure." She closed her eyes. "We should follow up with a call to his office in a few days to see if Taylor returns. Surely, he won't walk out permanently on a successful business."

Eli sniffed. "Unless he's fled the scene with money he stole from his dad's company. He could be lounging on some remote, exotic beach—someplace without extradition—if he's responsible for these two deaths. We should let Carlton or Wes do the follow up on that."

Her lips twisted sideways. "Taylor would have more to gain if he stuck around. Of course, if he killed Greyson and Tara, that would put him at risk for going to prison and losing it all. You're right about turning that part of the investigation over to Wes or his attorney. I want to get done here and get back home and get our renovation finished. This side job as a private investigator is starting to get old."

Eli groaned. "Glad to hear it. Let's stick to wrenches and hammers in the future. It's weird though. Who knows? The culprit could be anyone—the CFO, one of the junior agents, one of the assistants. Carlton hired a PI and a hacker to help Wes's CFO and forensic accountant find the missing company money. The PI can probably take over where we left off with Taylor."

Charli stood, as they arrived at their stop. "Do you think Wes is in danger? He's living with Gran, and she's helping him. Does that put her at risk?"

He grimaced. "Hell, I hope not. You live there too. I won't want either of your lives in jeopardy."

She shrugged. What was, already was. "No going back now. More the reason we need answers to these questions, and fast. Are we dealing with one murderer or two? Arsenic was used in both killings, but in different ways. It's similar but not consistent. Apparently, the stuff is easy to obtain."

Eli put an arm around her shoulders. "I'm worried about you, Babe. I get you wanting to protect Irma and to help her out in this investigation. As exciting as it is to be involved in something like this, you seem extremely invested in proving Wes is innocent. What's really going on?"

Closing her eyes, Charli winced then met his stare. Mixed emotions hammered at her chest. As much as she had longed to share her newfound joy with the man she loved, she had promised Irma to keep the information to herself.

Eli had done everything in his power to support Charli in this quest, without asking why. He'd been working on the assumption it was important to Charli because it was important to Irma.

It wasn't a lie, but it felt like one. Omission came with guilt.

Charli planned to marry Eli and spend the rest of her life with him. She trusted him above all else and owed him the complete truth. "Learning Wes is my grandfather has changed me. I want him in my life, but we still can't tell him."

Eli's head tilted toward the floor, not meeting her eyes. She silently let that sink in. When he met her gaze, a sweet, understanding smile engaged dimples as it spread on his handsome face, the same sexy dents well known to dampen her panties.

"I had a feeling. Why the secrecy? When does it end? Do you have a plan for when to tell Wes?"

She closed eyes and shook her head, sadly. "I don't intend to tell him . . . yet."

His chin lifted an inch. "I get why Irma kept something so important from him all these years, but I'm not sure he will be so understanding."

She exhaled some tension in her chest. "They'd split up. He'd moved on by the time she discovered she was pregnant. He was solely dedicated to his career. Gran figured if he didn't want her, he wouldn't want her child. I'm not sure that was accurate, but it's what she thought at the time. He seems a different man than the one who tossed Gran to the curb without discussion way back then. He might not have been ready for a family at the time, but I hope he will welcome one now."

Eli grimaced. "He talks like a man who is just now realizing what he missed out on. What about your dad? He had no father all those years."

Charli sighed. "It was his choice. When he was old enough to understand, Gran told him. He never contacted Wes—didn't want to."

Eli stroked her hand. "But you do? Yet you still haven't told him." The man knew her well.

She nodded slowly. "Yes. I like Wes. If he wants to be part of my life, I want that too. I'm at least going to give it a shot . . . but not now. He has too much on his plate. Maybe after— "

He drew her hand to his lips and kissed the palm. His breath was warm and comforting, seeping through her veins and wrapping her heart in his strength. "When?"

Not surprising, he didn't argue. Her eyes squeezed shut, willing the possibility of prison from the picture. "After he's free. I'll tell him then."

His brows crunched together. "Babe, what if he doesn't go free?"

She bit her lower lip and sighed. "He must, Eli. He just has to." She bit her lower lip and inhaled loudly. "Either way, it will be over. We'll tell him then."

"All right then." He stood, took her hand, and they disembarked. "Let's finish gathering what we can in New York and get our butts back to Kentucky. We'll save worrying for when we're safely home. Wesley and Irma can help sort it all out."

Geez! She loved this man. Thank the stars he'd come into her life.

CHAPTER TWENTY-FOUR

Charli and Eli arrived at Wesley's office building. Simone met them in the lobby and escorted them to the executive's office suites.

Once in her office, she turned toward them with a quirked brow and stern expression. "What's this all about? I thought you had everything you needed from here and figured you'd be on the next plane to Kentucky."

Charli was glad when Eli took this one, being a bit turned off by disdain in the assistant's tone.

He turned on that dimple display and sweet, masculine growl that never failed to turn the sternest of the fairer sex into a wilting rose, begging him for a drop of dew. "We thought so too. As much as Charli and I loathe interrupting your essential work, we've discovered we need another thing or two only available here. Your gracious assistance is much appreciated. I can't tell you how lucky Wesley is to have you on his team. Someone must run this place while chaos is in play."

Simone tried to hide a slight blush that swelled her cheeks, rolled her eyes, and smiled courteously. "What exactly do you need?" It wasn't a promise to help, but it didn't send them away either.

Charli didn't wait to explain. Best work their way in while Simone was under Eli's magic. "We need another look at Tara's office."

The starchy female's brows lifted, and her head tilted so she looked him in the eyes over her straight nose. "You already inspected her office and found nothing of significance."

He nodded, appropriately humbled. "We did, but after talking with Tara's sister, we felt another run-through would be diligent. You know how it is. The attorneys will question everything. If we don't double check every detail, a wrongful release or conviction could happen."

Simone eyes rolled upward with a double shake of her head. "Whatever." She turned and fished from the lap drawer of her desk and handed a ring of keys to Eli. "Only you and NYPD have been in there, not even the cleaning crew. I figured it would be diligent to keep it as Tara left it until the trial was over . . . or until someone else was in charge."

Charli reminded herself to be sensitive to the fact Simone might be losing her job. She'd called it retirement, but still. It had to be disturbing for the older woman. She'd been the queen bee around here for many years. At least, one of the two queen bees—Simone and Tara.

Eli flashed a winning smile as he took the keys. "Thank you, Simone. You are a blessing."

"Whatever." Simone strode to her chair and shot them one last formidable instruction. "If you need to take anything with you, please check with me first. I want a complete accounting of anything that is missing."

Charli frowned. "Has anyone taken any items from the room so far?"

Simone stared severely; lips pursed. "They have not."

A chill sped down Charli's spine. *Don't mess with that woman.*

Charli followed Eli across the hall, close to his back, as he unlocked Tara's sanctuary. The room had a slightly musty smell, having been locked up for a few weeks now without even a cleaning. She flipped lights on, hoping to ward off the stilted atmosphere.

Nothing sinister about the ultra-modern office space, with its thick, clear, glass-topped desk, supported by shiny metal pedestals on each side. Void of drawer or filing space, the desk was a mere workspace. To the side a heavily laminated credenza housed a built-in stainless steel mini refrigerator. A silver tray on top held a clear-glass water pitcher and four matching goblets. A matching table flanked the opposite wall, holding several silver framed photographs of Tara with major celebrities.

The wide window, void of curtains or blinds, allowed the small room to become a tiny part of the vast city enveloping it. A glimpse at the ocean peeked between buildings to the right. The Statue of Liberty as background, guarded her citizens from invaders.

Thick, navy carpeting provided a luxurious feel and set the tone of success, against ivory walls graced only by one sizable flash of color in the modern-art painting, bringing multiple shades of blue into the space.

Charli sighed. "Not much to see here."

Eli knelt before the credenza. "Nope." He opened the refrigerator. "Let's see. Four bottles of water. Sealed." He held up an emerald-green bottle so he could read the label in a better light. "Expensive champagne."

Charli snickered. "Probably for celebrating big contract signings." She flipped open the double doors to the side of the fridge. "Wine flutes are in here. Hand wipes, tissues. Not much else." She pulled the single drawer out. "Ink pens, stapler, paper clips, lip gloss."

Eli stood and took a photo of the credenza with its drawer, doors, and cooler door open. "Not much here. Maybe take a sample of the lip gloss . . . just in case."

Charli nodded and pulled a zip-lock bag from her backpack. Stripping a sheet from a notepad, she rubbed a generous application of the lip gloss on it, folded the paper and sealed it in the bag. "I doubt this is important, but it can't hurt to have it tested."

As she stood. Eli closed the cabinet doors, as she moved to its side. A stainless-steel trash can in a corner behind the cabinet held a handful of envelopes and a long, white carton. "Looks like Tara did receive flowers. Let's hope they were from Tee."

She took a photo of the box sitting as they found it. Then she lifted it out and sat it on the desktop.

Eli did the same with the envelopes from the trash. He took photos of each of them and their contents. "These are mostly advertisements for services. Nothing personal or particular to Tara and Wes's business. Just junk mail." He tossed them back into the trashcan.

Charli opened the box. "Roses. Must've been here awhile. They're all dried up." She fingered one of the brown, crusty blossoms, and it disintegrated into dust at her touch. "Looks like they were red, before—"

"There's a card." Eli pointed to the small envelope tucked among the stems.

Charli took a picture of the card where it lay. Then she placed it on the desktop. She photographed the envelope and the card and exhaled her disappointment. "It reads *I'll always love you. T.* That doesn't exactly identify Tara's mysterious lover."

Eli moved some of the tissue paper packing in the carton. "Stalker is more like it. This guy is giving me the creeps." He turned toward the box. "There's a receipt." He lifted the paper out. "Fern's Florals. There's an address."

She turned to the paper in his hand. "That's only a block away. We need to check it out."

Eli laid the packing slip beside the card and took a photograph with his phone. He placed them inside the box and returned the package to the wastebasket, as they'd found it.

Charli rolled her shoulders and moaned. "There sure isn't much here to look at."

Eli walked to the painting. "Really nice artwork." He ran a finger across the rippled canvas surface. "It's an original, signed. I know this artist. It's very expensive." He removed the painting, revealing nothing hidden on the wall but a sturdy hanger. He sat the painting on one of the two white, leather guest chairs, flipping the backside toward them. A manilla envelope was attached to the paper-sealed backing. His head turned to her. "Get a shot of this."

She took the photograph. "Weird."

Eli shrugged. "Not really. I'd hoped there was a safe or something behind the painting, but this might be important." He opened the clip and pulled out a piece of stationery. "Oh, hell, it's just a short note from the artist, authenticating the painting."

She took a shot of the letter. "What do you think it's worth?"

Eli looked at the ceiling pondering then met her gaze. "I'd guess a couple of hundred-thousand. One of the artist's smaller works went for a hundred-fifty grand at auction last year."

Charli snickered. "I had no idea you were such an art nerd."

Eli's head tilted toward a shoulder that lifted. "Your man is full of surprises, Little Lady."

She stood on tiptoes to meet his bend and receive a peck on the lips. "Well, Mr. I'm okay with that, long as they're good surprises."

Eli's hand slid farther into the envelope. "There's something else in here." He lifted out a folded paper then opened it. "Tara, enjoy this token of appreciation for your twenty years of dedication. You admired this painting when we were in Italy. I hope it brings you joy. Wes."

Charli snapped a shot of the note. "It must have been an anniversary gift. I suppose her sister will inherit it, along with everything else Tara left behind."

"Yeah, guess so." Eli returned the notes to the envelope and placed the painting on the wall.

She opened the door. "Let's get out of here and go visit that florist."

♥♥♥♥

After returning keys to Simone, Charli and Eli walked the short distance. She smiled, as they neared Fern's Florals, her small hand engulfed in his broad one. His warmth seeped through her, warding off the slight chill in the fall air. "It's a glorious day, even in New York City." She smiled, as they neared Fern's Florals.

Eli chuckled. "Spoken like a true country girl."

She smiled. "Guess it's true. You can take the girl out of the country, but you can't take the country out of the girl."

As he held the door open for her to enter, a bell tinkled above them. The fragrance of blossoms throughout the small room filled the air. "Wow." Charli inhaled the magnificent perfume slowly, relishing the experience. "Now, I could live here happily."

A dark-haired female with a green apron over her tee shirt and jeans entered from a back room. "May I help you?" She smiled.

Eli stepped to the counter where she stood in front of a cash register, a computer and displayed gift cards for every floral occasion. "I hope so. We're trying to identify the sender of a dozen roses that came from this store." He flipped his phone out and stroked the screen to the packing slip they'd found in Tara's discarded flowers. "This was in the carton. Is there some way you can determine who sent the roses?"

The woman flipped down a pair of glasses she'd worn as a headband. Adjusting them to her eyes, she stared intently at Eli's phone. With a raise of a brow, her head lifted. "Let me check." She clicked a few keys on the computer keyboard and then turned to Eli. "Before I provide this information, may I ask what this is about?"

Eli put on his business expression. "No problem. This is part of a police investigation. It is likely something minor, but a detail we've been asked to follow up on."

Charli recognized the ID card he flashed in front of the woman. He slipped it into his back pocket and placed his hands on the countertop.

Clearly, the woman didn't catch the card identified Eli as a Sweetwater Chamber of Commerce board member. She turned the computer screen toward Eli and glanced at the clock on the wall above her, as though anxious enough to get rid of them that she'd give them whatever they needed.

She probably had orders to fulfil. "Here you go. That receipt is from a standing order from T. Corbin at Taylor Printing. We were to deliver a dozen red roses to this address weekly." She pointed to the display.

Charli's heart skipped a beat. She gasped an inhale and tiptoed to glance around Eli's shoulder at the information. They were getting somewhere.

The woman pointed to another line on the screen. "After three deliveries, we experienced a refusal. At that time, the sender changed the delivery address to this one. The order stood for another four weeks until he called to cancel. That was a month ago." She stood erect, shoulders back while Eli photographed the computer screen with his phone.

Charli stepped out of the way and spotted a display along one wall. Captivated, her voice grew soft. "Could you tell me about this bouquet?" She pointed to the lush arrangement at the center of several on a nearby shelf. "It's so beautiful."

The woman walked around the counter to stand beside Charli, her expression softening. "This is our premium wedding spray presentation. The one you're pointing to is very modern. Twenty-six cascading, snow-white Calla

Lilies; eight white roses; baby's breath; pearl broaches and Gypsophilia together create a in a magnificent, upscale, floral waterfall. It will dazzle your guests and perfectly accentuate your bridal gown, no matter its style. You will look elegant, noble, and sophisticated."

Charli bit her lower lip as she listened raptly.

The woman continued, acting as though she was sure of a lucrative sale. "We can create similar but smaller bunches for your bridesmaids, incorporating the color of your choice. Also, church displays, table centerpieces, hair combs or clips, corsages, flower crowns and boutonnieres—any floral needs you have for your wedding and reception." Her smile was warm and enthusiastic, giving Charli her clearly rehearsed sales pitch. "You'll need flowers for your shower, rehearsal dinner, bachelor and bachelorette parties, bridesmaids and bridegrooms' luncheons, and of course a welcome party for out-of-town guests." She was on a roll, moving on to adjacent sale territory.

A vision of the store's cash register dinging over and over came to mind. Overwhelmed by the magnitude of planning in her future, Charli blushed and snapped a quick shot of the arrangement she'd indicated before the woman could complain. "I'm sorry. We're not from the city. Our wedding will be in Kentucky. We're just here on business . . . working a case."

The florist's shoulders dropped. Her lips pressed together. Her face resumed the earlier 'get these people out of here' expression. She returned to her spot behind the counter, slowly shaking her head. Turning toward them, chin tilted down, she frowned. Then she forced a smile.

"Well then, if that's all you need from me, I've got work to do."

Eli flashed her a winning grin, engaging those irresistible dimples. "You've been helpful, and we appreciate the information. Thank you for your time. We'll be going." He backed away, and Charli stepped to his side. He slipped a wide hand around hers.

She gave their hostess a friendly smile. "Thank you for your time." They exited with the ding of the door chime.

On the street, Charli's eyes met Eli's. "She was clearly fishing for an enormous order. I hated to disappoint her."

He winked. "No worries. There's no loss for customers in this vast city."

She shrugged, pursing her lips. "I suppose so."

He took her chin in hands and tilted her face toward his. "You looked so dreamy when you spotted that bundle of flowers. I wanted to snatch you up right then and run to the closest justice of peace." He waited as she giggled. "Does that mean you're ready to plan our wedding . . . set a date?"

It was impossible to miss optimism in his tone. Her voice was gravelly. "I want that so very much."

She fought down a thick lump in her throat. He stroked her cheek so tenderly his touch was barely felt. Tears filled her eyes. She swallowed hard and turned away. After a few seconds and a fortifying breath to stall the thought train breaking her heart and threatening a full-blown blubber fest, she turned toward him.

Time to change the subject before she had a meltdown right here on the streets of New York City. "The first address the florist showed us was Tara's home. The second was her office. The billing address was Taylor's printing company. He and Tara were involved."

She watched as Eli replaced his look of disappointment with his 'all business' face. "Yes, it sounds more and more like Taylor could be the culprit. He's still missing and was during the murders. He stands to inherit his father's estate, and he was obviously stalking Tara and must've been bitter about her breaking up with him."

"We need to tell Wesley and Carlton about this, and we should investigate more before returning home. I'm exhausted, and it's late. Let's get some rest and call them in the morning." As much as she hated hurting Eli, Charli just wasn't up to planning her future now. At least they had a strong distraction.

CHAPTER TWENTY-FIVE

Eli woke before Charli that next morning, sated from an amorous evening of lovemaking. They'd slept curled around each other in various positions, never losing contact with each other's flesh. His heart was filled to the brim as he watched his woman begin to stir, a sign she was waking.

Her pert breasts rose and fell at a steady, faster pace. He fought the urge to take the rosy buds into his mouth and gently suckle them. Her copper curls splayed across the pillow his elbow rested on in a random way that no designer could've made more perfect. Charli was a work of art, and he could hardly contain emotions filling his rising chest with love for her.

Admiration for the petite contractor had grown even more than he'd thought possible as they'd gone about this search for clues to prove her grandfather's innocence. It was risky work, but they'd been sure to minimize the risk. He wasn't about to let anything happen to the amateur sleuth—not on his watch. Charli had come to mean everything to him, and he'd centered his life around her.

She stirred and smiled up at him—that smile that filled his veins with burning lava and stirred his joint to rise as though filled with molten rock as it rubbed against her thigh. He fingered a tendril lying on her forehead. "Morning, my love. Sleep well?"

Her shoulders rocked upward. Eyes closed, as she stretched her arms upward. Those firm mounds squeezed together deliciously, causing his mouth to water with anticipation. "I'm getting spoiled, sleeping with you at my side. It makes me dread heading home. I know you don't want us to live together until we're married because you're afraid it will set a bad example for Kyler, but I could get used to waking up with you in my arms. What would you say to setting a date for our wedding?"

A sudden, strong blink and slight jerk of her head, and her smile changed to one he knew as forced. "Now?" Her whole body tensed as she lay beside him.

He'd obviously hit a nerve. "Now would be good, but if you want, we could wait until we get home. Irma might have some input." She was hesitating for some reason . . . but what?

She squirreled out from beneath the sheet and slid off the far side of the bed. Without facing him, she strode quickly toward the bathroom. "We can discuss it at home." As the door shut behind her, he barely heard the rest. "After Wes is cleared."

His phone rang on the bedside table. Amanda's image appeared on the screen. He hit the Send button. "Morning, Sis. What's up?"

"I'm calling to ask you the same thing. What's up with you and Charli?" His sister smiled into the screen from across the miles.

"We're coming to the end of the line for our little sleuthing exploits. I've got us booked on an afternoon flight home."

She frowned. "You don't sound too excited. What's wrong?"

He didn't want to get into the tons of clues they'd dug up with Amanda. "This whole investigation is just wrong. We've just breached the edges of this convoluted mess. It's time to turn everything we've discovered over to the professionals. We've learned enough here so the PI can take over. I'm almost certain Carlton can now entice Sheriff Gordon to dig deeper into suspicions we've been checking on. I know Wyatt Gordon. He wouldn't want to let a killer run free and wrongly convict an innocent man."

She squirreled her mouth up and shot him a pointed question "What's really going on—with you? Your voice and face give me the idea something awful had happened. When you talked about the work you're doing in New York, you acted normal. What aren't you telling me, Bro? You might as well spill it. You know, I'll get it out of you."

Amanda knew his moods and 'tells' well. She should. He'd practically raised his younger sister. They'd remained close even when she'd married Dr. Bill Frank and moved to Sweetwater. When Bill was sent to the Middle East to treat wounded warriors, Eli had sold his successful construction Cincinnati company and moved to Sweetwater to help her care for his young niece, Abbe.

It was the best thing he'd ever done. Not only had he been burnt out from twenty-four-seven dedication to his business. He'd discovered what he'd been missing out on once he'd settled in.

He enjoyed the physical craftmanship of low-key renovation. Now that he and Charli were business partners, he preferred letting her run things, giving him time to do what he loved. He was thrilled about living close by and being able to be an integral part of Abbe and Amanda's lives. He and Bill had grown even closer, now the congenial doctor had returned home from service.

And he'd met Charli. The spunky renovation expert who had spun a web of gold around his world. Once they'd gotten past their initial misconceptions about each other, he'd gladly allowed her to own his heart. They had much in common, worked well together, wanted, and valued all the same things. The day she'd accepted his marriage proposal had been the highlight of his life. Now he wasn't so sure.

Amanda gave him one of her cockeyed frows. "Spit it out, Eli. Come on. Abbe will be back in a minute. You need to tell me what the heck is going on before she returns. She's dying to talk to you."

He puffed out an exhale. "It's Charli. She's acting strange. Every time I bring up the subject of our getting married, she gets all tight and sometimes teary. She changes the subject and can't get away from me fast enough. She must be having second thoughts about marriage. I get the feeling she wants to wait until we return to Sweetwater before breaking up with me."

Amanda rolled her eyes and let out a 'tsk'. "Eli, that's the most ridiculous thing I've ever heard. Charli is head over heels. The woman literally radiates love for you. There must be something else going on with her."

Eli's brow rose, and he glared at the phone. "She is worried about this case, about Wes, and Irma."

Amanda chewed the side of her lip. "Yeah, sure. Charli is deeply involved in solving this murder fiasco; but if she's putting you off, there's something more personal happening."

His brows furrowed. "But what?" Hopefully, Amanda was right; but he didn't think so.

Amanda gave him a wide-eyed, stern glare. "Sorry, Bro. That's a mystery only you can solve. She's your woman." Abbe's entering the room sounded behind Amanda's dialogue.

He ended that subject line. His niece required attention. "Yeah. So, I thought. Now I'm not so sure."

Abbe's gleeful voice bolstered his temperament. "Is that Uncle Eli?"

No time to dwell on intimate issues with Charli now. "Hello, Abbe. How's my best girl doing?"

Abbe's face came on the screen. "I'm missing you and Charli. When are you coming home?"

"We miss you, too; and we're leaving later today. I will come by to see you tomorrow."

The adorable six-year-old cherub's lower lip pushed forward in a pout. "Why not today?"

He laughed, pushing his problems down to be solved later. "We'll be home way too late for a little gal like you to stay up. You get some rest tonight, and I'll come to have breakfast with you tomorrow morning. Deal?"

She smiled, melting his heart. "Deal. We've got important stuff to talk about."

His brows rose. "And what might that important stuff be?"

Abbe nodded as though doling out an assignment to a subordinate. "I'm the flower girl in your wedding. That's an important role, you know. I need to go shopping. Mommy said we must wait for Charli to tell us what color dress to buy."

He chuckled, hoping Abbe's dreams of leading the procession down the church aisle wouldn't be dashed. "I see. Well, little one; I'm sure there's plenty of time for all of that. Don't worry your little red head about it."

She let a heavy sigh out and rolled her eyes. "Okay but tell Charli to get a move on. Will ya?"

He couldn't help but laugh. "Sure thing, Sweetheart. I'll see you in the morning." Hopefully, he wouldn't have to break her little heart over a bowl of oatmeal.

Charli sat on the edge of the tub. She unplugged her phone from the charger on the vanity and hit Send at Jaiden's name. Her best friend's perky voice and adorable Texan accent helped Charli's racing heart to slow. "Hey, Girl, how's it going in the Big Apple?"

Charli inhaled more calmly. She needed a girlfriend chat to get her out of the pity party she was experiencing. "All's good. I'll fill you in when we return. We're heading home today."

Jaiden chuckled. "Okay, if you're not spilling the beans about your little investigation, what's this call for?"

"I just needed a friendly voice."

Jaiden never let her get away with ambiguity. "What's the prob?"

"Eli keeps pushing me to set the date?"

"And . . . you don't want to? I thought you were hot for that stud. What are you waiting for?"

Charli winced and closed her eyes tightly. "Every time I think of walking down the aisle, I picture Dad at my side and Mom sitting in the first pew."

Sympathy and understanding embroidered Jaiden's words. "I get you, gal. I'm no different. Clay and I keep letting work get in the way of tying the knot; but I can't help wishing my dad was still around to walk me down the aisle too. All I can tell ya, Gal, is you love that man and want to spend the rest of your life with him. You believe in marriage. Don't let what you don't have stop you from savoring what you do have. Don't throw away this chance at happiness. Your parents would want that for you. They'll be there in your heart."

Charli smiled, opened her eyes, and dried her tears with a tissue. "Thanks, Jaiden. I knew you'd know just what to say. Love you, Gal."

"Back at 'cha, Charli. See you soon."

CHAPTER TWENTY-SIX

When Charli had emerged from her shower, they'd gone about preparing for the day like nothing had happened. Had Eli imagined Charli's panic?

They tossed their meager belongings into suitcases, and then made the phone call to Wesley to report their newly uncovered information.

After sharing what they'd learned, Wes led the discussion. "Grey's attorney left a couple of messages for me . . . while I was detained. I talked with him today. Apparently, Greyson left me some token in his will. I won't know what it is until Taylor surfaces and the will can be read. He's been trying to no avail, to reach Taylor since his father died."

Charli frowned at the visual of Wes and Gran on Eli's phone. "You can't leave Sweetwater until the trial."

Wes scowled. "No. Greyson's attorney is going to link me in via video conference."

Eli lowered his voice. "An inheritance from Greyson could look like motive. That's all the police need—more incriminating evidence against you."

Wes shook his head. "Doubtful it's anything valuable, probably a small item of remembrance. Grey might not have been on good terms with his kid, but he was crazy about him. I'm certain Taylor stands to receive the bulk of Grey's assets."

Gran looked at the screen. "No sense wasting energy worrying about Wes's inheritance until we know for sure what it is."

Charli grimaced with concern. "It looks to us like Taylor murdered his father for the money. Taylor could've killed Tara because she rebuked him. That's motive. We need evidence he was in Sweetwater at the time of her death. Also, he would've needed access to her room to plant the poison and have means. We've been unable to track his whereabouts."

Gran bit her upper lip and spoke resolutely, "Sounds about right. Carlton's private dick should take it from here. He needs to track down where Taylor was when both murders occurred, how Taylor obtained and administered the poison, and find the man so he can be arrested. Surely, if the PI and Carlton can dig that up, the police will realize Wes is innocent. Is there any indication Taylor could've also siphoned the missing money from Wes and Greyson's company?" She placed a hand on Wesley's and leaned her silver head against his.

From the expression in Gran's eyes as she stared at her long-ago lover, the contact was more than a compassionate interaction. Obviously, she was still in love with Charli's grandfather, whether Gran had shared that fact with Wes or not.

There was nothing Charli could do about that until their job was done here. Her brows rose, glad Gran had given them a segway to a more currently productive direction. "What is the status of your search for the missing funds?"

Wes licked his lips restlessly, looking hopeful. "I spoke with the hacker and my CFO today. The bogus invoices were electronically deposited into a New York City Bank account. The guy traced a phoneline used to transfer company capital from there to an off-shore account in the Caymans. The same phoneline URL used that phoneline to move the money from that island account to another one. They're trying to determine the destination. So far, we only know it's somewhere in the South Pacific. They're still working on that. I'm hopeful they'll at least be able to locate where the money landed. Whether we be able to eventually get it back is another question."

Charli's confident smile met theirs. "Sounds like you're making incredible progress. That's got to be a difficult task. Not many have the skills to pull of such a heist."

Wes nodded with less enthusiasm than his granddaughter. "The bad news is the transfer was made from the land line in Tara's office."

Eli's eyes widened. "Tara stole the money?"

Wes pursed his lips and rocked his head sideways. "Impossible. She and I were traveling together when the transactions were made."

Gran steeled her eyes. "That narrows suspicion to the few who had access to Tara's office when she was out of town."

Eli's jaw set. "And that is?" Charli slid a hand around his tightened fists. They relaxed in her grip.

Wes lowered his head. Shoulders sagged in defeat. Lips pressed tight. "I hate to say it. Simone and Greyson were the only ones who had access to all the office keys. I didn't realize she had such skills. One never knows."

Eli frowned. "Maybe she didn't. Who knows what else Simone is hiding. From what you've learned, she's been less than forthcoming. There's a possibility she gave Taylor access to his father's office for some personal reason. If she trusted the young man that much, she might've left him alone, giving him access to using the key to Tara's office as well."

Charli's eyes widened in excitement. "He could've used some ruse, telling her he was doing his dad a favor. The four offices—yours, Greyson's, Simone's, and Taras—are all in the same suite. When Simone let us in, I noticed the keys were all on one ring."

Eli picked up that line of thought. "If that's what happened, Simone might've trusted Taylor enough to leave him alone in the office suite, which would've given him opportunity to access Tara's office with the keys."

Charli hummed in. "Maybe Taylor set the whole thing up, making Tara look like the thief . . . before he killed her."

Wes's head hung as it lolled from side-to-side. "Damn, I can't believe all of this was going on while I blissfully went about running my own end of the business. I'm a complete fool."

Gran stroked his upper arm. "Don't go blaming yourself for the shenanigans other people were up to."

He gave her a sad, sideways smile; but regret cracked his words as they came out of his deep voice. "I can hardly believe Simone betrayed us . . . especially Grey."

Gran's eyes remained on Wesley. "She could've been innocent. Greyson might've instructed her to give Taylor access. No telling what people will do for money . . . or love." She pressed her lips and eyes together. Opening them, she moved restlessly. "It's time for Carlton and his PI to take over this investigation. You two might as well head home."

CHAPTER TWENTY-SEVEN

Charli woke in her own bed jet lagged, frustrated, and exhausted after arriving home late the prior evening. The impression of Eli's head remained on the rumpled pillow beside hers where he'd spent the night in her bed one last time before life returned to normal—as normal as possible with all the fuss about Wes.

Her belly knotted. The aroma of bacon frying drifted in from the kitchen area but failed to entice her nervous stomach's appetite. She squeezed her eyes shut and gave a heavy sigh trying to hang onto the comfort his body next to her had provided.

Eli had had stayed with her—something she'd rarely allowed. With Kyler away at college, it wouldn't set a bad example. Gran had said she was a stick-in-the-mud and old fashioned, but Charli was determined to teach the boy to respect women.

Infinitely considerate as he always was, Eli had let her rest, stealthily leaving without waking her. She made the bed, brushed her teeth, and pulled her messy mop into a fresh ponytail. Charli entered the great room. Gran, Eli, and Wes sipped cups of coffee at the kitchen counter.

Gran hopped to her feet and went to the counter. "Morning, Sleepy Head. I'm sure glad you're back home safely. You and Eli worried the daylights out of me, roaming around New York City and looking for a murderer."

Charli snickered. "Better me than you. You know Eli wouldn't let anything happen to me."

At her grandmother's casual shrug, Charli accepted Eli's sweet peck on the lips and sidled onto the barstool beside him. She took a sip of the hot brew Gran sat in front of her. Closing her eyes, she allowed the strong, silky flavor to coat her dry throat and firm her resolve to get on with her day. "Thanks, Gran. We're glad to be home."

Gran resumed her seat suspiciously close to Wes's side. "I know, but it's a grandmother's prerogative to worry."

Eli stroked Charli's forearm casually. "Wes was telling us the latest."

Wes turned to Charli with a nod, and she couldn't help but note his striking resemblance to her father. "It's exciting news. It seems Carlton's hacker tracked down the actual computer IP address that made the money transfers. The IP address is tied to a specific computer—not one owned by my company. The investigator and the FBI agent in charge of our embezzlement case have been watching for it to go live for a couple of days. Apparently, it must be in active use for them to track its whereabouts. Carlton didn't reveal that to me until now, not wanting to get my hopes up. He said it could take months to trace. He called this morning to tell me they got lucky. The IP was in use at a New York apartment. The FBI and NYPD were preparing to make a raid."

"When was this?" Charli glanced at the wall clock. Ten o'clock. She must've been wiped out, sleeping so late.

As if on cue, Wes's phone rang, lying on the countertop. "It's Carlton." He tapped the send button and informed his caller, "You're on speaker with me, Irma, Eli, and Charli. Anything you need to tell me can be shared with them."

Carlton Farmer's familiar voice came from the cell. "Hello all. I'm calling to tell you the raid was a success. NYPD has apprehended the thieves. They are being booked as we speak. As we suspected when we spoke earlier today, Simone Claiborne was involved. Her wife, Aria Clemmons, embezzled your company capital. Ms. Clemmons was the brain and technical skill behind the operation. Ms. Clayborne provided access and opportunity. They moved the funds to an offshore account, then transferred it from that island bank to one in the Cook Islands."

Charli broke in, her eyes wide. "Simone and Aria have a home in the Cook Islands. They plan to retire there."

Carlton chuckled. "Apparently, their intention was to retire wealthy with Wesley and Greyson's money."

Gran's head tilted. "Does this mean they're responsible for Greyson's and Tara's deaths? If the two of them were aware of Simone and Aria's scheme, they could've been killed to prevent them from going to the Feds?"

Carlton's face went blank on the phone screen, as a good attorney should, not allowing emotional implications to taint the conversation. "It is evident these women stole from the agency. It's not so clear whether their theft led them to commit homicide. I advised the local district attorney of the New York case. He agreed to investigate the matter, to see if there's sufficient evidence to tie the women to the killings."

Wes groaned. "So, what you're saying is, I'm not off the hook for murder."

Carlton nodded. "Right, but we're on the trail of your missing funds. The court will go easier on the them if they cooperate and return the money. If not, we will involve the government in the Cook Islands."

Eli's face hardened. "Isn't the idea of hiding money in a numbered account a way of protecting assets one doesn't want revealed?"

Carlton's head rocked upward. "It is. However, once money is discovered, it's no longer protected by anonymity. The Cook Islands government should be willing to work with the FBI to return the funds, though it will be on their own discretion and timing. They're notorious for stalling. It could take a while."

Gran clapped her hands with a smile. "Well, hell, at least we have one thing to celebrate. You will eventually get it back one way or another."

Carlton smiled. "You do that. Things are looking up. My guy is hot on Taylor Corbin's trail. He's also looking for a lead on that odd waitress Charli and Eli were pursuing. Nothing so far, but I'll let you know what comes up as things develop."

Wes picked the phone up. "You do that. Thanks, Carlton." He clicked the call to an end. He turned to the threesome in the room. "I'm stunned. Never thought I'd see the day Simone would betray Greyson."

Charli stood, resolved to find some semblance of normalcy. "Eli, we'd best get dressed and go check on our project house. We've ignored our work long enough."

CHAPTER TWENTY-EIGHT

Eli moved back to their renovation building, leaving her bed with a vacancy. Charli and he went back to work. Wes was occupied on his computer in Kyler's bedroom.

Irma had grown used to having Wes in the house. It was nice, peaceful, and they lived well together. She had to continue reminding herself it was merely a temporary situation, but she couldn't help wishing it would last forever.

It wasn't to be. The s… was going to hit the fan at some point. As manure does, it would ruin her serene homelife with the man who held a permanent spot in her heart.

Wes could end up spending the rest of his days in prison. Even if he got off, Charli needed her to reveal to him he was her grandfather. Wes might never speak to Irma again. It wasn't all about her. Irma owed Wes and Charli that confession—that chance to bond as family. One way or another, Irma's heaven was about to spin into turmoil.

The house was quiet as Irma cleaned up the kitchen after breakfast. This was no time to end things. It was time for festivity. The four of them needed to celebrate the little victories. It was her responsibility to ensure they did.

Checking the refrigerator, an idea came to her. They needed a special meal to commemorate the first of what she hoped would be multiple wins on Wes's part. With any luck, the news he had a family would be one of them—but that wouldn't be anytime soon. That little tidbit must wait.

She patted her chest, to make sure she'd remembered to don her concealed pistol, a habit she'd acquired while on the road as a rock singer. Though she'd tried her best to convince Charli it was a good idea to carry heat, her granddaughter wasn't diligent about it like Irma was. A gal never knew when she might be in a bad situation. One couldn't be too careful.

Hell.

When she was on tour, a stalker had once climbed up two balconies and snuck into Irma's hotel room while she slept. Poor dumbass now walked with a limp, courtesy of Irma's little Glock 26.

The automatic pistol was easily concealed but came with fewer rounds on tap than a 19. The 26 might not be as accurate, but she was proficient with it and practiced occasionally at the firing range with the sheriff's wife, her friend Lemon Sage Gordon. The little pea shooter gave her a measure of satisfaction she could handle herself in a dire situation.

She tapped on her grandson's bedroom door and slipped quietly in at Wes's, "Come in." The sight of him sitting at the small desk typing on his laptop gave her a warm feeling all over. She could hardly believe how much she enjoyed sharing her home with him.

"I am going to the market. Want me to pick up some of that beer you like?"

He stood and ambled toward her, gently taking her hands in his. Bringing one to his lips, he planted a soft kiss on the top.

Her flesh sizzled at his heated breath. She inhaled his heady scent. It oozed through her like a warm internal blanket.

"Thank you, Babe, that would be nice." One hand reached up to stroke her hair, fingering a loose tendril. "You're way too good to me. I want you to know how much I appreciate you."

Not showing passion welling up in her chest was becoming increasingly more difficult. "Not a problem. You'll always be welcome here. I enjoy your company."

Keep it lighthearted. No strings attached.

He backed away releasing her, leaving the sensation of his touch branded on her skin. "Right now, I can't imagine life without you in it."

He failed to mention the mule in the race—the fact he might live that life behind bars. If it weren't for his trial looming over their heads, their future together would have a longshot at being damn near perfect.

She sniffed, rocking her head back to keep from letting his words fog her brain. "Well, no need. I'm here for you, Wes. I always will be." Truer words were never spoken. He wouldn't read the full meaning of what she'd said aloud. That didn't keep her from voicing it.

He reached toward his hip for his wallet. "You need money for groceries?"

Her hand went up. "No, I'm good. Still got some of what you gave me a few days ago."

He'd been adamant about paying his way while he stayed with her, taking over cost of utilities and food bills. Not necessary, but it was the noble thing to do; so, she didn't object.

He reached forward and stroked a solid hand tenderly down the side of her face. Her head leaned into his caress. Then he moved toward her and planted a gentle peck on her cheek. His breath hinted at coffee and something delightfully minty. It moistened her cheek. Warmth left there by his affectionate touch remained as he backed away.

Her chest rose. Nipples tingled with a craving to be touched by that hand that had unintentionally set off a tirade of desire in her. A twitch deep in her core ignited a flame begging to be extinguished by his powerful body.

A deep inhale as she turned away, but the separation did nothing to douse longing in her soul to connect physically with the man. She quietly shut the door and went for her purse, blowing out a sound exhale.

Whoa there, girl. Pull the reins back. We're in this race for the long stretch.

CHAPTER TWENTY-NINE

Half an hour later, Irma pushed a half full cart through the aisles of White's Market. Her phone buzzed. Pulling it from her purse, she smiled at Carlton's name on her screen, as she clicked it on. "Hi, Carlton. I didn't expect to hear from you. Are you looking for Wesley?"

The attorney's tone was unusually stern. "I have been trying to reach him. He's not picking up his phone."

"I'm at the store. He's working at home, probably on a conference call and can't answer."

Carlton must not have been satisfied. "It rings and then finally goes to voice mail. If he were on the line, it would immediately go to his mailbox."

"He could be on a video call on his computer." She tried to tamper down the nervous beasts starting to stir the bile in her gut.

Carlton still didn't sound convinced. "Possibly. I have important information he needs to hear right away. My PI called. Dana Sue March's mother was found dead. He spoke with a neighbor who reported the woman's mail piling up for a few days. She'd seen no sign of Jodi March during that time. She told police and my man a few days prior, she'd heard Jodi and Dana Sue arguing. It seems, the walls of their homes are adjoining. Anyway, after that, there was no sign of either of them . . . until she called the Police. They suspect foul play and are looking for Dana Sue as a person of interest. I spoke with the officer in

245

charge of the case. They won't say why. The neighbor told my guy she overheard someone from the coroner's office whisper something about poison."

Irma's breath caught. "Tell them to check for arsenic."

"Already did. I told the officer at NYPD, and I called the coroner myself. He said that was helpful. It is sometimes difficult to determine which poison was used. He refused to divulge information, however, on the on-going case."

Irma shoved items from her cart into the trunk of her car. "No sign of Dana Sue? I don't get it. Why would she kill her mother?"

"Who knows what hell goes on inside families?"

She couldn't argue Carlton's words, recalling what Eli and Charli had learned about the waitress's relationship with her drunkard of a mother. "Right."

Carlton persisted. "So, will you tell Wes to give me a ring? I'd like to talk more with him."

"Will do." She pushed her cart to a safe location, shoved her phone into her purse and climbed behind the wheel of her automobile.

Racking her brain, she recalled a couple of strange cars on the street as she backed out of the garage. One had an Ohio license plate. The other was from Missouri. At the time, she hadn't given it much thought, assuming one of the neighbors had out-of-town visitors. She took a cleansing breath, trying not to panic.

I'd best get my ass a shaking and get home to Wesley.

CHAPTER THIRTY

The bedroom door swung open. Wes spun around, expecting to see Irma's beautiful form standing behind him.

Instead, a rag-tag looking Dana Sue March glared down the barrel of a pistol. "Get up, you son-of-a-bitch. We're going to have a little chat."

Apprehensively, Wes stood, hands in the air. "Why? What are you doing here? What do you want with me?"

"Let's just say, I want more from you than you ever wanted from me." She motioned him through the doorway with the revolver.

He followed her directions, and she shoved him with the barrel through the hallway to the great room. "I don't want anything from you. I don't even know you."

"Yeah, well, fuck you. You never wanted me. Nobody ever wanted me. You didn't want my ma either, especially after you got a taste of her. Now, you're going to pay."

Wes's voice trembled as he spoke slowly and carefully. "Ms. March, I can give you money, if that's what you're after. I can have it deposited anywhere you like. Just tell me how much and where you want it. I just don't have much on me."

She poked him hard in the back with the nose of her weapon. "I don't want your dough, you dumb-shit."

He squinted and bit the side of his lip in consternation. "What then? I have no clue what you're talking about. I never met your mother. I do recall your face; however, from that airport tavern. You waited on me and my partner."

"Sit down and shut up. Put your hands behind your back. Don't try anything."

He complied by sitting in the dining room chair she indicated. She bent forward to tie his hands. His elbow swung up and clipped her chin. She jolted. Her firearm slapped hard against the side of his head. He blinked. Stars blurred his vision. Hot goo drizzled down his jaw from the wound at his temple. Brunt of the barrel jammed against the nape of his neck.

Her raspy voice grumbled. "Careful there, Daddio. This thing has a hair trigger."

Plastic zip ties tightened around his wrists, securing his arms painfully behind him. A belt slipped around his waist and was quickly cinched, strapping him to the chairback.

"Feet apart," Dana Sue snapped. Her stringy, mousy brown ponytail flopped to the side as she bent forward.

He glimpsed the tattoo on her neck. His skin crawled with an involuntary shiver, recalling the meaning of a capital V marked through with an identical upside-down letter.

Vengeance.

His knee jerked upward. She rocked back, avoiding it connecting to her nose. Her pistol slapped him again. This time, it slammed into his other temple. Biting back the bile rising in his throat, he closed his eyes, forcing himself to remain conscious.

"Stop fighting, you dumb shit. It's time you paid for your sins. You're mine." She chuckled, a satisfied drivel.

"What do you want with me? Why me?" Fighting nausea threatening to blacken his world, he focused on taking strengthening breaths.

She slid ties around his ankles, tying his legs to those of the chair.

It was baffling. Why was he was involved with this strange female? He needed to reason with the crazy bitch. Hopefully, she was at least lucid enough for him to reach her.

"Aren't you going to tell me what this is all about?" He'd heard somewhere that criminals liked to boast.

Dana Sue hopped her jeaned bottom onto the tabletop and laid the handgun beside her. "Sure, Daddio. I'm gonna tell you everything. You and ma—you're both paying for your crimes. You deserve to know exactly how badly you hurt me. How you destroyed my ma. I hate your fucking guts. I'll explain it all, cause clearly, you're clueless. Then I'll watch the lifeblood flow out of you, like it did Ma. That bitch finally got what was coming to her. Now it's your turn."

"Your mother is dead? I'm sorry for your loss, but I didn't know her. I don't know you." He racked his brain for why she thought he did.

She snickered. "Don't waste your breath. I loved watching that old battleax go. Course, she died the way she lived. Stone, cold drunk as a skunk. I laced her gin bottle with arsenic. Sat right there on the coffee table and watched her puke up foam from poison as it ate her insides to shreds."

Lightbulbs went off in his head. "How does one get arsenic? I thought it was outlawed?"

She laughed the kind of cackle that only a deeply deranged person could make. "Yeah, well, lots of folks think that. Ain't so. It's easy. I just ordered a shitload of fly paper online, soaked that shit in water to dislodge the poison, and let residue dry in the bowl. Then all I had to do was brush that sweet powder into a container. Course, I wore protective gloves. You know, you can absorb that crap through the skin. Right?" She laughed like she'd told a world class joke.

Wes measured his words and kept his tone slow and smooth, not wanting to send her into a rage. "I've heard that." It was how she'd killed Tara.

"Why did you poison Greyson that day in the tavern? What did you have against him?"

She snorted, swiped her nose with the top of a hand and glanced away and back. "Yeah, well, I didn't mean him any harm. Hell, I didn't even know the bastard. Good tipper, that one." She emitted another insane chuckle. "You killed him, not me. You're the one who gave him the bourbon meant for you. Guess you're guilty. Right? Just like the cops think." She giggled at her pun.

The loon was certifiable. "Right. So, did you follow me to Sweetwater and kill Tara to make me look even more guilty?"

Another snort. "Nah, that was another foul up you caused. You did that little bitch in, too."

He was a man putting together a puzzle, one piece at a time; and his life depended on it. "How so? I didn't even know you were in town, much less working at the Sweetwater Hotel." He needed to keep this wacko talking for as long as it took to figure his way out of this mess.

Her wild eyes glistened with what appeared to be pride. "Yeah, I pulled that little stunt off by taking the name Sue March, with the help of a choppy platinum wig. I kept an eye on you from afar. I about shit myself that morning when your spunky assistant ripped you a new one in the restaurant."

He hadn't seen her that day. "You were there?" Irma had learned this from her research. "I didn't see you." Had she been trying to frame him for the murders?

Her eyes sparkled. Where had he seen those eyes before? They looked familiar—not from their casual interaction in the airport tavern, but from much farther back.

"I was behind you, tending bar in the back of the room, just laughing it up. Your girl put on quite a show."

A little praise might help spur her on and keep her rambling. "That was clever of you, but I don't understand how you did it or why."

Her shoulders rolled backward. "I looked your room number up when that flirty desk clerk wasn't watching. There was a request for towels, a perfect excuse for someone to enter your room. I laced them when I delivered them. Also coated the toilet paper and a couple other items in the room with powder, then sprinkled the bulk of it on the sheets. You're the one who switched rooms with the bitch. Serves her right. She got what she deserved for screwing up my plan. The bonus is it makes you look guilty as sin. Which you are, of course. Tisk, tisk, tisk."

"So, Tara went to bed and absorbed the poison through her skin in her sleep . . . , but you meant it for me?"

"Yep, and she got an eternal rest." Laughter blurted from her pale lips. This dingbat thought she was hilarious.

Keep her thinking that.

"I'll give you this. You're a hard son-of-a-bitch to kill." Her head lolled from side-to-side.

"You are wicked-smart to come up with a way to secure poison and methods of dosing it. Why me? Why were you trying to kill me? Far as I know, the first time we laid eyes on each other was that day at the airport."

"Nope, Daddio, you and I have a long, disgusting history.

CHAPTER THIRTY-ONE

Irma drove as fast as she could. Her phone rang in her purse. She clicked Send on the dash connection to her phone, and the line connected. "Hello."

Carlton's voice sounded strained. "Are you home yet?"

"No, but I'm on my way. What's up?" She hesitantly slammed on the brakes at a stoplight.

"I still can't reach Wesley." The urgency in his voice made her skin crawl.

"You can tell me anything. Wes told you so." Her heart was inching upward toward her windpipe. Panic rose with it. Something was horribly wrong.

"NYPD has been looking for leads on Dana Sue March without success. My PI has been searching as well. He learned Jodi March's credit card had been used yesterday to purchase gas in Columbus, Ohio. The Columbus station surveillance camera captured the vehicle but not the woman's face. My guy ran the license plate number and found the car to be stolen from the Bronx the night the coroner pegs as her mother's time of death. The card was used again last night in Louisville. He reported this to NYPD, the police in Columbus and Louisville, and then called me. The Louisville station's security camera was on the fritz and got nothing. It looks like March is on the run. Likely killed her mother. Must've thought using her mom's card so far from New York would be safe. I updated Sheriff Gordon and the Sweetwater prosecuting attorney. They promised to investigate the March lead further. Not sure what will come of it. They're satisfied with what they have against Wesley. Can you have Wes call me when you get home? He needs to know this ASAP."

Her heart sank. She gunned the engine. A vision of the Ohio license plate on the strange vehicle parked on her street when she'd left sent her straining to recall the make and model of the sedan.

She peeled away as the light turned green. "Holy hell, she's heading to Sweetwater. Wes is in danger."

"You both are. Don't do anything stupid. Let the sheriff handle this. I'll call Wyatt again and send him to your house right away. He might want to set up a protection detail."

"I've got to get home." She tapped the phone dead.

CHAPTER THIRTY-TWO

Dana glared down her nose, one surprisingly like his own. "So, Daddio, it's time to get this over with, before the slutty senior cow you've been shacking up with returns."

Disgust in her voice chilled his bones, but he forced his voice to be congenial. "Ms. March, I get that you're angry with me and feel I've wronged you somehow. I had no intention of doing so, and apologize, if I have. It's not clear what you're so upset with me about."

She cackled in a way any witch would've been proud of. "You make it sound like a minor indiscretion—angry, upset just don't get measure up. You have not just wronged me. You ruined my mother's life and mine as well."

"Ms. March, I assure you. I don't even know your mother. I have never mistreated a woman in my life. You and I have merely had a brief encounter. Surely, you have mistaken me for someone else.

She snickered evilly. "Unfortunately, not."

He makes the connection that he is the jilting lover who left Jodi pregnant and Dana Sue in her mother's snare. She spouts how he's responsible for her miserable life, and she wants vengeance. The only way to get it was to kill her mother and kill him. Why Greyson and Tara? Got in the way. You're a hard man to kill, or the luckiest son-of-a-bitch ever walked free of responsibility. She wants him dead.

CHAPTER THIRTY-THREE

Irma had tried Wes's phone several times as she'd made the mad dash home. Like Carlton, she'd received no answer. She arrived on her street. One of the strange vehicles she'd noticed earlier remained a couple of doors from her house. Another car had parked too close to its rear for the plates to be visible.

Instead of pulling into her garage as usual, she left her automobile in the open spot in front of the unknown sedan and backed so close to it the driver would be unable to leave without hers being moved. It was rude . . . if the auto was there innocently. Until she knew for sure, an unscrupulous visitor would not be leaving easily if she could stop it. It would be easier to apologize than to regret the indiscretion.

Leaving her purchases inside, she walked around to check. Sure, as she'd thought, the car had Ohio registration.

Suspicions heightened; she answered the chirp of her phone. Sheriff Wyatt Gordon's deep-throated, Southern drawl filled her ear "Irma, I just got off the phone with Carlton Farmer. I spoke with NYPD and the New York City Coroner. It seems you and your family have stirred up quite a row with your sleuthing. Hon, you know better. These are police matters, best left to professionals."

Her voice was raspy with adrenaline fueled excitement. "Wyatt, I don't have time to chit chat. There's a suspicious vehicle near my house. Wes is not picking up his calls. He's alone and could be in danger."

Behind his voice, rustling movements were audible. "Hon, that's what I was calling to tell you. Where are you?"

"I'm on the street in front of my house." Her heartbeat so hard and fast, she felt like a thoroughbred about to cross the finish line in the derby. She breathed slowly and deeply, trying to ward off hyperventilation. Stealthily, she crept around the house to the side. Glancing inside the open blinds of Kyler's bedroom window, Wes was nowhere to be seen. His computer remained on the desk where she'd left him working.

As she strode quickly back to the front of the house sounds of Wyatt barking orders to his team came through her phone. She started around the other side, hoping to glimpse Wes relaxing in the great room through the patio doors.

Wyatt's attention returned to her. "Irma, this is likely nothing, but I'm on my way there now." The sound of a car door slamming and an engine roaring to life came through the line. "I want you to get in your vehicle and stay there. We'll be there in less than ten minutes. We're going to put a protection detail on your house until Ms. March is apprehended—just in case."

The private patio surrounded by hedges made it difficult to see into the house. The only way would be to peer over them through double French doors that opened to the courtyard. She scanned around for something to stand on, so she would be high enough to see over the bushes. "Wyatt, I hear what you're saying, but Wes might not have ten minutes. If he's in trouble, he needs help now. I'm going in."

Spotting a skateboard on her next-door neighbor's porch, belonging to his son, she tip-toed into his yard and took it—another thing she might end up apologizing for. She intended to return it in good shape, soon as she'd used it as a stepping stool. Guilt still flowed through her for using someone else's belonging without permission.

Wyatt remained his usual persistent self. "Now Irma, you can't be playing SWAT on my watch. It's likely nothing. If it's not, I don't want you putting yourself in harm's way. Wes is a smart fella. Whatever the situation is, he can handle himself until help arrives."

She soundlessly placed the skateboard on the ground, pushing it as tightly as possible against a hedge trunk. "Hon, I hear you, but I'm not hanging around and doing nothing. Wes needs me."

Wyatt's usual calm demeanor ruffled. His voice took on a demanding tone. "Dammit to hell, Irma. Get in your friggin' car and stay there."

She let out an exasperated sigh. "Wyatt, my dear friend. I'm putting your sweet ass on MUTE. There ain't a man alive who can tell me what to do. I'll keep the line live, but I'm doing whatever I have to do." She clicked the phone into silent mode and pushed it down the front of her shirt into her bra. Wyatt would be able to hear, but she and whomever she had to deal with, would not hear him.

Stepping carefully on top of the skateboard and holding onto a branch, she peered over the foliage barrier concealing her private, outdoor sanctuary. Stifling her gasp, she gulped.

The backside of a female sitting on her dining room table came into view. Wes was not in her line of sight. The woman's shaggy, brown ponytail waggled, as she hopped off the table to the floor and moved to the side. A pistol lay on the table.

Wes came into view. His arms appeared in an uncomfortable position pushed tightly behind his back.

Her heart stopped beating for a full breath. *He's tied to the chair.*

She sucked in a deep breath. Her mouth hung open. Deep purple swelling on both sides of Wes's face forced tears down her cheeks. He'd been beaten. The urge to tear the woman's eyes out filled Irma's chest with rage.

The skateboard slipped with her sudden movement, slid from its stable position, and flipped into the air. Her feet hit the ground with a snap. She bent forward in a flash and snatched the item just as it slammed into her shin.

Biting curse words back to a whispered, "Son of a bitch," she laid it carefully, wheels up, on the ground. "Wyatt, I'm okay. I just stumbled." A little white lie would sooth Wyatt's fears and was easier than taking time to explain to her listener her ridiculous, cartoonish escapades. Her eyes closed momentarily to calm herself before she steeled around to the back of the house. She wasn't sure what, but she had to do something.

She pulled the phone from her breasts. Whispering, she spoke as she reached the back door. "Wyatt, Wes is in the great room with an armed female. He's been beaten and looks to be tied up. I'm going in to try and diffuse the situation. I'm also putting the phone on record, just in case. I have a weapon; and, Wyatt, you know, we don't lock our doors. There's usually no reason to, in Sweetwater. So, come on in and join the party when you get here. Love ya, hon."

She clicked record and reset the silent mode to the tune of the sheriff's distressed tone. "No, Irma. Don't—"

CHAPTER THIRTY-FOUR

Dana Sue sat on the countertop. Her gangly feet dangled above the kitchen floor. "So, Daddio, it's time to get this over with before that bimbo you're shacking up with comes back. I'd hate to have to kill her, too. You've already caused the deaths of two innocent people. Besides, I need to hit the road and disappear forever. Once you and that hag of a mother you gave me are out of the picture, I can create a beautiful new life for myself – a fresh start. Know what I mean? All the ugly will be behind me. I'll be able to do anything I want. Life's going to be amazing."

Wes's jaws tightened. Could this maniac be his daughter? "Look, Miss March, I understand why you hated your mother. It sounds like she was a miserable, desperate woman and took it out on you. I might've been the sperm donor for your birth, but I assure you, I never mistreated any woman, including your mom. I barely even knew her."

"Sure, thing, Daddio. Clearly you knew her intimately enough to produce an offspring. She said you were the love of her life, and you used her and tossed her aside."

His head hung as he rocked it side-to-side. "For that indiscretion, I will be eternally sorry. I never meant to hurt her or you. You must understand. I didn't really know your mom . . . Jodi. She was a quiet girl, awkward and shy. Kept to herself. Lived in the neighborhood and went to my school, but we never interacted before. She came to me that night. I never pursued her."

The wacko made a sound resembling spit but didn't interrupt him.

"I was in a bad place . . . distressed. My steady girlfriend broke up with me after the prom. We were heading to different colleges far away from each other, and she said she had no intention of trying to have a long-distance relationship. She claimed to care for me but not enough to put herself through that. She wanted to be free to explore 'her options' at her new school."

Dana Sue let out a bawdy laugh but didn't stop his rambling.

She avoided his gaze when he tried to look her in the eye. "Anyway, I was crushed and drinking heavily sitting on the football stadium bleachers. Jodi wandered over, sat beside me, and pulled the bottle from my lips. Taking a long drink, she climbed into my lap, straddling me. She bit my ear and whispered for me to take her right there. What could I do? I was just a kid—seventeen. Guess we both were."

Dana Sue glared. "So, you did. Wham. Bam. Thank you, Ma'am? Just like that, and then you ditched her. Broke her heart."

He sighed, closed his eyes, opened them to meet her scowl with a slight shrug. "I guess so. It must've seemed that way to her. I never thought about it. Look, Dana Sue, kids make mistakes. We move on and learn our lessons. Life goes on."

A snicker and huff came from her. "She sure as hell never moved on. It was just about all she thought about, far as I could tell. Ma was broken, so she broke me."

"I didn't know. Never even saw her again. I left for school the following day."

Her brow lifted. "She looked for you. Tried to find you. Your parents left when you did. No one knew where they disappeared to."

He nodded, letting memories mill around in his saddened mind. "Yes, my foster parents retired to Florida." He'd been fond of the people who he'd been finally placed with—the only ones with tenacity enough to keep him long enough to let him finish school before he aged out of the foster system. If it weren't for those kind, stubborn folks, he never would've been able to stop screwing up his life, buckle down and win the scholarships. They'd changed his miserable life and given him hope for a real future.

It sounded like Dana Sue was the product of Jodi March's turning point in life, too. Clearly, the mousey girl down the street who had so easily offered herself to him at his lowest point, had taken a different direction after their brief encounter. It had, obviously, meant more to her than it had him.

How had she known he'd be at the deserted stadium that night? He'd gone there to lick his wounds, get stinking drunk, and forget his sorrows. Had she been following him? Jodi must've already been an emotional mess to do such a thing. She'd gotten what she wanted that night, but she must've expected it to lead to greater things.

"Ma tried to locate you at the school. The Harvard people said you never accepted their scholarship."

His head rocked back. "I turned it down and took the scholarship from Oxford instead. So, that's why she never told me about you. She couldn't find me." He paused, looked away and then back. "I'm sorry. If I'd known Jodi had a child, I would've done right by you. I would never shirk such a responsibility."

She stared daggers down her nose. "You'd a married her?"

He blinked as his head shook at the obtuse idea. "No, but I would've provided financial support for your care."

Her snickered said it wasn't enough.

"Look, I couldn't marry your mother. I barely knew her. Truthfully wasn't even sure what her name was. She came on to me. I did not force myself on her or try to seduce her. I don't even know why she was there." It sounded as though Jodi had been obsessed with him.

"Ma said she and you were in love. Said you went everywhere together."

His head shot upward. "We did no such thing. I never dated your mother or went anywhere with her. Was she stalking me? Is that how she found me that night?"

Dana Sue shrugged, as though it was irrelevant. "Who knows. Maybe. She was a nutcase. It's possible, she was the one who was delusional."

He nodded, hoping she believed that. "Maybe. Even so, I shouldn't have taken advantage of her. I'll be eternally sorry for taking part in that. It sounds as though Jodi had severe emotional issues. Maybe she'd suffered some trauma to make her that way. I can't believe that our encounter caused her to be the sick person who raised you. It had to be something else." He sighed. His only hope was to convince her he wasn't responsible for turning Dana Sue's mother into a nut job. "You need to believe me. I'm not the bad guy you believe me to be."

She shot him a glance that could've burned the hair off a grizzly bear. "I 'believe' you deserve to pay for what you did. It's the only way. Ma paid her debt. You're going to die. I'm going to move on. It's simple." She jumped down from her countertop perch.

CHAPTER THIRTY-FIVE

Irma crept around to the rear door and into the backroom laundry. She eased the latch on the holster of her little Glock 26 pistol, easily concealed beneath her heaving breasts and took one last cleansing, calming breath before she opened the door.

Hopefully time hadn't diminished her skill for playing a part and working under extreme stress. She'd had plenty of practice with acting during her many years on the stage.

As she stepped into the great room, she purposely avoided looking toward where she knew Wes to be confined and hoped the female holding him hostage had remained close by him. Instead, she strode toward the far end of the bar facing the kitchen sink and tossed her purse casually onto the countertop.

She glanced toward the hallway leading to the bedrooms and bath and raised her voice. "Wes, I'm home. Sorry to bother you while you're working, I forgot my shopping list. I'll just be a minute." Irma put hands on her hips as though searching for the missing paper and faced the female pointing a gun toward her. The older woman faked a shocked expression. "What on earth? Who are you, and what are you doing in my house?" She allowed a hint of indignation to show in her voice.

Wesley's forehead had turned a bright assortment of beautiful greens, blues, and purples, as though struck by a blunt instrument. A drizzle of blood had started to crust on his cheek.

The younger gal sneered and waved her weapon up and down, pointing at Irma. "Well, now, this is a special treat for you, Daddio. You get to watch your latest piece of ass die first. Then you can follow her to hell. Only fitting since your sins have caused me to live in hell on earth my whole life."

Irma sucked back panic with an inhale and glared at the female holding her man hostage. "Who in tarnation do you think you are, calling me a piece of ass? I'll have you know, I'm a well-respected member of this community—not some bimbo. Mr. Drake is a guest in my home, and you were not invited. From what I see, you're not welcome here. If you're smart, and I doubt you are, you will head for the hills right about now . . . before the police arrive."

Wes flinched and shot Irma a probing gaze. His words came out as stiff as his posture. "Irma, please don't antagonize her. She's dangerous, and I don't want to see you hurt."

A wild chuckle erupted from Dana Sue's pinched lips. "Don't try my patience. I don't have any. You and I both know the Fuzz isn't coming. No one is. You had no idea I was here. Why would you have called the cops?"

Irma let one brow lift high. She glowered at the stranger. "You're wrong and need to leave immediately."

Dana Sue laughed. "Yeah, right, Sister. Or should I call you Star Bright? From what I see, you're nothing but a dried-up, old prune—a has-been, rock-n-roll slut. This little baby gives me invitation to enter anywhere I please to be."

She waved her pistol around in front of her. "Until my business is concluded, it says I'm welcome in this shit hole of a town."

Adrenaline pulsed through Irma's veins like ice water. Where the hell was Wyatt? Her heartbeat so loudly the maniac in the room probably heard it. She inhaled, spoke slowly and deliberately. At the same time, her hand eased to her hip, slipping fingers beneath the bottom edge of her waist-length shirt.

Was that the slightest sound of a door opening behind her inside the laundry room? Her imagination ran wild. She couldn't count on it. It was up to her, whether she and Wes lived or died. She snarled at the intruder daring Dana Sue's eyes to leave hers, and let venom flow with her words, hoping poison would somehow infect the crazed bitch. "What do you want?"

Dana Sue's head rocked slightly, and she snorted. "Justice. Revenge. I want to see this ridiculous excuse for a sperm donor dead. That's what I want." She swung toward Wes.

Irma took the opportunity to ease her hand beneath her shirt upward toward her Glock. She turned slightly so her opposite side faced the assailant.

Maybe pleading would do the trick. She allowed honey to coat her words. "Look, Dana Sue, we know who you are and what you've done. Please, don't do this. You've already killed two innocent people. Wesley is likely going to prison for the rest of his life if he's convicted of your crimes. Isn't that enough for whatever sin you feel he has committed against you?" Irma silently edged toward the bar, away from the laundry room door, keeping her unarmed side toward Ms. March, taking advantage of every second the gal's eyes weren't on her.

Dana's head rocked side-to-side, staring at Wes. "Nope, but I'd figured to get this over with before you returned. Your death is your own damned fault. You're too frigging stupid to take your shopping list with you." She glinted over her shoulder at Irma for a second before returning attention to Wes, apparently oblivious to Irma's having moved. "What are you, senile or something? Dementia? Whatever! You're here. You'll just have to join Loverboy."

Irma's fingers coiled around the butt of her pistol, and she slipped it free of her clothing, pointing it toward Wes's daughter.

The front door slammed open. Dana Sue reacted to the thud by aiming her weapon at Wes. Simultaneously, Irma and Dana Sue fired their weapons. The laundry room door thudded open. Footfalls thumped behind Irma. Wyatt's voice boomed, "Police, stop. You're under arrest."

Dana Sue whirled sideways from impact and fell backward against the dining room table, as the shot penetrated her chest. Blood surged from her back. She clunked against a chair as she toppled to the tile floor. A puddle of red goo pooled from beneath her still frame.

Fire singed Irma's left shoulder, knocking her backward into a sturdy body. Her head tilted to the right. She smiled into the grim handsome face of Deputy Leo Sanders that sported an array of freckles across the cheeks and nose. His dark eyes glistened with what looked like a smile. His strong arms encircled her firmly. Her head rested against his solid, broad chest.

Sexy blonde, grown up Opie Taylor.

The room went black.

CHAPTER THIRTY-SIX

Irma's eyes fluttered open to pale blue, sterile looking space. Dimmed lights, pristine sheets, and tubes connected at one end to her body and the other to several blinking machines to her sides.

Stiff and numb all over, consciousness crept into her being. It awakened sensations of exhaustion, and slight nausea. Red-hot pain seared in her left shoulder.

Awareness dawned. She'd been in a gunfight with an insane murderess. "Wes!" She jolted upward in the hospital bed, intensifying her agony.

A firm hand coaxed her down. "Stay still, Gran. Wes is fine. Don't try to move too quickly. You've been shot."

Irma blinked, trying to clear tears clouding her vision. "He's okay?"

Charli nodded, bitterness in her voice. "He's good. Just a little bruised and banged up. A couple of black eyes. Maybe a concussion. Nothing serious. That wacko pistol whipped him."

Irma rocked her head in understanding. "Yeah, she did that before I arrived."

Eli walked from where he'd been waiting in the corner and stood at the foot of Irma's bed. "Irma, what were you thinking? You knew Wyatt was on his way. Why did you go inside and face that mad woman?"

Charli gave her a piercing stare. "Yeah, Gran. You could've been killed."

Irma sighed. "I couldn't wait for Wyatt and his team to show up. I had to do something. That insane female was going to kill him."

Wes rolled his wheelchair into the room through the open door. His head was bandaged. Both eyes were swollen and darkened from the beating. He wore a neck brace. "I was terrified when you arrived, afraid you'd become another victim. The truth is, if you hadn't arrived when you did, I would've been dead. She was ready to end the game."

Irma grinned, grateful at the sight of him alive and breathing, no matter his shape. It was well worth the headache scrambling her brain and blazing fire in her shoulder. "See, Charli, Eli. I told you so."

Wes nodded. "Your grandmother is a hero, the bravest, most tenacious person I've ever met. Woman, I'm glad to see you're still kicking. When gunplay between the two of you began, I feared the worst. My world would've ended had anything dreadful—more dreadful than a shoulder wound, had happened to you."

She shot him a rocking head, swaggering glare, and chuckled. "If that bitch had a better aim, I would be toast." One of her brows lifted, and she glared. "What do you mean your world would've ended? Wyatt and his people would've stopped Dana Sue from shooting you, too."

Wes shook his head to the side. "That's not what I meant. Woman, it's high time I told you what I came to town to say. I'm so deeply in love with you. Always have been. I've tried to live without you. Tried to replace you with one incredible lady after another. It never worked. None of them were you. If that sick creature had killed you, everything in this world I care about would've been buried with you."

Was her hearing affected by the gunshot? Drugs? Was she hallucinating? "Wesley Drake, did I hear you right?" She couldn't take her eyes off him.

His head nodded. A smile crossed those luscious, kissable lips. "Yes, Ma'am. You heard me."

Her chin rose, and she stared down her nose. "Say the words, Old Man."

"I'm head-over-cowboy boots in love with you, Irma Owens. I would've had nothing to live for had something happened to you." His face radiated a glow from his heart proving his words sincere. Then he snickered. "Now, who the hell are you calling Old Man?" He cackled.

Irma's gaze raked over Charli and Eli's faces. Each had a broad grin plastered across it. Clearly, she wasn't having a psychotic episode, a drug-induced bender or flashback from the 1960s. This wasn't a dream. Wes loved her.

"Not everything." She scoffed.

This was the opportunity she'd been waiting for. Would he ever speak to her again, after he found out what she'd hidden from him for so long? Could she tell him and wreck the love he'd professed for her?

His head cocked slightly, and his brows furrowed. "What do you mean, not everything?"

Charli took the decision out of her hands. "She meant me. You have me, Wes. I'm your granddaughter."

Wes's mouth opened in an expression of awe they'd expected. His eyes widened. He sat prone for a second. Slowly his arms spread wide toward his grandchild.

Charli's eyes filled with tears as she stooped and stepped into them. The two embraced for what seemed an eternity. When Charli stood, Eli came behind to steady her, wearing a broad, pleased smile.

Charli dabbed at tears streaming down her cheeks. "Wes, I look forward to getting to know you better."

"Absolutely." He wiped at the only tears Irma had ever seen him shed, using the back of his wrist. Eli handed him a box of tissues. He took them. "I know enough about you already from the way you treat your grandmother, the way you've watched over and taught your brother to be an upstanding young man, and how you and Eli stepped in to help me . . . someone you barely know. You're an incredible young woman. I'm proud to . . . know you."

Charli sniffed to clear her nose. "There's a question I've been dying to ask you. Eli and I want to get married just before Christmas. Would you consider giving me away?"

His brows came together like he was fighting a floodgate. "I'd be delighted." His lips tensed, and his jaw locked tight. He whirled the wheelchair around and shot out of the door into the hallway.

Charli started to follow him, but Eli held her back. "Let him go. It's a lot for him to digest. Give him time."

The weight of Irma's sigh broke her heart. Anxiety swelled her chest to its capacity. Pressure nearly stopped her heartbeat. She'd finally done it. The secret had been revealed to end any chance at a relationship with the only man she'd ever truly loved.

The only bright spot—he didn't look appalled at the idea of Charli being his granddaughter. Maybe the two of them could forge some good out of this fiasco.

CHAPTER THIRTY-SEVEN

Wesley spent the better part of the day alone in his hospital room staring out the window at the river, licking his wounds and feeling sorry for himself. He could hardly fathom that Irma had never told him he had a son. Tucker wasn't the product of Irma's next relationship, as Wesley had always assumed. She'd been pregnant with Wes's child when he'd panicked and tossed her aside like yesterday's garbage.

Early in the evening a knock came on his door. Eli peaked around it. "May I come in?"

Wes waved him in.

Eli took a seat beside Wes's wheelchair. "How are you doing, Man?"

Wes snorted. "Let's just say the last few days have been full of surprises. I spent my whole life not knowing I had a child." He gave a harrumph. "Not just one. I'd fathered two kids, a boy, and a girl, both out of wedlock. I never bothered to give children to any of my wives. Of course, they didn't want them either, like me. It was part of their allure. They didn't mind my sole dedication to work and expected nothing more from me than stability of marriage and financial support."

Eli nodded and sighed. "Could it be Irma realized you didn't want children? She knew, like your wives, you constantly traveled, committed to a career that took you all over the globe. Irma lived in that world when she was singing. She gave it up when Tucker and her daughter-in-law died. It's not the life she'd wanted for her boy. She left Tucker with her parents when he was of school age, so he'd have stability of a home and a normal childhood. She wanted him to have friends, play sports, and sleep in the same bed at night."

Wes snorted. "She gave him up?"

Eli nodded. "In a manner of speaking. She didn't relinquish parenthood. Irma supported Tucker and her parents, so they didn't have to work any longer. Every break she had between tours, she spent with him. If she played concerts anywhere within driving distance of Sweetwater, either she'd come visit or they'd meet her in that city. She kept in constant touch with Tucker. That boy meant everything to her. They talked frequently, right up to her last tour when the fatal accident occurred. Tucker was the only one who knew her whereabouts. He died with that information. It took the townspeople some time to track her down. Then she had to complete the tour, though her friend, Senator Madison, hired attorneys to try and get her out of the contract. Irma loved Tucker. Loved them all dearly. She told me leaving her son was the hardest thing she'd ever done. She just figured it was the best thing for him."

Wes blinked, moving his gaze away from the young man. "I suppose she was right. She was a much better parent than I ever would've been. It sounds as though Tucker turned out to be a good man. He raised a delightful daughter. I can't wait to meet my grandson, Kyler. Does he know?"

Eli's head shake confirmed the negative.

Wes nodded. "To be fair, I was in no shape to be a father back then. If I'd known Jodi had produced my child, I would've sent her money and kept in touch; but I wouldn't have been the father a young girl needed. I couldn't have been a part of her life."

"From what I gather, Jodi wasn't fit to raise a child either. She must've had some serious mental issues." Eli's head rocked upward. "So, why would Irma think you would want her son?"

Wes snorted. "Yeah, especially the way I treated her at the end. It was unforgiveable. I guess she assumed if I didn't want her, I wouldn't want her kid either." Another snort. "I'd have been a lousy father back then . . . to any kid. I suppose she made the right decision."

Eli scrunched his lips together. "Sounds that way. Regardless, it is what it is."

Wes grunted. "Still stings."

"I suppose it does. At least you got a family out of it, and you never had to change a single diaper."

Wes snickered. "There is that."

Eli gave him a half smile. "Any chance you can forgive Irma?"

Wes shrugged, his head turning away. "Not sure."

"What will you do now?" Eli's eyes penetrated Wes's silence.

He rocked his bruised, swollen head sideways. A bandage still covered one cut that had needed a few stitches, and it tugged uncomfortably with his movement. "What can I do? Until the judge drops the charges against me—and I assume he will at some point—I'm in her hands. I don't have much choice. The doctor wants to release me tomorrow. The bullet's out of my shoulder. My concussion is under control. I look like hell, but I'm not in such bad shape I can take up a hospital bed some other unlucky son-of-a-bitch might need. They want me to go home . . . guess that still means Irma's house."

Eli's eyes brightened. "If you are sure you don't want that, I could probably convince her to let you stay with me. I could put up another bunk in the house Charli and I are remodeling."

Wes smiled, liking the idea this upstanding young man would soon become part of his new family, and looking forward to getting to know Eli better. "Thanks, man. That's generous of you. Would you mind if we wait and see what tomorrow brings? My life is changing at whirlwind speed. I need to sleep on all of this. Let it sink in and figure out how to move forward."

Eli stood and slapped him gently on the back of his uninjured side. "No problem. I'll come to pick you up tomorrow. You have my number. Ring me and let me know what time they're releasing you."

Wes's chin lifted. "What about Irma?"

Eli leaned on the door as he opened it to go. "She's heading home tomorrow as well."

CHAPTER THIRTY-EIGHT

Wes's phone rang. It was Greyson Corbin's attorney. "Mr. Drake, I wanted to let you know, I've finally been able to reach Taylor Corbin. He has returned home to N. J."

Wes wasn't sure what to expect. "Is that right?"

The lawyer continued, "Yes. It turns out he's been in Las Vegas the whole time. He and his girlfriend flew there to be married."

Wes frowned, holding the phone to his ear. "Girlfriend? I thought he was seeing my assistant Tara Bonner."

"I don't know anything about that. Taylor married a young woman he met at a strip club in New Jersey. Apparently, she worked as an exotic dancer." A couple of lap dances and Taylor had forgotten all about his heated pursuit of Tara.

At least Taylor didn't kill her . . . and his dad. Wes would've hated his best friend's son committing those murders.

The attorney went on to schedule an on-line visual conference call for the reading of Greyson's will. Wes agreed to attend, as Grey had left him some token of their friendship, sure it couldn't be anything significant. He was certain the bulk of Grey's estate would go to Taylor. Taylor had also verbally agreed to sell his part of the agency to the person Wes had received an offer from, and papers had been sent to Taylor to sign his rights over to her.

Soon after he hung up the phone, a knock came on his hospital door. Sheriff Wyatt Gordon's head leaned in. "Okay for me to chat for a few?" The big man's deep, Southern drawl sounded casual.

This wasn't just a friendly visit. Wes would need to explain his part in the fiasco that had occurred. "Sure, Sheriff." He waved the silver-haired lawman in.

Wyatt's handsome face held a pleasant smile as he took a seat beside Wes's bed. "Please, Mr. Drake, call me Wyatt—everyone does."

Wes hoped the friendliness was sincere. He liked the sheriff, despite their relationship so far having bounced from one state to another and back again—hopefully to stay. "Make it Wes. How can I help you, Wyatt?"

"I've talked with Charli, Eli and your attorney, Carlton Farmer. Their stories all coincide with what they all told me prior to your attack. Can you clarify exactly what happened yesterday for me?"

Wes nodded, folding hands in his lap. "Certainly. I was working on my computer in Kyler's room. Irma left for the market. I'd been distracted by a conference call, and as I concluded that meeting, the door slammed open. That young woman, Dana Sue March burst in. She forced me at gunpoint to the great room where she secured my feet and hands. I resisted, and she pistol-whipped me. I believe I blacked out for a short time. When I came to, I tried to reason with the woman. She was crazed and fiercely angry. I recognized her as the waitress who had served me and Greyson at the New York airport. She had that tattoo on her neck. After my arrest for Grey and Tara's murders, Irma learned she had followed Tara and me to Sweetwater and taken a job at the hotel we were staying at. I'd been

282

unaware of that at the time. Charli looked it up online and told me the tattoo signified '*vengeance*.' Anyway, Dana Sue confessed to me she had murdered not only Grey and Tara, but also her mother, Jodi March. It seems Jodi bore my child after a brief encounter we had in high school. I didn't know about the baby—barely knew Jodi. Dana Sue told me about her mother's abuse of her during her lifetime. She wanted vengeance for her suffering, blaming me and Jodi. Dana Sue inadvertently killed both Tara and Grey, in attempts to poison me. Dana claimed I was responsible, because I offered Grey the tainted bourbon, she'd served me. She stated I'd killed my assistant by giving Tara the deluxe room reserved for me, where Dana coated the sheets with arsenic in her attempt to poison me in my sleep. I tried to stall Ms. March, keeping her talking for as long as possible. I never found a way to escape her, however. Out of the blue, Irma sauntered in like she was unaware of what was going on. They argued. Dana Sue pointed her weapon at me. I'm sure she would've killed me, had Irma not been armed and fired her pistol. Hell, I didn't even know the woman carried." He snorted.

Wyatt grinned, what looked to be a genuine expression. "Yes, Irma called me before she came in. Carlton had alerted me of Jodi March's death. NYPD told me they believed Dana Sue March to be responsible for toxin in her mother's liquor. I tried to convince Irma to wait for me and my team to show up, but she was adamant you were in imminent danger. It appears she was correct."

Wes's head hung forward. "How is Irma taking it, having killed that woman?" That woman had been his illegitimate daughter—the daughter who lived only to murder the man who fathered her. That woman had wanted him dead. Instead, she was the one to be heading six-feet under. "It's just a sad thing, all around."

Wyatt nodded agreement. "Yes, it certainly is. Irma is a strong woman. It's not the first time she's had to defend herself, but it is the first time her shot was lethal. Maybe you should ask her yourself."

Wes winced. "I'll do that."

Wyatt's chin rose, and his eyes met Wes.' "Dana Sue died in the ambulance but lived long enough to own up to her crimes to Deputy Jaiden Coldwater, on the way to the hospital. We have the confession on recording. Irma is a quick thinker. She'd set her phone to record before she entered the house. Irma had left the line live, so I'm also a verbal witness, and we have her recording. I've handed over copies of both conversations to the District Attorney and to Carlton Farmer. They're meeting with the judge on this case as we speak. I'm certain you will be vindicated, and all charges will be dropped."

Wes heaved a heavy sigh of relief. "Thank goodness." He shook his head. "I'm still having a hard time wrapping my head around all of this. It's such a crazy story."

Wyatt snickered. "Yeah, well, real life is much more complex than any story. That's been my experience."

"Guess you're right, Sheriff . . . Wyatt. Now you know the whole story, I guess you're as appalled as I am. I can't believe I spawned such a person."

Wyatt's lips curled. "Everyone has a story. Some are worse than others. Perhaps madness runs in Jodi March's family. Maybe it's not hereditary. Abuse is generally passed on from one generation to another. People live the way they're brought up most of the time."

"I suppose so. It's heartbreaking . . . tragic." Wes sighed.

Wyatt stood, towering over Wes's seated position. "That it is. I hope this doesn't dissuade you from considering retirement in Sweetwater. I'd enjoy having you as a neighbor. I know Irma and her family would love to see you settle nearby."

Wes snorted. "Think so, huh." *Not so sure.*

CHAPTER THIRTY-NINE

Recovering from a restless night flipping from restless sleep to soul searching, Wes was ready to check out of the facility when Eli arrived.

"You're looking stronger," Eli chuckled. "Though, your eyes have turned green and yellow, versus black around them from yesterday. "Ready to blow this joint?"

"Yes, I need to go somewhere a man can get a good night's rest. Nurses give you something to sleep. If you're lucky enough for it to work, soon as you doze off, they're back to check your vitals. Up and down, nightmarish naps, and then awake again seems to be the rule around here."

Eli laughed. "Hospitals are no fun—not meant to be. Let's get you home."

Home? The only foster parents who gave a crap about Wes had passed away long ago, but he'd never forget their kindness. Wes hadn't felt at *home* anywhere since he'd been in high school and lucky enough to finally be placed with them. That is, until Irma had made a place for him in her home.

An aide pushed a wheelchair into the room. He checked to be sure Wes was the patient he'd come for, helped him into the rolling limo, and ushered him slowly toward the exit. Eli followed, carrying a sack of Wes's belongings. He'd parked beside the entrance.

Once loaded into Eli's truck and driving toward the lot's exit, Eli glanced sideways. "Are you bunking with me for a spell, or sticking with Irma?"

Wes had rolled those options around in his brain all night, back and forth. It was time for a decision. "Guess I'll stay with Irma. After all, until I'm released by the court, she's responsible for keeping me from fleeing the country."

Eli snickered. "Yeah, like that would ever happen. You have too much going on here to take off like that. It's good. Either way, we'd have to stop at her place to get the rest of your things."

Wes frowned. "I hope she sees it that way. That lady knows how to make a man's life hell if she's not happy." He'd rather live in an Irma-made hell than never see her again. Would the love she'd professed for him withstand what they needed to settle between them?

Eli snorted. "I can imagine. She's the gutsiest female I've ever met. I wouldn't want to be on her bad side." He pulled out onto the main street and drove toward Irma's house. "Look at it this way. Irma barged into the house yesterday because she knew you were in danger. She put her life on the line. The woman took a bullet for you."

Wes winced. His heart ached that she could've died trying to save him. "How's Irma doing? It must be hard on her, knowing she killed a woman."

Eli's head rocked back in admission. "Not just any woman—your daughter."

Wes cringed. "Damn, it's hard to believe I spawned someone like that. Dana Sue was more of a progeny of Satan."

Eli pulled in beside her, as Charli parked her truck in her driveway. He stepped out with a smile for his fiancé.

Charli rounded the vehicle and slipped into his open arms. "Everything okay?"

He released her. "We'll see."

She turned to help Irma out of the passenger side. Eli came around to assist Wes. Irma shot him a questioning look—one brow raised. What it meant, he hadn't a clue. Was she upset he'd returned to stay at her house? Did she wonder whether he'd forgiven her for denying him his son all those years? He wasn't sure how he felt about that either. Who knew what she was thinking? Irma was anything but predictable. Once they were inside, she might tell him to hit the road and find other accommodations.

They walked in, Irma and Charli first, closely followed by Eli and Wes. Shouting came from all areas of the great room. "Welcome home!"

A crowd of Irma's friends and neighbors filled the large space. Streamers and balloons strung from corner to corner and surrounded the kitchen's center bar. Cake and a floral arrangement sat on the dining room table. A beverage station had been arranged on the countertop. The bar space was covered with what appeared to be homemade delicacies of all sorts.

Charli beamed and slipped an arm through Irma's and Wes's, so they flanked their tiny granddaughter. "Everyone insisted we have a celebration to welcome you both home. I baked a cake. They each brought their cuisine specialties. I hope you're starving. I know I am. Eli and I didn't have time for breakfast."

Irma hugged her granddaughter and turned to the gathering. "Thank you all for coming. It's so good to have you here. It's been a long time since I've hosted a party. We have lots to celebrate."

She glanced at Wes. He couldn't read her expression. "You folks know Wes. Most of you met him or know of him by now. The Sweetwater Grapevine and the press have had a field day with the story. What happened at the Sweetwater Hotel and with his partner in that New York Tavern were not his doing. As you know, Wes was suspected of both crimes. Yesterday's chaos proved he was innocent. I'm certain he'll now be vindicated of both allegations. I hope you're here to welcome him to Sweetwater, and not just to celebrate that the crazy woman who abducted him wasn't a good shot. Both of us are going to be fine."

Physically? Yes. Mentally? To be determined.

Attendees applauded and shouted, "About time." "Wonderful." "Good to know." And "Great."

As the loud commotion of comments ended, Irma smiled. "Thank you for that and for putting this party together. It means a lot to me. There's something more we should celebrate."

She shot Wes a peripheral glance. "Wesley Drake is the father of my son. He's Charli and Kyler's granddad."

The gathering gave another rowdy round of applause.

As they quieted, Irma turned toward Charli. "I believe Charli and Eli have an announcement worth celebrating today."

Charli's lovely face held a beaming glow. She slid her hand into Eli's open one. "We have finally set a wedding date. You're all invited. Mark your calendars for a Christmas Eve wedding. Also, Wes has agreed to give me away."

Eli glanced at the sheriff. "Wyatt, would you do the honors and officiate the wedding?"

The broad-shouldered giant of a man nodded his silver head. "I'd be delighted."

A sleek, dark-haired woman clung to the sheriff's arm. Wes recalled having met Wyatt's wife briefly. Who could forget a woman with the name Lemon Sage Gordon, even if she wasn't stunning, with her ponytail hanging across one shoulder and nearly to her waist?

The group began milling about, mixing drinks, and nibbling. Scanning, Wes recognized most faces. He didn't recall all their names. Hopefully, he'd have a chance to get acquainted with them—if Irma didn't toss him out on his behind.

Irma waved toward the buffet with the arm not in a sling. "Well, let's get this party started. I'm starved." She looked up at Eli. "Would you make your granny-to-be a Kahlua and soda, sweetheart?"

Eli nodded, "Absolutely. Charli, I'll get you a spiced rum and soda."

"Thanks, Eli." Charli waltzed toward a group of young women.

Irma eyed Wes with a critical gaze. "I suppose we should talk."

Charli joined her friends chatting near the fireplace. "So, Jaiden, will you be my Maiden of Honor? Chloe and Sage, would you consider being Brides Maids, or is that Maidens? You're both married." She chuckled lightheartedly.

"Of course," came the chorus of female voices.

World-renowned chef and restaurateur, Dovie Farmer, strutted over and gave Charli a hug. Her red hair tickled Charli's cheek. "I checked when you made the announcement. My banquet hall has that date open, but it won't be for long. You interested?"

Charli let out a sigh. "That's a relief. I was afraid with only two months to plan the wedding; we might have problems finding a venue. Your place is tops on my list, so the answer is absolutely. We want it. We will have the wedding there and reception immediately afterward."

Riley Powers-Madison smiled. "Why don't you let me, Sage, and Corrie host an engagement party-slash-wedding shower at Mane Lane Farm? We can do it in the mansion ballroom."

The advertising agency owner was married to Levi Madison, a world-famous horse breeder and trainer. His parents were Senator Garrett, and Adele Madison's son, one of the families who had hosted Charli and Kyler when they were orphaned. They lived at Mane Lane Farm, and her husband, Levi, ran the multi-billion-dollar facility.

Corrie Madison-Henderson grinned and lifted her champagne flute. As Levi's sister, the attorney served as CEO of their family conglomerate, Adele Industries. "That's a fabulous idea. Don't worry about a thing. The three of us have it covered. Right, Sage?" Corrie pointed her gorgeous blonde head toward the stunning brunette.

Lemon Sage Gordon beamed at her friends. "I checked your horoscope. Stars are aligned for wedding date for bliss during the holiday season. This is going to be the wedding Sweetwater will never forget."

Sage was known for being a danger magnet, but Charli adored her mystical friend. Having been born in a commune, Sage's parental hippies had moved to the New York suburbs to give their daughter a proper education. After years working at the FDA and living the high-life with her first husband, Sage had left the city in her tracks following his tragic death and pursued her dream of getting back to her roots by running an organic farm.

Her move to Sweetwater and eventual marriage to Wyatt had done nothing to keep the spicy brunette out of trouble. Hopefully, she wouldn't draw some horrible fiasco their way.

Real estate agent, Chloe, changed the subject. "Say, did you hear about the auction scheduled to sell that old mansion on the hill?"

Corrie frowned. "Neighbors say that place is haunted."

Deputy Jaiden snickered. "So, they say. We've had several calls to investigate phenomena but never found anything. It was part of the pre-Civil War Underground Railroad. It stands to reason, if ghosts are there, they likely met tragic ends."

Sage smiled serenely. "No problem. With a little burning of sage and some direction, I'm sure Charli and I can rid the place of any spirits lingering there. We'll simply direct them to the light."

Charli bit her lower lip. "I doubt Eli and I could afford that place, but it would make a fantastic renovation project. I'd love to bring that old gal back to her former glory."

Chloe told her specifics about the auction, including the seller's bottom bid price, and scheduled an appointment to give Eli and Charli a pre-auction tour.

Charli smirked. "Awesome! I can't believe it's within our budget. We'll likely bid on it. Thanks, Chloe."

CHAPTER FORTY

Irma walked toward the French doors and out to the secluded patio with Wes on her trail. Settling into two comfy chairs, they faced each other. He was at a loss for what to say.

Irma swallowed every doubt she's been focusing on for the last few decades and gulped in what energy and gumption a deep breath from the universe could provide. It was time to face the music. Do the thing she'd dreaded for so long.

"Wes, I must apologize. You're probably shocked learning Tucker was your son. You have every right to hate me for keeping that secret."

He bit his lip before speaking. "True, but if I've learned anything, it is not to jump to conclusions. That was my mistake when I broke up with you without giving you the opportunity to explain. To be fair, I was running scared. I loved you so much, it frightened me. Everyone I ever cared for deserted me. My mother dropped me off as a toddler at a fire house. Every foster home I lived at either didn't want to be bothered with my needs, or they needed a slave or someone to abuse. Finally, a wonderful couple took me in and helped me graduate high school. They too are long gone. I was terrified of loving too much and losing— petrified enough to avoid it all together. That didn't work either. No matter what I did or how hard I tried, I never stopped loving you.”

Hardly believing her ears, she let out a sigh of relief. “The same here.”

Wes' head rocked up and down. “That's a major surprise—a good one, but still a shocker. I figured you hated me, hated me enough to keep my son from me.”

She shook her head. “Never, not hate. I was angry at first. I tried to forget you. That didn't happen. Your rejection stung like a knife in my heart. When I found out I was pregnant, I considered telling you. You didn't want me. By that time, you were all over the press with a new lover. I knew how focused you were on your career. Your life didn't include me. You didn't want it to. Why would you want my son?” She paused for a breath. “Truthfully, I didn't want to share my boy with you. I was afraid you would reject and hurt him. I refused to risk you scaring him the way you did me. I couldn't put Tucker through that.”

Wes gave a snort with a bob of his head. “You might've been right. I wouldn't have been a good father back then. I never considered having kids, not even when I was married. My wives didn't want or have time for children either. It just never occurred to me until lately. As I began contemplating retirement, I longed for something more—family, friends, to be part of something and a place to belong.”

Irma glanced around her. “I can understand that. Being part of this community is hardwired in my genes. It's a wonderful thing, to belong. Even after all the years I traveled for my career, these people welcomed me back as one of them.”

Wes smiled. "I can never thank you enough for taking me in during this mess. You made me comfortable in your home. You, Charli, and Eli stepped up and did what I couldn't do myself to help clear my name—I'll never be able to repay that debt."

Irma smiled as she shook her head. "No thanks needed. It's what we do for family."

He snickered with a backward rock. "Family . . . I've never had one."

She slapped her knee with her good hand. "Well, Wesley Drake, now you do. Like it or not, we are your family."

Wes gazed down. "I wish I'd known Tucker. You raised him well, from what I gather. He sounds like a wonderful man." His eyes met hers. "How are you fairing, Irma? I see you're physically as well as possible, considering you were shot."

She smiled in lieu of throwing her good arm around the man she loved. "Not bad. I have pain meds in case I can't sleep. Doc Barnes—you remember Clay Barnes, right? Anyway, Clay said I might need a bit of therapy as the shoulder heals, but I should be fit as a fiddle before long."

He snickered. "It's cute how you picked up all those little country sayings and southern accent, since you've moved back to Sweetwater."

She shrugged, not having noticed it herself. "Only natural. I was born and raised here, at least until I was sixteen and went on tour."

Wes smiled. "I was asking about your mental state. You fired the fatal shot yesterday. How are you handling that?"

Her head rocked to one side. "I made a split-second decision, knowing in the back of my mind when I went in it might come to a gun battle. Still, there's this thick, dark pressure in my chest when I think about killing that woman, regardless of the psycho she was. I didn't see any way around it. If I hadn't you wouldn't be here now. It was you or her."

He pursed his lips. "And I'm grateful you made this choice."

Her brows shot up. "Are you really? What about you? That gal was your daughter, another child you had no idea about."

He winced. "Yeah, that's a bitter pill to swallow. I can't believe I could be party to creating such a person."

She sneered sorrowfully. "I'd say Jodi March was responsible for how Dana Sue turned out. Your seed might've sprouted in that garden, but you didn't cultivate the crazy in her child. She did. You dodged a bullet not being part of that demented gal's life."

Sorrow filled his eyes. "Dana Sue was completely irrational. I tried, but there was no reasoning with her. She lived only to see her mother and me dead—said that was the only way she could move on and have the life she wanted. It's so horribly sad." His eyes met Irma's.

She pursed her lips. "Sounds like we both need professional help."

He chuckled and winked. "I know a good psychologist. I practically paid for her yacht."

She laughed. "Sounds good." She stood and reached a hand toward him. He followed suit and took it. His grip was warm and comforting. It felt right. "Right now, we've got a party to attend and a wedding to help plan."

CHAPTER FORTY-ONE

Sam sauntered to where Wes stood watching Erma chatter with her friends. His head tilted toward the gathering and then met Wes's gaze. "She's one hell of a gal. Don't you agree?" Did he detect a hint of pride? Maybe a bit of protectiveness? He couldn't blame Sam. The guy had to know Wes was trying to step into a position Sam clearly wanted badly to occupy with Irma.

Wes beamed, ruing the day in 1970 when he had he'd rudely walked away from her in a theatre parking, crying her heart out in front of her best friend's motor bus. Guilt hit him like a punch to the gut. He swallowed his stomach back into place and donned the smile he'd perfected over his years in business. "She certainly is. Irma is one of a kind." He gave the doctor his hand in greeting. "Good to see you again, Dr. Baker."

"Might as well call me Sam. Everyone does—either that or Doc. It appears you'll be sticking around Sweetwater."

"I believe I will, as soon as I clear up some loose business ends in New York." Wes hated the idea of leaving Irma for even a short while. Maybe he could talk her into going along.

"I wanted to tell you how sorry I am that you lost your two friends. It was awful what happened to you and Irma.

I'm glad you both survived it." Sam's eyes beamed genuinely.

"Thank you, Sam. That means a lot to me."

He eyed the doctor who couldn't seem to take his eyes off of Irma. "Does she know you are in love with her?"

Sam snorted. "She knows. The problem is, she built a big 'ole impenetrable wall around that generous heart of hers. That didn't stop me from trying. In the meantime, I was happy with what I had with her. When you arrived, it was obvious you and she had history. Now I know why she kept her heart at bay. She never stopped loving you."

The little guy was more perceptive than Wes had assumed. "It may have been apparent to you. Not to me. I figured our past relationship meant more to me than it did to her. When we split, it looked like she had no problem moving on. I thought she found a fella she was wanted to raise a son with. Publishing rags showed her with many famous men over the years. Surprisingly, she didn't marry one of them. I truthfully had no clue she still cared for me."

Sam solemnly nodded. "She's a keeper—that one. It seems that barrier came crashing down when you showed up."

Without words, Wes nodded, astonished he had been able to reach her veiled heart.

Sam's eyes left Irma and glowered at Wes with one brow high. "It's only fair I warn you. If you break her heart, you will answer to me."

Heat from Sam's stare burned his message into Wes's ears. With a snort, his head rocked backward. "Thanks for the warning, pal. That's the last thing I want."

Sam appeared somewhat appeased. It was evident he cared deeply and meant what he'd said. "Good to hear." He shook his empty bottle. "I'm going for a beer. Want one?"

"Thanks, Sam. I'm good."

With a nod, the coroner walked toward the refreshment cooler. Wes' redheaded attorney, Carlton Farmer, pulled him aside from the party. The lawyer's husband and firm partner, Howard Ross, moved their threesome to a quiet corner. "What's up?"

Both men smiled, but Carlton took the lead. "I've spoken with the judge. He listened to both recordings of your conversation with Ms. March and read your testimony. He spoke with Irma and Wyatt, getting their take on the situation. The judge signed papers to release you from suspicion in Tara's murder."

Howard put a hand on Wes' shoulder. "I spoke with NYPD. They've done the same, concerning your partner's death."

Carlton grinned. "You're no longer required to stay in Sweetwater. That is, unless you want to."

Relief flooded Wes's body. It was over. He could move on.

His corporate theft was being managed and funds reimbursed . . . eventually. Murders had been solved. Attorneys were working on the sale of Greyson's share of their agency to Wes' new partner. He would soon be able to execute his plan to retire within the next few months.

Wyatt and Irma's friends seemed genuinely pleased he was acquitted. They'd acknowledged him as part of their group. Was there a remote possibility he could settle in or near Sweetwater?

Wes had a family who seemed to want him. Charli acted as though she was thrilled and had asked him to be part of the nuptials. Eli had welcomed him with open arms. Irma had forgiven him, as he had her. He had talked with Kyler over the phone and had high expectations for a relationship with the young man. He and Irma were planning a visit soon, so Wes could meet his grandson.

Miraculously, Irma loved him. He could hardly fathom it, even in his wildest fantasies.

Wyatt came over and stood, both hands on hips. "It seems you're free to go, Wes. Charges against you have been dropped. Congratulations. I hope this incident doesn't put a sour taste in your mouth about our little community. Sweetwater is a wonderful place to be."

Wes smiled, surprised at the display of welcome he was receiving from the township. "Thank you, Wyatt. No, not at all. I'm finding Sweetwater delightful and appealing."

The big man's head rocked back. "Wonderful."

Irma looked stunning as she joined them, regardless of her injury. A fuchsia, silk tunic hid the shoulder bandage. Slim, white linen slacks showed off her sleek figure. Her long train of silver locks were braided and cascaded across the arm protected by a black shawl that served as a sling. "It's good to see you enjoying yourself."

His head tilted. "Sweetheart, didn't the hospital supply you with a proper sling?"

Her eyes rolled upward. "Heavens yes, but this silk scarf looks more fashionable and serves the same purpose. Don't you agree?"

Wyatt chuckled and kissed her cheek. "You look lovely, as usual, Irma."

Wes smiled and slipped his hand around hers. "Wyatt, Howard and Carlton were just assuring me I'm no longer a suspect and am a free man."

She beamed, and the light caught her eyes with a sparkle. "Good to hear, but it was inevitable."

Wes lifted his chin in relief, blinking away the hint of tears. Her faith in him was immeasurable. He was so blessed. "I'm glad someone was sure. I had my doubts. Wyatt, how did Dana Sue obtain that poison? I thought arsenic was outlawed and hard to obtain."

Wyatt nodded toward the coroner. Sam Baker stood a short distance away and chatted with Sadie Carson, the owner of The Royal Diner. "Doc told of the three most common arsenics; gray is the most stable form when it becomes a soft, waxy semiconductor. It is the easiest to obtain and the most commonly used."

Sheriff Gordon's head leaned back. "There is nothing illegal about having arsenic in your possession. It's a naturally occurring mineral rock found in volcanic ash, weathering of minerals and ores, and mineralized groundwater . . . also food, water, soil, and air. It is absorbed by plants—especially leafy vegetables, rice, apples, and grapes—even seafood."

Irma's eyes went wide. "Yikes."

Wyatt snorted with a grimace. "The EPA rules it as Number 1 on its Priority List of Hazardous Substance, classified it as a Group A carcinogen. All forms of arsenic pose a serious risk to human health."

Irma wrung her hands in her lap. "If it's so damaging, why is it broadly available and used?"

Wyatt's lips curled. "It has wide-ranging forms, primarily in alloys of lead, and serves diverse purposes. For example, car batteries, ammunition, or semiconductors in electronic devices, such as computer chips. It's instrumental in the production of pesticides, treated wood products, herbicides, and insecticides."

Wes cringed. "So, don't burn pressure treated wood?"

Wyat shrugged. "Right, unless you're trying to collect poisonous ash." He exhaled loudly. "Usage is declining due to increasing recognition of toxicity; but hamsters, goats, chickens, and some other species need trace quantities of arsenic in their diet."

Irma expired a heavy breath. Her head rocked back, as though in disbelief. "Chicken feed? I assumed that wacko got it from fly paper Charli discovered in her room in New York."

Wyatt smiled with a nod. "That's what we've concluded as well. I just wanted you to understand how widely available arsenic is."

Wes exhaled a huff of air, recalling the terrifying events of the prior day. "What you're saying is it didn't take a genius to obtain the poison." He was having a hard time coming to grips with having fathered a monster who lived only to see him dead. "That agrees with what Dana Sue said while she held me hostage. She dosed the bourbon and served it to me. Unaware, I swapped drinks with Greyson. When that didn't work, she coated Tara's bedsheets with deadly powder, thinking I would be the one dying in my sleep." He shook his head in wonder.

Wyatt stared at them for a few moments of silence.

With frazzled nerves Wes clutched his hands in his lap. He needed to get a grip. It was over. Only fallout remained.

Finally, the sheriff broke the silence. "Arsenic can be inhaled with atmospheric gases or dust. It can be dissolved and ingested in food or drink, like the liquor Greyson consumed. Tara Bonner absorbed it through her skin."

Irma frowned. "So many ways to kill a person! It's shocking. I figured her lotion, shampoo, or body wash was dosed with poison, until I pulled the truth out of Sam."

Wes shook his head. "This whole thing is just freaking crazy."

"I'm just glad it's over." Wyatt shook Wes's hand. "We'll leave you two to let it soak in." The three men walked toward the drink station.

Wes and Irma sat alone for let a long, uncomfortable, quiet few minutes. As her trembling hand relaxed in his, time came to finish their talk. Wes feared letting go of his hold on her. It might be his last opportunity to touch her. "Do you want me to move my things out? Eli invited me to stay with him for a while if you do."

Her chin rose, and her eyes seemed to scour his. "Not necessary. Stay as long as you need." She paused with a dip of her head, then met his gaze. "I suppose you'll return to New York soon."

He nodded. "Guess so. Pressing business requires my presence."

She nodded but didn't speak. Her hand remained in his, though he sensed the barest of quivers. His heart raced like a thoroughbred on the homestretch.

He let silence settle before continuing. "You wouldn't consider accompanying me. Would you? I'm not sure I can bear to leave you for long."

Her brow knitted, and she glared down her nose like a Sunday school teacher preparing to reprimand him. "Just what are you suggesting, Wesley Drake?"

Placing hands on her shoulders, he leaned forward, nuzzled her ear, and slipped the lobe into his mouth. The taste of her sent tingles throughout his body. His rod filled with a surge of hardening passion.

A tiny shiver escaped her as his words breathed heated passion into her ear. "I'm saying I can't live without you, Irma Owens. I won't waste another day being apart from the Starr of my life, my one and only love."

She answered with a turn of her head. Her lips demanded his in a kiss they'd each waited a lifetime for.

THE END

DEAR READER,

If you liked the ***Rock Starr Baby Daddy, A Flip or Flop Mystery***, I'm sure you're going to love reading more from Lynda Rees. Here's a sample to get you started.

FLIP OR FLOP

MURDER HOUSE

CHAPTER ONE

Charli Owens strode a few feet from her pickup to where the auction would be held. A few characters she knew casually waited for the Sheriff and County Clerk to exit the Sweetwater courthouse. A couple of insurance agents, a boring, grey-suited guy studying his clip board—a bank representative monitoring the sale, and an older couple, made up the group.

A pickup truck with ladder racks on top pulled to the curb and stopped. Buckets and equipment filled the bed—a contractor's work vehicle. A too-hot-to-be-loose on the street guy stepped out of the driver's side and rounded the truck.

Trouble.

Shaggy blonde hair draped his neck, framing a swoon-worthy face. Light eyes glowed from his smile, noticeable from the distance. It lit up his face, causing adorable wrinkles at their sides. A slim waist joined long, slender legs in tight-fitting jeans. He dwarfed the petite, blonde with cropped locks, who climbed from the passenger side. The female reached in and helped a miniature version of her out.

Bouncing red curls topped the toddler's head, and she wore overall blue jeans with a red tee shirt. Her father took her hand. The mom tiptoed to kiss his cheek, bent to do the same to their daughter then strolled around, jumping into the driver's seat then sped away.

Lovely family. No danger there.

A pang hit Charli's heart, having hoped to have a household like that by now.

Hunky Daddy ambled slowly, so his daughter could keep up as they walked. Petite like her mother, the imp looked about four or five. Dad stood six-feet-four inches tall at least, probably more like six-foot-six. Broad shoulders strained fabric of his black tee stretching across a rolling chest and rippling abs.

Stopping at the rock wall by the courthouse steps, he squatted and whispered to the little one. She slipped behind him, and tiny arms surrounded his neck. He grasped the pudgy hands, lifted her onto his back then positioned himself to allow her to step onto the wall. She sat with legs dangling. He hopped to land beside her and put an arm across her shoulders, giving her a sweet hug.

Charli pushed away jealousy gnawing at her and waltzed toward a familiar couple. "Hi, Sandy, Mike. Are you looking to buy?"

Twenty-something Mike Carey shook her hand. "Not sure we're in position to purchase at auction."

Sandy Carey slid a palm across her protruding tummy and shook Charli's hand "Mike and I don't understand the process."

Mike nodded. "We decided to observe, though we'd love to bid on the Blossom Lane house."

Charli swallowed a lump lodged in her throat. "You aren't swayed by—"

Mike interrupted her bumbling attempt at posing the question tactfully. "Not a bit. It had nothing to do with us."

Charli exhaled relief and inhaled hope, nodding at Sandy's belly. "Congratulations, I didn't realize you were expecting. Is that why you're in the market?" There was the green-eyed monster again. Charlie pushed it down.

Sandy beamed. "Our daughter is coming in September. We've prequalified for an FHA mortgage, but there's nothing on the market we're interested in. Blossom would fit us well, but we're not sure about tackling a fixer upper."

Mike's faced reddened. "I'm not helpless, but a lot needs to be done to that house. You're an expert and a real estate agent. Maybe you can help." He pulled out a paper and handed it to Charli. "This is our mortgage approval letter."

Relieved she wouldn't need to compete with the young couple for the property, she reviewed the document then handed it to Mike. "You won't be able to purchase a house needing renovation. FHA strenuously inspects your purchase to ensure it won't require major improvements for a long while. They don't want to put you in a position where they might need to foreclose."

Mike solemnly nodded. "I was afraid of that."

Charli smiled warmly. "I'm bidding on that property for my next rehab."

Sandy frowned. "Don't you remodel more expensive houses?"

Charli put a happy face on. "I'm taking the company in a different direction. There's a vast market for reasonably priced housing." They didn't need to know about Charli's effort to salvage her company and make a mark on her own.

Mike folded the sheet and stuck it in his pocket. "We're having trouble finding a suitable home."

"If I'm successful and get Blossom Lane, my intention is to bring it to perfect condition. I'll give you first crack at it if you want."

Sandy's eyes grew wide. "Yes, absolutely, we want to take a look when you're ready."

Mike grinned at his wife then turned to Charli. "Thank you. That would be perfect."

Charli cocked her head and eyed the handsome father and his child. She had hoped to be the only contractor bidding. "Pray I win at auction."

The strange man's head lifted, allowing a better view of his face. A square jaw eased into a grin, showing off glistening whites. Amusement appeared in almost iridescent gray eyes. Tiny wrinkles formed on outsides as he nodded pleasantly in Charli's direction.

Damn. She'd been caught gawking. Just what a good-looking guy needed, a stroke to his ego.

The antique, double doors opened. Sheriff Wyatt Gordon stepped out with a woman. He scanned and welcomed the crowd, introduced himself and the clerk and explained the process. The auction began.

An agent Charli recognized purchased a couple of city plots for his out-of-town insurance company. Bidding started for a laundromat. The older couple upped the banker's offer. A man in a business suit made a competing proposal. They countered a couple of times until he gave a resolved shake of his head.

Hunky Daddy sat quietly observing. That didn't bode well in Charli's mind. She'd hoped to avoid competition. His vehicle screamed contractor, someone who might bid against her. Blossom was the only property left.

Charli took a final look at figures in her notebook, reminding herself to stay within budget. She'd carefully inspected the house earlier in the week, gotten accurate pricing data together and assessed renovated value based on market data. Her bottom dollar was enough to satisfy the mortgage holder. It might not stand up against an aggressive bidder.

This guy better not be here for her house. The place had good bones. She needed it to keep her company afloat but didn't have money to get into a bidding war, not if she planned to keep a cushion to deal with unforeseen issues.

It wasn't simply her need to eat and provide shelter for her family. Self-esteem had suffered a deafening blow during dissolution of her partnership. Her pride was the size of a two-penny nail.

Damn it to hell.

That son of a bitch, Thompson Shade, wasn't about to end her. Shoulders rocked back. Her chin shot high. Resolve eased her rigid jaw.

She'd bought many a house at auction, designed, remodeled and successfully sold million-dollar residences at major profits. This dinky, three-bedroom pit wasn't about to get the better of her.

Wyatt opened the bid. The bank rep's hand shot up. The elderly couple upped the price a thousand dollars. Charli's hand went high, accepting the auctioneer's offer a thousand more. Next submission increased another grand. Hunky Daddy's mitt rose into the air. Charli took the next grand. The old couple's eyes met, and they dropped out. Hunky Daddy and Charli went up a thousand a time, playing against each other.

Charli gaped at her scratchpad. She lifted her paw and shouted a proposition five-thousand dollars higher. Hunky Daddy grimaced then shrugged as he shook his head.

Wyatt's announced, "Sold to Charli Owens."

Relief flooded her lungs and swilled into her gut. She smiled pleasantly toward Hunky Daddy.

He'd already hopped down and was lifting his child to her feet. Without a gaze Charli's direction, he took the girl's hand; and they strolled from Town Square.

His fine ass moved side-to-side. Broad shoulders shifted with ease of his stride, as those lengthy legs took him and his daughter down the street. Sandy, shaggy hair was chin length and might look lazy on some men but enhanced sex appeal to a peak on this guy. She sighed when they rounded the corner and disappeared.

With nothing left to watch, Charli waltzed into the courthouse to finalize the deal. She'd searched the title, having done it many times before. Paying cash, the title company was prepared to close in three days.

Afterward on the street, Charli whipped out her phone and dialed. Her best gal pal, Jaiden. "So? Did you get it?" Deputy Jaiden Coldwater's Texas drawl was nearly identical to local, Kentucky twang.

Charli chuckled. "Yep, I figured Wyatt would've filled you in."

"Nope, information is confidential until closing. The boss said if you wanted me to know, you'd tell me. Congratulations. Your business is on track. We need to celebrate and then find you a decent fella. You need to get that fine tush of yours back out there." Since Jaiden had gotten engaged to handsome surgeon, Clay Barnes, she'd been on a mission to fix Charli up.

Charli's eyes shot toward the heavens. "Hell no; I've sworn off the male sex, at least until I finish this rehab and sell the property."

"Whatever you say, but you can't stay off the market for long. Your love life needs a total rebuild."

"Don't I know it. The finest male specimen I've seen in a long time showed up at the sale today. The dude was eye candy, palpitation worthy and sweating testosterone clear across the courthouse lawn. It literally made my thong wet when his dreamy peepers met mine. I was perspiring blood; my face went so red."

"You don't sound sure about this temporary-celibate thing." Jaiden chuckled. She hadn't masked her relief when Thompson had tossed Charli aside like yesterday's takeout, and she wasn't on board with Charli's *no men for a while* choice.

"Honey, I'm not dead. There's nothing wrong with my sight. I might not be shopping, but I can view the merchandise. That boy was too hot to ignore. I had to soak up some of that sex appeal while he was hanging around. I can tell you my libido is fully intact."

"So why didn't you hit that?"

Charli tucked away in her mind the male vision causing her to perspire like the morning dew. "The guy is taken, married. They have the most adorable, little girl."

"Got 'cha," Jaiden groaned. "Oh well, at least, what's his name hasn't ruined you for other men. There's a deserving, guy out there for you, Charli. You'll find him when you're ready. Speaking of ready, when are we going to celebrate?"

AUTHOR'S NOTE:

Get *Flip or Flop, Murder House* at
https://www.lyndareesauthor.com
<u>For more from this author, consult the list of published books in the following pages.</u>
I hope you enjoy my work, and we become life-long friends. Please join my **VIP** group. Get the latest book **deals, exclusive content**, and **FREE** reads by joining my **VIPs**. Email for a **FREE** copy of *Leah's Story* at
https://preview.mailerlite.com/t1a6j6
Website: http://www.lyndareesauthor.com
Email: lyndareesauthor@gmail.com

Lynda Rees
The Murder Guru©

Love is a dangerous mystery. Enjoy the ride!©

BOOKS BY LYNDA REES

Historical Romance:
> *Gold Lust Conspiracy*
> *Write to Murder*

Mystery:

> ***The Bloodline Series:***
> *Leah's Story*
> *Parsley, Sage, Rose, Mary & Wine*
> *Blood & Studs*
> *Hot Blooded*
> *Blood of Champions*
> *Bloodlines & Lies*
> *Horseshoes & Roses*
> *The Bloodline Trail*
> *Real Money*
> *The Bourbon Trail*

Reggie Chronicles:
> *Hart's Girls, #1*
> *Heart of the Matter, #2*
> *Magnolia Blossoms, #3*

Flip or Flop Mysteries:
> *Fresh Start, Dirty Money*
> *The Attic*
> *Rock Starr Baby Daddy*
> *Cold Case*

Single Titles:
> *Fresh Start, Dirty Money*
> *God Father's Day*
> *Madam Mom*
> *2nd Chance Ranch*

7 Book Anthology: *Sacrifice For Love:*
Second Chance Romance, Lynda Rees
Children's Middle Grade:
Grandma Is An Alien
Freckle Face & Blondie
The Thinking Tree
Children's PictureBooks:
The Lost Dragon
NO FEAR
No Fear Learning and Activity Book
Find information about these books at website:
http://www.lyndareesauthor.com

ABOUT LYNDA REES

Lynda Rees, The Murder Guru, is a storyteller, an award-winning novelist, and a free-spirited dreamer with workaholic tendencies and a passion for writing.

A diverse background, visits to exotic locations, and curiosity about how history effects today's world fuels her writing. Born in the splendor of the Appalachian Mountains as a coal miner's daughter and part-Cherokee, she grew up in northern Kentucky when Newport prospered as a mecca for gambling and sin.

Lynda's work is published in cozy mystery, historical romance, romantic suspense, middle-grade mystery, children's picture books, non-fiction, and self-help non-fiction.

Made in U. S. A.

© 2025

Sweetwater Publishing Company